The Quiet Man

Fear not the stillness; for doubt and despair shall cease
With the gentle voices guiding us into peace.
Our dreams will change as they pass through the gates of gold,
And Quiet, the tender shepherd, shall keep the fold.

—Æ

By Patrick Purcell

HANRAHAN'S DAUGHTER
THE QUIET MAN

THE

Quiet Man

BY PATRICK PURCELL

G. P. PUTNAM'S SONS
New York

TO ANNE
WHO HAS NO BOOK
NOR NEED OF ONE

ACKNOWLEDGMENTS

The author wishes to thank the following publishers for permission to use material from their publications:

Coward-McCann, Inc. for some lines from *The Collected Poems of Francis Ledwidge.*

E. P. Dutton & Company for some lines from *The Thrush and the Jay* by Sylvia Lynd.

Funk & Wagnalls Company for some lines from "The Cold Sleep of Brighidin" which appeared in *The Four Winds of Eirinn* by Ethna Carbery.

The Macmillan Company for some lines from "The Silence of Love" from *The Collected Poems of Æ;* and the first verse from W. B. Yeats' "Red Hanrahan's Song about Ireland" from *Collected Poems 1933.*

Contents

Old King Coady

The old brown thorn trees break in two
   high over Cummen Strand
Under a bitter black wind
   that blows from the left hand;
Our courage breaks like an old tree
   in a black wind and dies,
But we have hidden in our hearts
   the flame out of the eyes
Of Cathleen, the Daughter of Houlihan.

                  —W. B. YEATS

Chapter One

FROM his lonely perch on the high seat of the swaying sidecar, he stared down at the narrow road that straggled on before them up the low hill. Pearl-white the road was here in the early moonlight; mud-grey there where the dusk had gathered thick beneath the trees.

He sat silent, his loneliness wrapped around him like a cloak. He saw the first stars blink above the laggard moon and grew more lonely as the thought came to him that these self-same stars were winking down tonight on his own Burren—Burren, bare and bleak, half Ireland's breadth behind him now. Yet, louder than the click-clack of the horse's steeled hoofs on the rough roadway, he seemed to hear the hungry breakers roar and seethe and fret and fume against the rugged coast of Clare; seemed to see, reflected in the velvet mirror of the darkness, his father's white-walled house, crouched high on the barren hillside above the clustered roofs of Ballyvaughan; and he wondered at feeling more homesick tonight than ever he had felt when first, half a dozen years ago, he had gone from the family hearth to the training college in distant Dublin. . . .

The driver's elbow came jolting sharply into his ribs to rouse him from his reverie.

"Do you see them few lights above us, there on the hill?"

"I do."

"That, now, is the street of Carriglea." The jarvey flicked his whip. " 'Tis there we're goin'. To the teacher's house, you said?"

"To Mr. Coady's house."

"An' I suppose you're another new assistant for him," surmised the driver, suddenly grown garrulous. "Bedad, I hope you stomach th' oul' impostor better nor his last curate did. Six

3

months of the bould Jer Coady's carry-on an' me poor youngster had more than a bellyful of botheration an' flew back like
the wind to wherever he came from. Aw, unless he's rubbed
the right way, Coady is harder to handle than a horseload of
thorns."

. . . To his loneliness a dead weight of dread was added now,
filling him with the emptiness of fear. Yet must he test the
matter further and know his fate in all its bitterness. "That's
not a very pleasant prospect," he observed, careful of his words.
"Perhaps you should have told me all this before we left
Waterford and so spared us both a journey. What's wrong with
this man Coady? The letters he wrote me seemed very
friendly."

The jarvey spat out sideways, well clear of his mare's bob-
bing haunches. "Bedad, 'twould be easier for me fly off up to
the moon than give you a straight answer to that question. One
man will tell you he's the learnedest scholar from this to Cork
an' the grandest gentleman you could wish to meet. You'll ask
another an' be told there's no more cracked oul' eejit walkin'
Irish ground."

Having waited in vain for further enlightenment, the passenger spoke again. "And your own opinion?"

The carman chuckled, clucked to the mare. "Not bein'
obliged to live near Carriglea I don't have to have any opinion,
barrin' that the man is mad. Oh, from what I do hear, there
was never hare in March could hould a candle to him for madness. But, mad or mad not, you'll travel far an' wide before you
meet another character as quare as Masther Coady. If you're
able to bear up at all with his antics, me young man, you'll
never see the day that you'll be short of amusement. Jer Coady
would sooner a long laugh than a long life."

They pulled up opposite an iron gate. Timorous now, he
stepped down, took his valise, paid without haggling the high
price asked. He waited till mare and car and man had departed
at a gallop off into the night. Then he went stumbling up the
path, knocked gently on the door.

Very timidly he waited for a response, wondering what kind
of monster this man could be under whom he had come to

4

serve, very conscious of how the day's journey must have greyed the virgin whiteness of his celluloid collar, very sensitive of his new-grown moustache.

The light that poured out through the opened door blinded him for a moment, so that, before ever he saw his host, he was conscious of a feeling of friendship and warmth and homeliness, so that he was undaunted by the great voice booming in the great beard, "You're welcome this night to Carriglea, young Peter O'Dea from County Clare."

Peter O'Dea sat, happy, on the low chair in the chimney corner and watched the gay flames dancing on the stone hearth. He found himself smiling at the very thought of the huge bulk of bearded man who sat opposite, merriment ever agurgle in that hidden throat. He could have laughed aloud at the memory of all his own fears and loneliness—and how groundless they had been and how quickly they had vanished.

The big man smoothed down his black beard. "Speaking, Peter, as a wise man and as a pedagogue, I'll have you to know that the eighth wonder of the world was the achievement of Arthur Guinness in wedding the tawny waters of Dublin with the mold of the barley-mow, thus giving back to mankind the elixir of life, the nectar of the gods, the Cadmean honey, the lost secret of the Pictish brew. The grey juice of the long-haired barley, Peter, is at once an oil for the tongue, a lubricant for the brain, and a grand aid to the digestion."

Jer Coady paused to refresh himself from a pewter tankard of stout, sucked his whiskers thoughtfully.

"But glad I am to hear, my young Peter O'Dea from County Clare, that you yourself are no drinking man. In our profession, sir, in the noble art of pedagoguery and the general and particular instruction of the young, it is strongly to be recommended that those whose bounden duty it is to hammer the rising generation into industrious, cultured, and civilised habits should shun intoxicating liquor like the devil himself shuns my old friend Canon Costigan. It is regrettable that any man should dare to preach temperance, sobriety, and total abstinence with a large black bottle peeping out from under the

5

coattails behind and a large red nose peering out over the beard in front, as has upon occasion been the misfortune of one Jeremiah Coady."

He drank another draught.

"I am doubly glad to hear of your commendable sobriety, Peter, because my last villain of an assistant was born thirsty and liked no drink better than the drink I bought and paid for. 'Ah,' said I to myself, 'such a man is no fit person to be teacher in any school under Her Majesty's Commissioners of Education.' So I indulged in a few little stratagems of my own, and, by the lord harry, inside a few months he was only too glad to say a last good-bye to Carriglea and the blue sky over it. There's no doubt about it, Peter, but the Man Above is good to His own. Here I am tonight, blessed with a new assistant who is at the same time a teetotaller and a damn' good listener. You're a hero and a friend, sir. Oh, I think we'll get on very well together, Peter O'Dea."

At the door someone was knocking, as much in salute as for admittance. Jer Coady whistled in answer, loud and shrill. Familiar fingers fumbled at the latch, then a tall, thin man, dark eyes bright in his narrow face, came swaggering into the kitchen, the lilt of a song on his lips. He swung the door shut, turned to speak, stood silent at the sight of the stranger beside the fire.

Coady's beard shook with laughter. "The natives, the aborigines of Carriglea, Peter, are often friendly and sometimes almost human. Here we have a perfect specimen, Fonsy Farrell the rhymer, the most remarkable poet under the four winds of heaven. A sociable lad on an evening's revelry so long as he hasn't to pay for the refreshments."

Peter stood up. "I'm very pleased to meet you, Mr. Farrell," he said politely.

Fonsy Farrell winked across to Peter. "The jealousy," he exclaimed, shaking his head. "The green jealousy is at him again. He suffers from the jealousy like I do from the rheumatism."

"Peter O'Dea is the boy's name," interjected Coady. "Peter O'Dea. And he comes from Burren in the County Clare."

The tall poet bowed to the stranger. "I am very glad to know

6

you, Peter O'Dea, and sorry to see you in such bad company."

"Fonsy is a rebel too," Jer volunteered. "He takes the very poorest view of our Sovereign Lady the Queen, her crown and dignity. Oh, Fonsy is a right rebel! Aren't you, Fonsy?"

"Lingering to my grave," said Fonsy sadly, "just lingering to my grave, boy, a poor but faithful admirer of the late Charles Stewart Parnell. A follower still of Jeremiah O'Donovan Rossa, of John Devoy, of John O'Leary, and the rest of my old comrades, the bould Fenian men."

Coady crowed and chuckled. "You'll mistake your company some night, Fonsy, and you'll make that same speech to Lalor the Peeler, and then you'll have plenty of time to cool your chops, snug behind a sixty-foot wall in Ballybricken gaol. The least you might do, man, is make a song in honour of the visitor instead of standing there spouting out treason."

Fonsy sat down. " 'Tis easy make a song when you're sober, Jer. And many's the good song I made up when I was drunk. But when a man is betwixt and between 'tis mortal hard to woo the muses." He spread his fingers before his face, closed his eyes for a moment in a very agony of silence and thought. Then, triumphant, he threw his arms wide and declaimed in a high monotone:

"From Burren, bleak and bare,
In the far-off County Clare,
To the green, grassy fields of Carriglea,
There came a teacher bold
Whose fame must be extolled,
And his name was young Peter O'Dea."

"Oh, Fonsy! Fonsy!" Jer Coady shook his head sadly. "Such a way to disgrace me before the stranger, and I half the night here singing your praises to him! I have no child in Third Book who couldn't make up a better poem than that."

"I thought it very good, especially when it was composed in so short a time," said Peter timidly, not wishing to cross his principal, yet not desirous that Fonsy should feel hurt at the rejection of his poetic nosegay.

"To be sure it's good, Misther O'Dea." Fonsy Farrell was

7

not a jot perturbed. " 'Tis only the jealousy makes him deny it. He knows I couldn't make a bad poem if I tried. An' now, Jer, even a poet is worthy of his hire," smiling and winking towards the pewter mug. "I'm a thirsty soul an' a merry one, Misther O'Dea. No common clay, Misther O'Dea. A poet, I'll have you know, does be cursed with a drier throttle than your ordinary man."

Peter O'Dea had cycled up to Killrone, proud yet partly frightened of his new bicycle. He had parked his machine, safe from inquisitive small boys, inside the new, square, solid wall which caged in the Canon's new, square, solid house. He had been met on the threshold by the housekeeper and promptly ushered into the presence of the no less grim parish priest, who, reading his breviary, had signed to Peter to be seated but had not raised his head or said a word of welcome.

Somewhat awed by the silence, somewhat intimidated by the grey head bent in prayer over the well-thumbed book, somewhat overconscious of the stern furniture which filled the Canon's living room, Peter O'Dea sat silent and noted the small things which might help to interpret the character of the man he had come to visit. The carpet, long ago worn thin, told of poverty, of lack of pride, just as the well-fingered books on the table revealed the scholar, the lover of those older beauties which, if they change, but grow more mellow with the passing years. Virgil stood there, and Horace, and a great red-bound Dante in the original Italian, and the *Imitation of Christ*, square-set to stare every visitor out of countenance. There were solid tomes by Thomas of Aquin on the low shelf behind the pastor's chair, and in the far corner a grand piano, strangely incongruous amidst so much piety and learning.

Canon Costigan snapped his breviary shut, looked up at last, grey eyes peering weakly out over his steel-rimmed spectacles. "Well, young man, and what can I do for you?"

Taken unawares, never dreaming but that the priest would either have known him or known of him, Peter found his shyness shackling his wits while his mind fumbled for an answer. "I'm very sorry to intrude on you like this, Canon, but, you

8

see, I'm the new assistant teacher in Carriglea, and I thought it high time for me to call and thank you, as manager of the school, for appointing me to the post."

The Canon picked up a small bronze box from the table, flicked open the lid. "Oh, I see! I see! And what's this your name is?"

"O'Dea, Canon. Peter O'Dea."

"I see! I see! And do you take snuff, Mr. O'Dea?" He proffered the box. Peter shook his head. The Canon sniffed a huge pinch up each nostril in turn. "Well, Mr. O'Dea, it may be a very irregular state of affairs, a great admission of weakness on my part, but, in fact, you owe no word of thanks to me. Oh, I have very little say at all in such matters down at that end of my parish." He took another pinch of snuff. "For a trifle over fifteen years I have been parish priest here in Killrone. For five years, which proves me to be a stubborn man, I tried to gain full management and control over my own schools. I would have been better advised had I kept my breath to cool my porridge. Finally I got sense—or lost heart—you can interpret it which ever way you like. Since then Mr. Coady allows me to minister to the spiritual needs of his scholars, but in all matters temporal, whether it be an ultimatum to the commissioners of education, a reprimand to the caretaker, or the engaging of a new assistant, he gives the orders and I obey."

Peter, not too sure of his ground, forced a little smile, said hesitantly, "Mr. Coady seems to be a remarkable man."

"A remarkable man!" echoed the Canon. "Ireland has never seen his like before." The old priest stared sternly at his visitor. "You must remember, of course, Mr.—er—O'Dea, that you are not expected to retail those observations of mine to our friend Coady. I may mention, as a matter of interest, that, except on strictly business matters, Coady and myself have not exchanged a word for over ten years." The Canon sighed. "A temperamental gentleman is Mr. Coady and not given to respecting either persons or offices. He habitually refers to me, I understand, as 'that liturgical oul' cod above in Killrone.' Isn't that so?"

Peter, always a truthful young man, blushed and stammered, saw the pale eyes twinkle, said with what he hoped was not overmuch daring, "Well, he did mention when I told him I was coming here that he had crossed swords with you a couple of times."

Canon Costigan was human enough to smile. "I see! I see! Oh, you have the gift of diplomacy, Mr. O'Dea. Oh, you phrased that very well. I can easily imagine what our friend Coady actually said. But now perhaps we had better leave our great bluebeard and return to yourself. I suppose you're living below in the teachers' residence? Would you like me to get some other lodging for you? I'm told that place down there generally resembles a not too well-regulated lunatic asylum."

"Oh, I'm very satisfied where I am," stated Peter earnestly. "It's easy to grow accustomed to his little oddities. Besides, he feeds me well and I find him very amusing."

"Amusing! I see! You can thank God then, young man, for giving you a good sense of humour, because through the years the whimsies of Jerry Coady have managed to wear out the humours of most of the rest of us. Of course, he hasn't had time to try out his tricks on you yet. Has he held any washday since you came?"

"No, Canon. Not so far."

"Ah, you have a pleasure in store for you, Mr. O'Dea. Wait till you see him set about the washing! Wait till he wears the front out of your best shirt with his patent method of scrubbing! Oh, by the time you've lived a few years with Jer Coady, your sense of humour will have served a very stiff apprenticeship. But how are you getting on with the people? And with the pupils?"

Peter O'Dea's enthusiasm mastered his innate shyness. "I'm really amazed, Father, I mean Canon, at my own progress. I never expected to be anything but a stranger, a foreigner almost, among those people. Instead, I find them anxious to treat me as one of themselves. There seems to be a sort of fellow-feeling between myself and the folk of Carriglea, young and old. Their habits, their way of living, and their outlook,

10

even, are very similar to those of my own people at home in Clare."

"I see! I see!" said Canon Costigan. "Of course, there's a ready enough explanation for all that. Your people and these people both belong to the old breed of countryman. In Clare you have always been a bit isolated from what it is usual to call the blessings of civilisation. The Shannon and the mountains and the sea have done their best to save you. Here the river and the hills tend to have one and the same effect. Like you, the people of Carriglea are an old people and a proud people and a hospitable people. Is it any wonder, then, that you notice so strong a link between this breed and your own?"

"It's a very good theory anyway, Father, I mean Canon."

"Then consider the difference between yourself and our friend, our famous friend Coady. Down there in Carriglea they look up to Jer Coady far more than they look up to anyone else, priest, policeman, or parson. You met Fonsy Farrell, I presume?"

"I did, Canon."

"Well, the truest thing Fonsy ever said in his life was when he called Jer Coady the King of Carriglea. They honour and respect Jer Coady, in his saner moods, of course. They'd follow him to the death, the younger men would, if he decided to lead them out into a revolution, as he might. He was a famous Fenian, you know, in his young days. Carriglea never forgets that, and the police never forget it either. However, actually that's neither here nor there. Oh, they have a great regard for Coady. They never tire of telling stories about himself and his odd doings. They take pride in repeating the songs Fonsy Farrell makes up about him. And yet," concluded the Canon dogmatically, "he will never be one of them, even if he lives among them for a hundred years."

"And why do you say that, Canon?" Peter asked.

The Canon picked up his snuff-box again. "Fundamentally, Coady is both a mountainy man and a townsman. He was actually reared in the town of Wicklow. He has a townsman's quick mind and a townsman's quick judgement. He has a mountainy man's fine sense of values and, when he bothers to

11

have any such outlook at all, a mountainy man's farsighted outlook on life. He's a remarkable man and in his own way a great man, but a Carriglea man he'll never be."

Canon Costigan took snuff with a certain stately air of dignity before he continued.

"Whereas you, Mr. O'Dea, are a quiet man like themselves. And another important point: you seem to be the type of man who will settle down here and take root. You're the kind of man who, if God wills it and you yourself feel that inclined, will found a family here to carry on the name. Or am I being guilty of rash judgement?"

Peter smiled and said nothing.

"On the other hand," went on the parish priest, "Coady, whether he knows it himself or not, is in spiritual exile here. I believe that, on the day when Jer Coady retires, he will hoist his sails and shake the dust of Carriglea off his shoes forever and a day. And the legend of his name and his oddities and his sayings and his doings will never die in Carriglea. But you, before you're ten years in this parish—I assume, if you notice, that you will stay here—will be so much of themselves that, if you don't mind me saying so, you'll be just as ordinary as anyone else. They'll say, I should imagine, that you're a quiet, kindly class of a man; and I, for one, would ask no finer epitaph on my tombstone." Canon Costigan paused, smiled at his visitor for the second time. "Oh, but you must be heartsick listening to an old man's vapourings, Mr. O'Dea." He leaned back, tugged at the bell rope. "If my housekeeper is in good humour, I may, perhaps, prevail on her to provide us with a cup of tea."

Jer Coady, whenever he listed his own varied virtues and qualifications, was fond of describing himself as a bachelor from birth. On occasion he might even add that he was also a bachelor by conviction, maintaining strongly that, blindfold and with one hand, he could keep house better than any woman in the barony. In all his time there, no woman had ever crossed the threshold of the teachers' residence, and Peter O'Dea had not been long within the jurisdiction before the

12

older man set out to make his assistant as confirmed a bachelor and as able a housekeeper and as complete a woman-hater as he was himself.

The women of the parish, especially those who were young and eligible and unmarried, had no intention of letting such a fate befall a young and likable assistant. But even the hardiest of them feared to tangle with Jer, whilst Coady himself, by eternal vigilance, ensured that not even the most forward female could get within striking distance of Peter O'Dea. Nor is it probable that Peter missed the pleasures of feminine company, for it was a fine, fair and easy, happy-go-lucky life he was learning to lead down there in that high box of a house below Carriglea, where the ivy, like some untidy flag of freedom, was forever waving long tendrils high above the eaves.

On the last Saturday morning in that July, Peter O'Dea lay lazy in his bed, glad because it was the teachers' sabbath, happy at the thought of a long rest and an idle day to follow. Suddenly the battered alarm clock, jangling in the next room, roused him from his dozing. He could hear the big man growling and groaning, then there was a great outcry of tortured springs, followed by a solid thump as feet met floor. Came the thud of three short strides, a knock-knock on the wall.

"Hear yez! Hear yez! Hear yez!" Boomed the deep voice of Jer Coady. "Nine o'clock and all's wrong. Arise, arise O! The court of King Coady is now in vogue! Piping all hands to battle stations! Hear yez! Hear yez! Hear yez! That most mighty, most illustrious, and most puissant monarch, King Jer the First, is now in session. Awake, therefore, since morning in the bowl of night has flung the stone which puts the stars to flight. Arise, my little one, from out thy bed, or old King Coady will bite off your head! O'Dea, you big lazy, good-for-nothing Clare bosthoon! Will you get up to hell out of that until I wash your shirt for you."

Peter, happy at the thought of merriment in store, was quickly up, dressed, and down to the kitchen, there to find his principal busily quoting poetry, singing snatches of ribald songs, imparting stray scraps of assorted wisdom, and delivering short homilies on the folly of womankind, while all the

13

time the biggest and blackest pot bubbled merrily over the open fire.

"Now, Peter," Jer announced, breakfast over, "now, my lad, you will see your first demonstration of the Coady contrivance for whiter washdays!" Into the steaming pot he poured more boiling water from a handy kettle. "The witches' brew, the merry witches' brew, Peter," he cried, snatching a square of black soap from the mantelshelf, tossing it into the frothy water. "That will give a tang to the broth."

From the hearth where he had heaped them he bundled up all the soiled clothes, dumped them into the cauldron. "And now, Peter, wait till I lay hands on my washing machine and then we'll start on the A.B.C. of laundry-work." He departed to root out the heft of an ancient axe handle from some secret recess, pointed with it as if lecturing to a class. "To wash clothes, boy, you need three things and three things only: patience, perseverance, and ordinary, common, honest-to-goodness sweat. You boil up your clothes, Peter. You take a deep breath, like so," and he engulfed a huge mouthful of air. "You bring your machine to the ready." He presented the axe handle as though it were a spear. "And then you charge the enemy." Wedding words and action, he attacked the pot and its contents, poking the gurgling mass of clothes and water with reckless energy and enthusiasm.

For full twenty minutes he poked and boiled and preached, nor would he let Peter take any part in the ritual except, finally, to drag in the huge wooden tub which stood outside the back door. Hopping back and forth, Jer fished out garment after garment with the sharper end of his axe handle and dumped them in turn into the tub. When all were salvaged, he granted to Peter one lug of the tub, took the other himself, and they staggered out into the backyard with their burden.

There Coady began part two of his laundry lesson. "Do you know now, Peter, where all the women go wrong when they set out to wash clothes?"

"I do not, sir. It's a black art in which I never dabbled nor ever cared to."

"Well, then, cock up your ears, boy, because you're going

14

to hear a trade secret, every bit as important as how to brew good beer or how to make Beecham's pills. Some day I'm going to have the whole thing printed. And I'll have it bound up in red covers and sell it at a guinea a copy. 'Coady's Correct Washing Method,' I'll call it. 'Copyright reserved and patent applied for.' Yet here and now, free gratis and for nothing, I'm going to reveal to you the secret formula that has made Jer Coady the envy of Carriglea."

He came closer to Peter, lowered his voice to impress; but the twinkle in his eyes was merry as ever. "Don't wring out the clothes, boy! Never squeeze the good out of them! Poke them like the devil when you have them in the pot. Then up with them on the line where the water can drain from them in a natural way, and you'll find, when they're dry, that you've done a better job than all the so-called washerwomen in the ring of Ireland could do in a lifetime, despite all their squeezing and wheezing and wringing and whinging."

Peter stared at the sodden draperies, dripping sadly where they hung there in the sunshine. "The simple things are always the hardest to discover," said he, playing for safety.

Jer Coady tapped him on the chest with his closed fist. "I'll soon make plain to you, Peter, how effective the Coady method is. Every woman who passes down that road there is no sooner clear of the sight of my windows than she's ducking into the hedge, peeping out through the bushes, turning green behind the ears from jealousy because she recognises the excellence of Jer Coady's washing as compared with her own miserable, muddy efforts. Aye, and if she sees me watching her, or suspects me of watching her, she'll stick her nose in the air and march off down the road like a peacock among a gaggle of sparrows."

Coady unfurled his tucked-up shirt sleeves, the morning's labour done. "But just the same, supposing she were to put back her nose so far that she could see her heels, she knows and I know and everybody knows that Jer Coady can handle a week's washing with any man who ever made suds and is a greater master of the craft than any maid, wife, or widow." He groped for his pipe in a waistcoat pocket. "The most re-

15

markable poem, Peter, that ever Fonsy made up he composed about myself and my washing."

"And you kept it to yourself!" accused Peter. "Don't you know I'm only too ready to listen to anything Fonsy wrote?"

"This is the way it went," said Jer, heading back towards the house. "Oh, I'd have rolled it out to you long ago, but I thought that a practical demonstration should precede a metrical description." He took the pipe from his mouth.

> *"In the month of May, as I made my way*
> *Through fair Carriaglea,*
> *I did chance to meet with a hero neat*
> *Who to me did say,*
> *'I've been toiling hard in my own backyard,*
> *For 'tis Saturday,*
> *From my Sunday shirt, that was chained by dirt,*
> *To break the black bonds free.'*

"Bygor," said Peter, all admiration, "Homer is never dead while Fonsy Farrell is alive and kicking."

"Ah, but listen here to this verse," cried Jer. " 'Tis the masterwork, boy, of a master hand.

> *"First the pot he filled, and with fingers skilled*
> *On the fire did place.*
> *Then a stick he took and with stern look*
> *He began his toil.*
> *As with learned nods and judicious prods*
> *Jer his wash did boil,*
> *Every female maid fled away dismayed,*
> *Shamed to show her face."*

Before his own back door Jer Coady bowed low to his assistant. "There I am for you now, Peter O'Dea, immortalised for all eternity in the deathless poetry of Alphonsus Farrell, the rhymer." And the great laugh rumbled like thunder in the great beard.

"Carriglea? Oh, indeed I do know it. A dead-and-alive kind of a place at the back of God-speed. Not one thing has ever happened there since Noah's flood, and there will be no other

16

notable event in that part of the world until the Day of Judgement."

That opinion, from a commercial traveller, was the sum of Peter O'Dea's knowledge concerning Carriglea before he arrived therein; and he had, in his ignorance, consoled himself with the thought that there he would have peace and quiet and time and opportunity to prepare himself for better things, to read profitably in his empty hours, to study through the long nights, so that, thus equipped, he would speedily become a principal teacher or perhaps an inspector of schools. And it could even be, he promised himself in his wilder dreams, that he would rise to become an omnipotent commissioner of education, towering over the rest of puny mankind like an oak among buttercups, like a god among slaves. But yet even in Carriglea, dead-and-alive and all though it was supposed to be, never a textbook did he open, nor ever a line did he study, as the days and the weeks and the months went by.

Ah, but fine, happy, philosophic months they were, with Jer Coady, High King and Monarch of all, bubbling over with wit and wisdom in his chair by the fire; with Fonsy Farrell stringing rhymes together for hours on end whenever the fancy took him, singing songs that might be five centuries old or that he might have composed himself five minutes before as he came whistling up the road, the words scarce cold as yet from the anvil of his agile brain. Seldom a night passed by that the pleasant kitchen was not crowded to the doors, and after all the onward march of the years there's still many a white-haired man, nursing a quiet fire in one or other of the rambling farmhouses that dot the river glens, who could while away every sunlit hour of a June day tracing back those happy nights when the boys and young men, and some who were not so young, gathered in Jerry Coady's kitchen.

Coady himself would be enthroned before the fire, snuggled down deep in his sugawn chair, the curved pipe waggling amidst the square-cut beard as he preached his gospel for the night. There Fonsy Farrell would posture and pose, poeming to his heart's content, striding up and down the floor one minute, squatted on his heels before the blaze in a moment's time.

17

Young Peter O'Dea would be perched beyond on the settle seat, a melodeon sagging between his hands or Jer's own fiddle tucked snug beneath his chin, and jig or reel or march or horn-pipe was never noted that he could not play.

He would sit there silent, listening and laughing with the best of them, and maybe fingering a sprig of a soundless tune to himself, until Coady would suddenly call for silence and shout, "Give us a bar or two, Peter boy. A bar or two, till we get one of these young buckos to knock the dust out of the tiles for us and drive the hobnails home into the brogues at the same time." Then Peter would draw out the melodeon bellows or rake up the fiddle bow, and he would play, very soft and sweet, *The Flax in Bloom* or *The Miller's Courtship* or *The Road to Kilmeaden*, or that rollicking little tune he himself had composed, *The Creamery Manager's Daughter*. Soon some shy giant would be pushed out into the centre of the kitchen, bashful as a ghost at noonday until the rhythm conquered him and sent him footing it heel and toe, a frown on his face and a poem in his feet, while the sparks flew from the flagged floor and every man who watched was willing to swear with Fonsy Farrell that any step-dancer who was tutored in Coady's kitchen was well fitted to take turn and turn about with the best that ever tapped toe in Ireland.

Once in a way Peter's conscience complained, pointed out that he was squandering all the years of his youth, emphasised that this was no way for a man of his brains and talents to be letting his best days dribble away from him, lulled to laziness by the antics of fools and oddities. But, as Peter O'Dea was always quick to demand of his conscience, could it in fact be conceded that his time was being squandered at all?

Jerry Coady had a world and more of wisdom tucked away behind that black beard, and any knowledge which might perchance have strayed out of his head, he could always discover again in his books, for he possessed a library every bit as un-orthodox as he was himself: a library scattered higgledy-piggledy through a dozen old butter-boxes that were always being overturned and were forever wandering round into some part of the kitchen where they had no right to be. And yet, whether he sought information or enlightenment or merely amusement, Jer could without search place his hand on the correct butter-box and fish up therefrom the very book he needed.

And if it was a political education that Peter wanted, a few months in that house would have quickly qualified him to sit for his diploma. Many a mad hare of argument was flushed in that kitchen, to twist and turn through every tangled trail of politics and religion until half a dozen men would all be shouting angrily together, until Jer Coady would be driven to fetch forth his "washing machine" from its secret corner and pound and pound on the tiles before he could restore order. Though Charles Stuart Parnell was cold in his grave, still to one half of Carriglea he was a spotless saint and still to the other half he was the blackest of sinners. Many a night the high words roared and echoed round that kitchen. There was one night in particular when Fonsy and Andy Gorman from Ballyvarna grew so hot in their leather that they paid no heed to Coady's pounding stick and were still striving to push their respective opinion down each other's throats when the big man came thrusting between them.

"Sit down, ye nincompoops, with yer loud talk and yer dirty politics!" he roared. They sat down, sheepish and subdued. "Sit down and learn the first lesson on how to free Ireland. And it's this: to keep a still tongue instead of always roaring and bawling. To keep the tongue still in the head, to plot and plan in silence and secret until the day we're ready and then let the bomb and the bayonet and the bullet do the talking." He pitched the axe handle back to its corner. "I said no word against Parnell when he was up, and I said no word against Parnell when he was down. We were both Wicklowmen in the first place, and the mountainy men were always clannish."

He glared fiercely round the room, found no head raised save that of Peter O'Dea, neutral observer.

"In the second place, I said no word for or against Parnell because, although his way wasn't my way, he was hoping to free Ireland. He took over where O'Connell left off. He took over the ballot boxes, the speech-making, and the monster

19

meetings. Davitt and the Land League were solid at his back. Himself and the Party could always raise tallywhack and tandem in the House of Commons, the Holy of Holies. And always he could frighten the English Liberals by threatening to take his party over to the Unionists or vice-versa, as the need arose. And when he wanted to scare the lot of them he had only to threaten the English that if they didn't treat with him they'd have to face worse villians altogether, those murderous ruffians the bould Fenian men—Fonsy there and myself." There was a growl of laughter through the tensed kitchen. Coady crossed back to his chair, sat down.

"Well, when Parnell was at his highest, certain parties came to me and suggested that I fall in behind the band and follow him with the rest of them. But I reasoned this way: if all of us were to up and away after Parnell, where would any wicked Fenian men be found if Parnell ever were to need them? So I decided to stay at home for myself and play cute. 'You were a Fenian man, Jer, when Parnell was little talked of,' says I to myself, 'and you'll still remain a Fenian man in case Ireland ever needs the like again.' "

Massive behind his beard he frowned at them all, began to fill his pipe. When next he spoke his thoughts had strayed a little. "Eeyah, but what's the use in talking to ye? Ye moneygrubbers were busy stuffing golden sovereigns into the stocking up the chimney while we husbanded the flame of freedom in Wicklow's wild valleys. Aye, and if God spares some of us we might strike another stroke yet on the wet hillsides for the Green." He turned sharp on Andy Gorman. "And we mightn't wait for your approval either, boy."

"Approval!" cried Fonsy. "And what would he approve of but the one thing, slavery and subjectification for ever and always, the white-livered slob?"

"There's more Gormans than him alive," cried Andy's brother Ned, the firebrand of the family.

"Oh, there's no doubt," retorted Andy, bringing heavy sarcasm into action against superior numbers, "that if Lalor the Peeler ever gets his grip on ye fellows, ye'll make speeches from

20

the dock that will never be forgotten. All about how ye freed Ireland—in Coady's kitchen."

So the days drifted into weeks, and the weeks merged into months, and the months were slowly welded into years that slipped, almost unnoticed, past the strangely matched pair. For who would pay heed to so trivial a thing as the passage of time when your fingers could stray along the keyboard of a good melodeon, or your wrist could be moulding the flow of a fiddle's melody? When the lithe dancers were always ready to beat out a hornpipe on the tiled floor, when Jer Coady would read out from his well-thumbed books the wisdom of all the sages, explaining and expounding and enlarging on what they had to say, aye, and well able to refute their teachings too, if the knowledge of the bookmen and the learning of Jer Coady ever failed to agree.

Oh, it was easy to let time slip by like sea sand through a child's fingers, with half the rambling gamblers of the parish gathered there in the warm kitchen, and Fonsy Farrell at hand to play a rubber or construct a ballad according to the mood that ruled him.

Nor did life flow any less smoothly in the schoolhouse itself. Peter O'Dea had quickly discovered that, despite all his oddities, there was never better teacher than Jeremiah Coady, and never better scholars than the boys who sat beneath his ferrule.

Thus, while a new century came creeping from out its swaddling clothes, while an old queen died and an elderly king reigned in her stead, while in the world outside a whole age was passing away, while a new era dawned, Peter O'Dea and Jer Coady lived happy as sandboys, like two strange monks in some mad monastery. And never a care cared they if the rest of the world lay in ruins so long as Carriglea escaped, whole and entire, from the general catastrophe.

Chapter Two

THROUGH the leaves of the stout ash tree which shaded the house from winter's southwest gales, summer sunshine filtered into the teachers' kitchen. Jer Coady, breakfast down and done with, crossed one knee over the other, contentedly set about filling that first pipe which provided his peak point of pleasure on lazy Saturday mornings.

"Peter," he announced, ramming tobacco into pipe bowl with a blunt forefinger, "if I were ten years a younger man, I'd bid my quick good-bye to this damn' schoolteaching, and I'd off around the country with a little sideshow of my own, like Barnum and his circus beyond in America—only, of course, on a slightly more modest scale. Because, do you see, in my circus, Peter boy, there would only be the one exhibit; and that, God knows, the strangest thing ever known in this nation —an Irishman with no more politics in his system than Fonsy Farrell's old tomcat has morals. Oh, by the lord harry, Peter O'Dea, I'd make a rare mint of money exhibiting you through the country for a silver shilling a look."

A little lurk of a smile at the corners of his lips, Peter O'Dea sat down on the window ledge to consider his answer. Even as he pondered, the front door was burst open and an awkward, excited youngster of sixteen came panting into the kitchen.

"By the lord harry, Packey," cried Jer Coady, "but you bear a great resemblance to a man in a hurry."

"'Tis District Inspector Lalor an' the sergeant. They're comin' up the road. I was inside the ditch, an' I heard them talkin'. An 'tis up here they're comin'. 'An' you make no mistake, Din, about what you tell that ruffian an' the warnin' you

22

give him, because that oul' crackpot could make matthers very conthrary for us all,' the sergeant was sayin'.''

"Aha," crowed Jer Coady, roused, all delight at the prospect of conflict ahead. "So we're going to be honoured by a visit from the Forces of the Crown! Well, begor, I'd be the last to turn them away. Tinker, Turk, or Chinaman is welcome in Jer Coady's house, so why not Din Lalor and his minion? All I'm sorry for, Peter, is that old Din, the father, is retired. Ah, you could knock fire and brimstone out of him in an argument. There was good stuff at the back of all in that old blackguard. Close the door, Peter! At least we'll put them to the bother of knocking for their entry."

Peter O'Dea obeyed even as the two tall men in bottle green entered the gateway and approached the teachers' door with all the famed stateliness of the Royal Irish Constabulary. Behind him he heard Jer softly instruct Packey. "Out the back way, young Regan, before they lay eye on you. There's no sense in letting the huntsmen know the old fox has smelt blood."

Packey went as quickly as he had come, and the thunder of the official knock on the front door masked the sound of his going.

"The first shot! Bedad, Peter, they've fired the first shot," whispered Coady, overjoyed. "Open the door, boy, brazen as you like. 'Twill take more than a few whacks on a knocker to frighten Jerry Coady."

Peter swung the door open.

"Good morning, Mr. O'Dea," said the cold, polite voice of Inspector Lalor. "Could you inform us as to whether or not your colleague, Mr. Coady, is at home?"

Peter O'Dea got no chance to reply, for Jer, the very essence of geniality, shouted from his chair, "Oh, bedad, at home he is. Walk right in, Inspector! Ah, and how's life with you at all, Sergeant Dwane?" They came stalking into the kitchen. "Eeyah, by the lord harry, isn't it a heart-ease to lay eyes on a couple of fine, big, upstanding men after all the miserable alyawns of assistants that the Government persists in dumping

23

down on myself. How the devil are you, Din Lalor? And how's the father? Keeping well?"

"My father enjoys excellent health, thank you," replied Din Lalor without enthusiasm. By his shoulder the sergeant stood, silent as a shadow.

"Eeyah, but isn't he the hardy bit of flesh for a man long gone seventy! And him with his hands well full since he bought Moonbawn above. Eeyah, but he was a fine, active breed of a man always. And, 'pon my soul and honour, I never asked ye to sit down. Plant your weight on a chair there, Din, and give the sergeant an official order to do likewise. God knows but ye have weight enough on the feet already in yeer exacting profession without standing when ye can be at yeer ease."

The sergeant cleared his throat, looked expectantly at his superior. Din Lalor cleared his throat and tried, in vain, to ignore the sergeant. Peter O'Dea had slipped round to his favourite seat on the settle, whence he could watch all three men, missing nothing.

Lalor frowned at the window. "As a matter of fact, Mr. Coady, we thought we'd drop in on you in the course of our routine duty. Not altogether official, you see, and not, perhaps, from your point of view, altogether friendly. A modicum, you might say, of semi-official warning plus a favouring of friendly advice." He switched his frown from the unoffending window to the equally unoffending Peter.

"Oh, well, if I hear no state secrets I can't be accused of retailing any," said Peter, quick to take the hint that frown implied, rising from his seat, making to move out through the back kitchen. But Coady forestalled him.

"Stand your ground, Peter boy," Jer commanded. "'Tis only a little whim of my own, yet I always like to have a witness on hand when I'm dealing with the representatives of law and order. You know, Din, the memory is inclined to get a bit tricky with me now; and Peter here, a smart young fellow, might be a help to me at a later date in jogging my recollection if by any mischance myself and yourself and the sergeant here couldn't remember the same facts about our little interview."

24

"Please yourself, Mr. Coady." Lalor was still coldly polite, although an angry flush had warmed his pale cheeks. "Actually what we have to say is no state secret, nor is there much to it that can't be easily remembered." Peter slipped back to his settle. "I presume you have heard, Mr. Coady, that His Majesty the King will be paying a state visit to Waterford next month?"

"Of course I did," cried Jer, enthusiastic. "Didn't he send me a personal postcard, only the other day, telling me all about it? 'I'll be sailing to Dublin, Jer,' he says, 'the Wednesday, and then I'll be making a bit of a tour around the country for a day or two, and I'll be calling down to Waterford towards the end of the week, the Friday,' says he, 'or maybe not till Saturday. Be sure to call in, Jer,' he says, 'whatever day it is, and we'll have a few flagons together for the sake of old times. Hoping this finds you as it leaves me, Edward, Rex, etc.' And a fine elegant hand he writes too, Inspector. 'Tis pity I haven't the card here now to show you. I had it in state up there on the mantlepiece until yesterday when Peter, the scoundrel, so far forgot himself as to light his pipe with it. So, to make up for such a sad catastrophe, I was thinking of asking Fonsy to compose a bit of a song in honour of the event. Something with a swing to it, like:

> "Says Edward, King of England,
>   To the King of Carriglea,
> 'I'm dropping down to Waterford
>   So be sure and come to tea.'"

"Sergeant," ordered Inspector Lalor sharply, "you'd better keep your notebook ready to your hand. Mr. Coady seems to think he can talk treason under our very noses and get safely away with his cleverness."

"Treason is it? Was it treason I heard you to say?" Jer, in all his injured innocence, looked up to heaven as though expecting an angel, complete with flaming sword, to come down and testify to his loyalty. "Wisha, Din, but I thought you had more sense. 'Treason,' says he, when there's word, hand, and promise between me and the King!" He turned to his assistant. "Let

25

you repeat it to them, Peter, seeing as how they don't choose to believe the word from my mouth."

Poor Peter, anxious to avoid all taint of Fenianism, yet incapable of deserting old Jer in his hour of need, spoke up. "It may seem very strange at the first glance, Inspector, but Mr. Coady there is telling you the truth, He did indeed receive a fine, ornamental invitation to a tea party or a garden party or some other class of a party that's being given to, by, or for His Majesty below in Waterford to mark the occasion of his graciously condescending to come and open the new bridge."

Lalor raised his eyebrows. The sergeant cleared his throat and spoke for the first time since his entry. "I hope, then, that His Majesty will not be enthertainin' many other angels unawares."

"Thank you, sergeant," said Jer politely. "I must remember you very kindly to His Majesty when we get down to our little *tête-à-tête* among the teacups."

"Well, to come back to business." Lalor was a trifle brusque but otherwise unshaken. "All I wish to convey, Mr. Coady, is this: Even if His Majesty is after inviting Fonsy Farrell and yourself to spend the next twelve months in Buckingham Palace and to play Forty-five with the Royal Family for a month of Sundays, that doesn't affect what I came here to tell you." His voice became more its official self. "Ireland is struggling back at last towards peace, order, and prosperity. The forthcoming visit of His Majesty, King Edward, will be a great help in the consolidation of that fortunate state of affairs. Now, it is my duty to suggest to you, and through you to others, in a friendly way, of course, that it would be not only a great crime but a great pity if any unseemly incident during the royal visit should spoil the present peacefulness of our country. We, the police, will ensure that no demonstration or disturbances take place; but if none is even attempted it will make life much easier for all of us. What little nuisance a few malcontents can cause will actually hurt no one but themselves."

"By the lord harry, Inspector, you have an eloquent command of the King's English," admired Jer Coady. "Yet, if

26

you'll pardon me asking one small question, who would be so downright foolish as to stir up any trouble against Edward the Peacemaker? Isn't he, by all accounts, a wonderful man? Wasn't I reading in the paper, only the other day pages and pages about how magnificient a king he is and all the great favours he is going to confer on poor Ireland by his visit? And I was reading, too, about the steadfast loyalty Ireland has now for the Crown. So would you tell me who'd be so scatterbrained as to think of stirring up any trouble against so benevolent a man?"

"Nobody, I hope." Lalor laughed uneasily. "Nor will there be any trouble even if any body does think of starting same. I'll ensure that. I'm merely letting you know how things stand, Mr. Coady, for your private information. I trust that Mr. O'Dea here has got all I said off by rote in case that weak memory of yours might fail you on a sudden and that you might forget both the things I told you and the wonders you read in the papers."

Jer Coady rose up from his chair as Lalor, with the faithful sergeant at his heels, turned for the door. "And I," he promised, "won't forget you either, Din. When King Edward and myself are hard at work, drinking down the strong tea and snapping up the buttered scones, I'll speak out straight to him, and I'll say, 'Ned, my man, Your Majesty,' I'll say, 'you have a policeman working for you out in my part of the country, a man by the name of Din Lalor, and if ever a man was wasted in a backward country place, 'tis he. In charge of the police in London he should be.' I'll say, 'or at the head of an army, or administering some nice handy colony the like of New Zealand, or head boss over a sizable wedge of India.' Oh, I'll put in the good word for you, Din, never you fear."

Lalor smiled again, correct and polite to the last. "I'd take good care, if I were you, Mr. Coady, that I wasn't sitting amongst my good words one of these fine days, with the bars of a prison cell between me and Carriglea." And, courteously ushering the sergeant out, he slammed the door shut behind them.

Over the lush beauty of high summer and through the quiet of the twilight hush the south wind came sighing up the estuary from the distant sea, hinting in its own quiet way of romance and mystery, of fairy lands beyond the far horizon. But the soft south wind brought no solace to the heart of the angry Resident Magistrate, whose plans had been set askew, whose evening had been disturbed, who was now in some doubts as to whether or not he would be fully groomed in time to see His Majesty open the State Ball. And still he counted himself a trifle fortunate, if one must look for a silver lining, in having his old friend the colonel as his guest. This special charge against a ballad singer or travelling poet or rural songmaker, or whatever the fellow was, would surely amuse the colonel and would give the Resident Magistrate an opportunity of displaying his own wit, sagacity, and legal acumen in dealing with the wild Irish. . . .

The Resident Magistrate balanced his small body well forward on his toes and strove to have the watching colonel understand that, even while he so balanced himself, he was at one and the same time both deep in thought and yet aware enough to be master of the situation and of the little group gathered before them. With due deliberation he balanced back onto his heels again.

"Singing treasonable songs in the street, Inspector Lalor," chirped the Resident Magistrate. "Drunk and disorderly, Inspector Lalor. Inciting other drunken villains to congregate together to the general annoyance of our Sovereign Lord the King, his Crown and Dignity: These are grave charges, Inspector Lalor. Grave charges, Inspector Lalor. And what has the culprit to say for himself if the culprit has anything to say for himself? And what did you say this man's name was, Inspector Lalor?"

"Farrell, sir. Alphonsus Farrell."

"Fonsy Farrell the poet," enlarged the aforesaid culprit.

"Hem! Ha! A devotee of the Muses, eh, Colonel? Well, Mr. Fonsy Farrell, poet, and what have you to say for yourself? Is there any good and cogent reason as to why I should not consign you to prison here and now?"

"If I may make so bold, your honour," and the Resident Magistrate wondered at the resonance of the voice which came booming from behind the two policemen who guarded Fonsy. "If I may make so bold," and now that the speaker had come forward the great beard seemed even more alarming than the great voice, "I would like to point out that, while it is within the prerogative of Your Honour's clemency to dismiss this charge, this actually trifling charge, against Mr. Farrell, your power otherwise merely allows you to remand him, on bail or in custody, to the next Petty Sessions."

The Resident Magistrate frowned. He hoped the colonel had not noted the impertinence of the interruption. The Resident Magistrate turned on Lalor. "Er-em, Inspector! Inspector! Who is this man? What is his business here?"

"Those two men, sir, are friends of the accused who came to offer bail for him in case he is remanded to the Sessions. They are both schoolteachers, a Mr. Coady and a Mr. O'Dea."

"Hm! Hmm!" The Resident Magistrate went back to his heel-and-toe balancing, a bit uncertain now since Jer Coady had out-thundered his thunder.

It was the prisoner who broke the brief spell of silence. "Sure, what had I only a couple of bottles of bad stout?" demanded Fonsy, aggrieved. "An' what did I do only sing a few verses of a song that I was after makin' up myself in honour of such a famous occasion?"

"Silence in court," said the Magistrate sternly.

"But didn't Yer Honour ask me, there a few minutes ago, if I had anything to say for myself?" complained Fonsy, now more aggrieved than ever.

Peter O'Dea could have sworn that the colonel winked at him. "I think, Herbert," suggested the colonel smoothly, "if you don't mind me butting in, old man, that it would be a deuced sensible idea to have our bibulous friend, Fonsy, sing his song for us. The song must be, after all, the chief exhibit in the case."

"A very good suggestion, Colonel." The Resident Magistrate hoped that he sounded sufficiently patronising and yet justifiably grateful. "Highly irregular, of course. Highly irregular but quite feasible in the circumstances. Now, Farrell, my good man. Let's all hear this song of yours."

Fonsy, who seemed on the verge of tears, wiped the back of one hand across his mouth, raised his voice in a melancholy monotone:

> "Ye gentle muses, assist my genius,
>   While I endeavour for to relate,
>   The sights I seen by the sweet Suir River.
>   The Tenth of July was the date.
> There youth and beauty were brightly gathered,
>   The grandest sight any man could sing.
> And all the heroes of all the nations
>   Were thick as flies round our Gracious King."

"Bravo," cried the colonel.

"That doesn't sound at all treasonable to me, Inspector Lalor," announced the Resident Magistrate, who had high hopes of yet marrying his eldest daughter to the colonel's only son. "Nothing treasonable there, Inspector Lalor! As for the charge of being drunk and disorderly, any man, in the enthusiasm generated by such a memorable day as this, might very easily err in computing his own capacity. Eh, Colonel? Eh, Inspector? Therefore, Inspector, while I have nothing but praise for your zeal and attention to duty, I think that since our poet, Mr. Farrell, possesses an escort of two seemingly sober friends who will, I am sure, take him straight home if requested to do so, I think, therefore, Inspector Lalor, that, taking all the circumstances into consideration, I am fully justified in dismissing the case with a caution."

"I have further evidence—" began the Inspector.

"The case is dismissed," declared the Resident Magistrate, hoping the colonel was duly impressed by his firmness.

"As you wish, Your Honour," answered the Inspector, fully as tired by now of the Resident Magistrate as the Resident Magistrate was of him. "But, in strict fairness to myself and my men, I might mention that the words and sentiments of his song, as sung just now by the accused, were vastly different to those used and expressed by him below in the town."

"I have told you, Inspector Lalor, that this case is dismissed." Little red patches of anger flushed livid beneath the Resident Magistrate's cheekbones. "You may go, Inspector Lalor, and take your men with you."

The policemen saluted smartly, clicked heels, and departed, the stiff correctness of their demeanour a silent protest against the major's decision.

"And now," said the Resident Magistrate, "I have a warning for you two bailsmen. Get your friend outside the borough boundary within an hour. Because I promise you, Mr. Fonsy Farrell, poet, that if you come before me again, drunk, sober, or inspired, you will not find me as lenient as I have been this evening."

"Indeed and I'm very grateful to Yer Honour," averred the grateful Fonsy. "And if Yer Honour wishes, I'll sing another song for you now, a grand, entertaining song like *The Palatine's Daughter* or a sad one about poor Parnell such as *The Blackbird of Sweet Avondale*."

"We're going home now, Mr. Farrell," Jer Coady interrupted, cold, prim, polite. "If we don't hurry him up, Major, Your Honour, he'll still be speeching here when his hour's grace is ended. Good night to you now, Major, and to your kind friend." And with a polite, jerky little bow he hustled the wordy Fonsy out the door before him, while Peter O'Dea, silent and smiling, marched, faithful, at his heels.

The Resident Magistrate relaxed, turned to smile at his guest. "And there you see, Colonel, the way we handle our problems in Ireland. The human touch, Colonel, or rather, the humane touch. A little bit of fair play, Colonel. A modicum of broad-mindedness. A spirit of give and take on both sides, Colonel, and there we have three potential police-made rebels, loyal men for life, Colonel, by the quality of mercy unrestrained."

The colonel laughed quietly, chose a cigar from the box on the table, stared at it critically before he spoke. "Oh, well, Major, I told you before that it's not my line of country. I'm accustomed solely to dealing with men in the field. None of your civil administration for me, thank you! Now, not knowing our three departed friends, I can only rely on a quarter of an hour's personal observation. But in my opinion the prophet with the beard is not a loyal man and never will be a loyal man. He looks to me like a born rebel."

"That's perhaps the beard," suggested the Resident Magistrate sweetly. "That kind of beard always reminds me of Parnell."

"Then," went on the colonel, fondling his cigar, "we have the Shakespeare with the unlaurelled brow, our alcoholic Fonsy. I would have dearly wished to hear the song he actually was singing when your policemen picked him up. And I'll swear the King would enjoy it too. Damme, old Ned is a sportsman with a damn fine sense of humour."

"And the third?" asked the Major.

"The young fellow? A good-natured poor devil like myself, willing to run his head into a halter to oblige a friend. But I have one very good reason for thinking that the two seasoned Johnnies may be dangerous men. And why? Because, Major, they seem to be men of spirit, and yet they were more obsequious than Lalor's policemen. I always find a man of spirit is most dangerous when he cringes, Major. That shows he has made his pride a servant to his will. And when a man can make his own pride subservient to other motives and purposes, he is then a very dangerous man."

"They seemed harmless enough to me," confessed the Resident Magistrate, a little troubled now by his recent benevolence.

"The bearded gent, at least, had no desire at all to run foul of the law. I'll wager that he has read Fonsy a pretty severe lecture by this for opening his poetic mouth too wide." The colonel paused to light his cigar, then cheerily clapped a hand on the Resident Magistrate's shoulder, "Oh, buck up, Herbert, and don't take such trifles to heart. We'll have no rebellion yet, not in our lifetimes, and who are we to worry over what may happen when we're snug in our graves?"

32

Down the hill, on towards the new bridge that was still gay with bunting, the other three were marching, steadfast and silent. Only when they had crossed the bridge itself and left the gay and festive city behind them, did Jer Coady's anger at last come seething through his beard.

"Blast you and blast your drinking, Fonsy the fool! 'Tis through no fault of you and your black bottles that the whole three of us are not caged above in Ballybricken gaol this night with half the tinkers of the world and all the fleas of Ireland for company. Had you nowhere else to sing your illiterate songs only under the sniff of Lalor's long nose?"

"Am I a prophet to know he'd be listenin'?"

"And who do you think he'd be listening to? A few old dowagers chirping God Save the King? After I telling you and telling you again to play safe and innocent and steer clear of trouble! What's the sense in drawing suspicion down on ourselves before ever we're ready, before we're even started to get ready?"

Fonsy gave ground but counterattacked with a certain astuteness, "A man of a poetic frame of mind has to say out whatever he thinks. Sure I couldn't help but say what my genius called on me to say, not if there were two thousand Lalors listenin'."

"And I suppose it was the poetic frame of mind that had you down licking the fat major's boots above, with your, 'Yes, Yer Honour,' and your 'No, Yer Honour,' till you had my stomach sickened and the major's head was swelling as big as his fat belly, and he puffing himself up there like a toad, showing off before his old butty of a military man."

"Still, he gave Lalor a short knock," ventured Peter.

"He did," retorted Jer, "because he wanted to show the colonel that he could boss the police just the same way as he could lord it over us. Besides, the way our beauty of a little lap-dog of a Fonsy here was wagging around his toes was enough to wring a heart of stone."

"What else could I do?" queried the indignant Fonsy. "Didn't you say yourself, one single minute ago, that you wanted no trouble? And what else was I trying to do but taking the easiest way out of the trouble I was in already? Isn't it a feather in anyone's cap to have it to say that they codded the major up to the whites of his eyes? The fat little lump of consequence, thinkin' he rules the world, begor, and him not fit to stand straight before a middlin' strong breeze of wind! Aha, but the same major will long rue the day he left Fonsy Farrell go free!"

"Aye! You'll make up a rhyme about him, I suppose," said Jer Coady sourly.

"Listen," interjected Peter O'Dea, "we're far beyond the bridge now, and Jer and myself are bailsmen no longer. I think, Fonsy, you should do the decent thing and, after all the trouble you put us to, at least let us hear this famous song that Lalor took such a poor view of."

Jer Coady halted. "I'm shocked and outraged and scandalised, Peter O'Dea, to hear a nice, quiet, sensible boy like you egging on to his own destruction a poor, miserable fool of an idiot that can't drink a bottle without preaching all our secrets into the ears of the peelers. And how are we to know that Lalor and his bloodhounds are not sniffling at our heels this very minute?"

Fonsy raised a hand in admonition. "Order an' silence," he demanded. "A little bit of order an' silence! I am now composing a song to preserve for all posterity the history of myself an' the major."

"There you are, Peter," said Jer with all the fine resignation of a martyr on his way to the stake. "That's what you get for encouraging the fool."

"*The major stood in his castle hall*," began Fonsy.

"In plain fact," interrupted Jer nastily, "it was neither a castle nor a hall, but a mouldy old drawing room in his mouldy old house."

"All right! All right so!" Fonsy made a gesture of resignation. "I'll start it different for you if you're so particular.

"*The King was waiting to start the Ball,*
But the major stood in his parlour hall
For, on the spot, without rhyme or reason,
Alphonsus Farrell must be tried for treason."

34

"Good man, Fonsy," praised Peter. "You never lost the gift."

"God above," asked Jer Coady, "what had the man to lose?" Fonsy, in the embrace of the muses, paid them no heed.

> "The tall dragoons stood around in pairs
> And the big hussars lined up the stairs."

"The artillery, I suppose," said Jer, "were all in the ballroom waiting for the supper to begin."

> "And his brow was pale but high was his head,
> When bold Fonsy Farrell into their midst was led."

Jer Coady caught the bemused poet by the shoulder. "Peter, like a willing lad, would you take this madman under the other oxter till we cart him home to his bed before he persuades himself either that he walloped the whole British Army single-handed or else that, overpowered by legions of foemen, he was hanged, drawn, and quartered as another martyr for ould Ireland."

Chapter Three

I F, DURING all the happy years he spent in Jer Coady's company, Peter O'Dea had any grumble against the older man, such complaint was in no way related to Coady's cooking or Coady's washing, or any other of his odd ways around the house. These vagaries, though often uncomfortable, were never more than fit subject for joke or laughter. The one thing which irked Peter was the fact that, as the pair of them grew more friendly, the bearded one grew more and more obsessed by the dread lest some day a designing female would succeed in enticing his model assistant away from him into the bonds of holy matrimony.

Peter was the more hurt because the fear was so ill-founded; for he, in his own quiet way, was in as little danger of falling victim to any woman's wiles and charms as was old Jer himself. Peter O'Dea had been a shy boy. He had grown up to be a shy man in no way inclined to take chances with even the plainest female. Whether that was due to his nature or to his Clare cuteness, or to the fact that he had never yet met a girl worth wasting the second word on, remained an undecided question. Be that as it may, he felt a little aggrieved when, if ever he did happen to pass the time of day with a neighbour's daughter on the way home from school, or chatted a moment with some fair soprano after choir practice on a summer evening, inside two seconds Jer would come sweeping down on them, beard abristle, and tuck Peter in under his wing like a hen saving her lone chick from the questing hawk.

Therefore Peter O'Dea, after due deliberation, began to figure out and think over little plans for playing a small joke on Jer Coady and for hitting the King of Carriglea a hard blow where it would do the most good. And when opportunity knocked he was quick to avail of her offer.

The old schoolhouse, like some fading maiden lady, had for many a day been striving to hide the ravages of the years under coat after coat of the best paint. But when two rafters and part of a gable-end came down one night in a January gale, even the canon realised that no amount of renovation could stretch its life further. So a new schoolhouse was soon rising up on the top of the hill, just across the road from the old one. As the new school grew, stone by stone, so did the debt grow with it, until both Jer Coady and Canon Costigan, neither of whom were men to worry over trifles, became more and more dismayed at the frown which wrinkled the bank manager's brow every time they asked him to add a few extra pounds to the parochial overdraft.

Both being practical men, they ignored for the moment their personal feud and attacked their common problem in a variety of practical ways. For the best part of a year Carriglea was almost as gay as Dublin itself, there were so many concerts and raffles and card-drives and every other species of catchpenny organised to gather funds for the new school. Yet all too soon the day arrived when everyone, except the born gamblers, was sick and tired of the recurring card-drives; when there were more people willing to sell raffle tickets than were ready to buy them; when there wasn't step-dancer or singer left in the ring of the parish but their every note and caper was known by rote to the faithful few who could still be persuaded to attend the concerts. The overdraft had been greatly reduced, it is true, by such sustained effort, but still remained sizable enough constantly to bring King Coady and Canon Costigan groaning from their soundest slumbers.

Then it was that Peter O'Dea startled the staid school committee with a new suggestion. The people of the parish, he stated, might be tired of concerts, turned against card-playing, sickened by the sight of raffle tickets; but there still remained one method at least of attracting both themselves and their money. A good play, declared Peter, a play with as many characters in it as you could possibly find room for, a play in which you picked most of your actors from the more prosperous sections of the community, a play in which you got all the local funny men onto the stage at one time or another—such a play, Peter maintained, was the very thing that would bring the customers flocking up in hundreds so that you'd find yourself having to close the doors and turn money away before ever the curtain rose.

Jer Coady, willing to clutch at any straw, backed the scheme from the first. The canon proved harder to convince, for, if he had one eye on the red figures in the bank manager's ledger, he had the other eye fixed just as firmly on the bishop, who missed little above in his episcopal palace. To avoid any clash with his ecclesiastical superiors, Canon Costigan was more in favour of bringing over the Mooncoin champions to play a hurling match and charging a silver shilling at the gate. But the bishop was thirty miles away, while both the bank manager and Jer Coady were very near at hand, so in the end he had very little option but to give his sanction to Peter's play.

The whole affair being Peter O'Dea's unaided suggestion, it seemed only right and proper that he should be made responsible for transferring it from theory into practice. With the help of a few hindrances from Jer Coady, he selected a suitable drama. But when it came to choosing the actors his real troubles commenced. First there arose the problem as to which of the two Gormans, Andy or Ned, was to be included in the cast. Peter, who had long been friendly with Ned, argued that, man for man, there was no comparison between the brothers, and pointed out also that, when the good looks and the brains were being handed round, the Gorman fairy godmother had got a bit mixed up in her mission and, while giving Ned a double dose of both, had missed sight of poor Andy altogether.

Jer Coady agreed thus far, not being able to dispute known facts. But, possibly because he thought Peter was getting a wee bit uppish and needed to be shown who was master of the house, he argued round the point for a full hour. He emphasized that the Gormans, snug and well-connected, would object to seeing the younger son on the stage and the elder left to cool his heels amongst the audience. Many a one might think, he said, that Ned was chosen because of his friendship with Peter, while Andy was passed over because of an odd hot word about politics which had passed between Jer Coady and himself. If such an idea once got into people's heads, Jer maintained, the public would fight shy of the play from the first, lest they be accused of taking one side or the other. Moreover, argued the acute Jer, since there was no living man inside Ireland, or outside it either, who was less likely to make a good play actor than the same Andy Gorman, the mere fact of him being on the stage at all would bring in the whole countryside, if only to jeer.

Peter fought to the end, but the best bargain he could make was to confine Andy to a moderately small part in which he couldn't make too much of a fool of himself or a fiasco of the play, and to get Ned appointed as a money collector at the door, which was, as Jer carefully pointed out, a far more responsible position.

But not till the question of the female parts came up did Coady really kick the stars. No woman, he stated, should be allowed on any stage under any circumstances. Women, he said, were so goddamn' busy acting all day and every day off the stage that damn the one of them could ever do any bit of acting when and where she'd be supposed to do it. If they did in their folly select two or three girls who would air themselves on the stage, the other women of the parish would raise such a rumpus that the hard hand of jealousy would crush the play before even the first rehearsal could be held.

Peter, however, handled old Jer very craftily, answering all his arguments with courteous cunning. If they ignored the female sex, he pointed out, they would only succeed in making a general laughing stock of themselves and their play. And as regards the question of jealousy, Jer could rest easy, because Peter had found that ladies anxious to win fame as actresses were scarcer in Carriglea than strawberries in December. Only three, he said, were willing to face the wrong side of the curtain. The first was Mrs. Sullivan, the publican's wife, a big, jolly woman with a long string of a husband and a long tail of a family, who was friendly with everyone and everyone friendly with her. The second was Miss Sexton, the mistress in the Girls' School, who had not much of her youth left now except a few well-dusted memories and who was so much in awe of Jer Coady that she scarcely counted as a woman at all. The third, and here Peter burst his bombshell, was Julia, the widow Stapleton's eldest daughter.

That announcement fairly took Jer Coady's wind away from him. Rightly or wrongly, he had long suspected the same Julia of having an unhealthy interest in Peter's future, and so when his breath came back he strove tooth and nail to ensure she'd grace no stage that Peter trod on. But Peter, ready for just such an emergency, had all the right answers at the tip of his tongue. She was the daughter of the richest woman in Carriglea; she was convent-educated; she was a leading light of the Ladies' Altar Society; she had proffered her services; and, in Peter's opinion, if they should be so foolish as to slight her, the mother would head straight up to Canon Costigan with a complaint. Even if they could talk the canon over to their side, they couldn't stop Mrs. Stapleton from airing her grievances long and loudly enough to ruin their plans.

Were Jer Coady not so shrewd a man he might have fought to the death on this matter of Julia Stapleton. But if two other women were left in the cast, while Julia, who might be expected to make a better actress than either of them, was passed over, it would be obvious to Peter, and to more than Peter, that Jer had a personal spite against her over and above his well-known opposition to the sex in general. And the reason why Jer Coady had his knife in the widow's Julia would be shrewdly surmised and quickly belled through the parish. The wily Jer sensed that if he himself were accused of victimising the Stapleton girl, Peter, feeling she was wronged, would begin to feel sympathetic towards her; and Jer Coady believed that once a man began to feel sympathetic towards an acquisitive woman, matrimony stared him in the face.

So, with a great show of graciousness, breathing fair play and benevolence all over his beard, Jer Coady added Julia Stapleton to the chosen band of actors and actresses, vowing in his own mind that courting Peter O'Dea would prove no part of her official duties and comforting himself with the assurance that, after a couple of hours rehearsing with such a scatter-brain as the widow's daughter, Peter's own common sense would soon make a quick end of that young lady's ambitious ideas.

Peter O'Dea, for his part, was more than satisfied with the night's work. In his own quiet way he was tasting already the fun he hoped to enjoy, playing off Jer Coady against Julia Stapleton and Julia Stapleton against Jer Coady, and steering a nice straight line himself between the two of them. Being, too, a very prudent young man, accustomed from childhood to take a careful look before ever he leaped, he had examined his scheme over and over again and could find no possible danger in it save one. Overeager to tantalise Jer, he might venture too far into Julia's clutches and be enmeshed in the bonds of matrimony before ever he could shout for help. Yet, after a reasoned assessment of all Julia's charms and an equally careful consideration of her faults, Peter formed a convinced opinion that, short of suffering from any sudden softening of the brain, he had nothing to fear from the widow's black-haired daughter.

It so happened—whether by some strange chance or through some subtle design only Peter O'Dea could say—that at the climax of this play which was to charm all Carriglea the hero was supposed to kiss the heroine. The public, who knew the hero was Jer Coady's Peter and the heroine Mrs. Stapleton's Julia, waited impatiently for the night of nights until they could see with their own eyes the actual outcome. Nobody doubted, for instance, but that Julia Stapleton would be only too willing to do her share. On the other hand, long before the first rehearsal, bets were being freely made all over the parish as to whether Peter would have the nerve—or the stomach, unkind people said—to kiss his fair heroine; or whether, even if Peter was willing to go through with it himself, Jer Coady would ever allow such a sacrilege to be perpetrated.

A month went by, slowly enough for all concerned, and when at last every player reported, word-perfect and ready for action, the first rehearsal was held in the old schoolhouse. That same rehearsal gave satisfaction and confidence to all those, and they were many, who had wagered their good money on Jerry Coady. None had been admitted save the players themselves, but the news was soon broadcast that Jer, as stage manager, had ended the play a second or two before the actual kissing scene. Moreover, Fonsy Farrell, who might be expected to possess most of the old master's confidence, was remarkably willing to lay any odds, either in money or in black porter, against the embrace taking place even on the night of the performance. "What ye have to remember," Fonsy would say very wisely, "is that Canon Costigan, and the Lord knows what other clergymen besides, will be sitting up there in the front row. And would it be likely that any cuddling or courting, either play-acting or otherwise, will be allowed to be demonstrated under the very nose of the parish priest?" The wise men, therefore, suspecting that, although the voice was the voice of Fonsy, the words might still be the words of Jer, grew naturally reluctant to lay down their money on any side except one.

There the case might have rested and all curiosity and interest might have died an early death had not Packey Regan, who, young though he was, had bet a nice little bet on Julia Stapleton's ultimate success, decided he was not going to lose his money without a fight.

At the last rehearsal but one he gained a seat beside the fair Julia when their presence was not required on the stage. "Isn't it a terrible pity," declared Packey, all innocence, "that Jerry Coady, th' oul' cod, won't be satisfied to let the play end the way it should end? God knows but anyone would think a single solitary kiss would melt that big sugar-babby of a Peter O'Dea."

Julia Stapleton, petulant, tossed her head. "I think Mr. Coady is more than right," she announced. "Kissing and suchlike carry-on should not be encouraged in public, whether on a public stage or on a public road. Besides, even if you could kiss him a thousand times, what girl in her senses would want to kiss a molly-coddle like Peter O'Dea, who hasn't the grit nor

42

the gumption to know his own mind, but trots around like a little pet lamb, afraid to do anything except what hairy-face tells him to do!"

"Many's the girl," stated the wicked Packey, "would gladly jump a nine-foot ditch for the chance of kissing Peter O'Dea, even allowing him to have no more grit or gumption than would fit on the point of a needle."

Julia tilted back her head. "Their taste must be all in their teeth, then, like Bob Andy's drake."

"An' many's the girl I do hear sayin'," continued Packey, "that it mightn't be Peter O'Dea who's so lackin' in the grit an' the gumption at all, an' that if any girl with a spark of spirit were to be standin' in Julia Stapleton's shoes, she'd make no more bones about kissin' poor Peter than she would about eatin' her breakfast."

"You're a very sweet liar, Packey, for a lad so young"—ignoring the fact that she was only three weeks older than he—"but I'll make a suggestion to you now which will surely please everybody concerned. If you name out to me a few of those willing beauties, I'll go straight to the girls concerned and tell them that Julia Stapleton, who knows well what spite and jealousy she's up against, is only too ready to let one or all of them step straight into her own place and let them see for themselves how much of a shake they can take out of Beardy Coady and his tame assistant."

Packey took off his cap, scratched his head. "I always aimed, Julia, to live long an' die happy, an' there was never a man yet who named names between women an' lived after to comb a grey hair. But, mind this, name them all out to you I could, an' if you were to hear some of them names you mightn't be so content to let them get within a hand's clutch of Peter."

"Wouldn't I so?" asked Julia, and sat silent for a moment. "Well, let you, Packey Regan, carry back this message from me to all these brave girls of yours. Let you inform them from me, Packey, that I'm going to kiss Peter O'Dea forninst the whole parish the night of the play, and what's more the kiss I'll give him will rise blisters on him a foot high."

43

Carriglea has no June races and no August horse show where the ladies may air their finery and swop scandal with their friends, so that, although the coursing of the hare is not, when all is said and done, the most fitting sport for the female sex, yet the belles and beauties of the parish, if they were to show off their fashions at all, had no option but appear at the Carriglea and Killrone United Coursing Clubs' meeting, which was held at Moonbawn every Twelfth Day. That post-Christmas function was the biggest, and only, social event of the year, if one excepted the Barndarrig boat races in July. Therefore, every marriageable maiden, from Ballyvarna down in its glen by the river to Tubberjames snug above on the hills, craved and crimped and saved in order to appear in some new wearable at Moonbawn on the sixth day of January.

That long field, staked and wired down the centre lest the spectators, interested or otherwise, get mixed up with the running dogs, was always early athrong with earnest sportsmen; and it was not until midafternoon, when the dinner-delph had all been washed and the sun had aired the day, that the ladies ventured forth in all their glory. Then for an hour or two would they dominate the field, strolling up and down in pairs and threes and parties, waving to friends, nodding to relations, staring saucily at foes and rivals, all oblivious of the mud and the mire which was ever and always an integral part of that particular Moonbawn field in wintertime.

And there it was, on the afternoon of the very day on which the concert was to be held, that Miss Julia Stapleton staked her luck on a gambler's throw and, walking stiffly away from her two sisters, made so bold as to address Peter O'Dea where he leaned, lonely, against the wire fence.

Normally he would have shied away from her, panicky as a young horse who meets a steam roller face to face, but he knew full well that the details of this meeting would be quickly conveyed back to Jer Coady in Carriglea and would lose nothing in the telling. Such public action on Julia's part suited Peter's little schemes to perfection. Besides, he was long ago bored by the coursing, and Julia's chatter would at least while away the time.

44

"Good day, Mr. O'Dea," she greeted.

"Good day, Miss Stapleton," he answered.

She smiled up at him. "It's not every day, Mr. O'Dea, we see you loose in the great wide world without your guardian angel standing over you, beard and all."

"Jer doesn't like the coursing," said Peter gravely. "And although, the day being so cold, I'd have liked to bring the beard along, I couldn't very well do so when the boss himself was remaining at home."

Julia giggled, returned without a blink the haughty glare of two girls of the Mullalleys. "All joking aside, though, you don't often venture out on your own. Do you never think of going to a dance? There was a wonderful dance down at Mulhall's on Sunday night. Or was it on New Year's night? I've been to so many dances lately I forget which. No! It was Sunday night. At Comerford's the dance was on New Year's night. But any of the dances weren't a patch on Mulhall's. Such sport! There were lads there from Carrick and from Ross. 'Tis a great pity you don't dance, or don't go to dances, I mean. Sure, I hear you're a great dancer."

"Very little I ever danced," answered Peter, wondering how she could say so much and talk so quickly yet never lose breath. "I'm not much inclined for it, somehow. I'm fond of the music, you know, and I'm all for a good bout of stepdancing; but otherwise a verse of a song or a good game of cards, quiet by the fire, is more in my line."

"A quiet hand of cards!" She pouted. "And the brave Jer Coady hiding the ace behind his beard, I suppose. And the great poet, Fonsy Farrell, rhyming out of him with every card he plays, every bit as good as Shakespeare in his own opinion if in nobody else's. No wonder you're so dead in yourself on the stage when that's the kind of company you have to put up with in your free time from the school.

"Oh, now," said Peter, annoyed, "you can't expect any man to put the same heart into a rehearsal as he would into the play itself." He grew daring. "You might find your leading man a very different proposition tonight from what he has been up to this."

"I hope so, indeed," Julia tried not to show her elation at what she deemed a battle won. "And I'm sure you won't let our famous Jerry Coady ruin the play tonight with his foolishness, stopping it short before it reaches the artistic climax. That's what heart-scalds me. I was mad about the drama when I was at school in the convent; and now, when I do get a chance of appearing in a play, even if it is only in Carriglea, Jerry Coady, the old ignoramous, must make a mock of the whole thing by cutting the end off it and never letting it come to the artistic climax. Look at the way his codology is ruining the play and making mummies out of all the players! How can anyone be expected to act artistically when they know an old idiot is not going to let the play accumulate to its artistic climax?"

"The fact can't be disputed," Peter admitted, swamped by so much eloquence and such a profound knowledge of the dramatic art.

"Well, then," continued the temptress, "I think the solution to the problem and the end of all the difficulty is in your own hands, Mr. Peter O'Dea. Let you point out to old Coady that not to allow the play to proceed to its artistic climax will ruin the poor play altogether; and that, unless they know the play is going to proceed to its artistic climax, he can't expect the players to give an artistic performance." She smiled at Peter, her most charming smile. "You will point that out to him, Mr. O'Dea, won't you? He'll understand when you explain it to him. The only reason why I want to see the play carried on to its real finish is because I want to be able to do my best in front of my mother and all the friends she's bringing with her. And you see, having always been so fond of the drama, I can't really act unless I know there's going to be a proper artistic climax."

"Well, I'll do my best endeavours," stated Peter, committing himself to no definite promise.

"I knew you would," she said, smiling her gratitude. "I must fly now. Good-bye, Peter." She moved swiftly towards the two Mullalleys, who, their tour of the field completed, were again

46

passing by. "Good-bye now, Peter," she called loudly as she joined them. "Good-bye now, Peter, until tonight."

The shades of evening were thick across the valley when Peter, determined on having his joke out to the end, faced Jer Coady across their narrow teatable.

"I was above at the coursing," opened Peter cautiously.

"There was never man from Finn MaCool's time right down to the present minute was or is fonder of coursing than I am, but, since the meeting place was shifted from Ballyvarna to Moonbawn, I never saw two dogs slipped. When old Din Lalor, the big peeler, bought Moonbawn, I swore I'd never set foot on any land of his; and, much though it galls me not to see the running dogs race, by the lord harry I've kept firm to my word."

"There's not much sense in keeping up the bitterness now that the old man is dead."

"The old man, Peter, properly speaking, is not dead and never will be while seed or breed of his holds that house and land. Besides, bad an old blackguard as the father was, he was a straight, blunt man who did his duty as he saw it in a straight, blunt way. He was a tyrant and a renegade and a Queen's man to the marrow; but he was an enemy you could meet fair and square in the open, not like his foxy weasel of a son who will never do anything above-board if he can accomplish it under-hand."

"He was good enough to give you a warning all the same that time there when the King came to Waterford," Peter reminded.

"He was good enough to give me a warning," Jer thundered back, "because it well suited his own book to warn me. If anything did happen, do you see, his own slate was clear, because he had given ample warning to Coady, the Fenian. In the same circumstances old Din would have met me by accident on the road and we'd have had a nice, quiet private chat and maybe settled the whole matter. He'd never have done like the son—come marching into my kitchen in the full panoply of the King's law, with a henchman by his jowl, to peep and pry and pick up any information or suspicion that he could from every word and gesture." Coady busily brushed crumbs off his beard. "I'm telling you, Peter, the difference between father and son is this: Old Din was a renegade and a gentleman. Young Din is a renegade and a cur."

" 'Tis a wonder to me so," said Peter, "that, in the first place, he allows coursing meetings on his land at all; and that, in the second place, such a patriotic body of men as the Carriglea Coursing Club would be beholden to Lalor for the loan of his field."

"Patriotic! Patri—" Jer Coady choked a mouthful of tea back into his beard whence it spewed out in a fury of fine spray. "Patriotic, is it? You'll find goddamn few patriots around Carriglea when patriotism puts a strain on the pocket. Lalor gives them the field free! I can't very well call traitors to the Coursing Committee for accepting Lalor's offer when not a single nationalist farmer in the parish would let them have a field for their purpose unless he set own price on the privilege."

Jer snorted and glared at Peter as if he were one of the guilty ones. "By the lord harry, young Regan below, who hasn't a bite in his belly or a brain in his head, has more patriotism in his little finger than you'd find in half the big farmers of the barony if you pulped them all together. You can't instruct me, Peter boy, about the great patriots of Carriglea. Patriots indeed! I could name the patriots out for you and needn't take the second hand from my pocket to do so." He picked up his cup, wrinkled his nose at the contents. "Blast it, Peter, my tea is gone cold over yourself and your parlour patriots!"

Peter decided that now was the time to skirmish towards the play and its artistic climax. A certain panic descended on him at the memory of Julia's endearing farewell before the eyes of the two Mullalleys. If she did manage to kiss him on the stage it could be that, willy-nilly, a certain section of the parish would at once accept her as the logical suitor for his hand. And Peter, who had no intention whatever of venturing out on the sea of matrimony, had even less desire to begin such a voyage with the voluble Julia for his partner. Determined not to let his own joke prove his undoing and equally anxious to harass Jer to the last, he made his opening move.

"I think we're going to have a full house above tonight. The play was the principal topic at the coursing."

"Was it so?" asked Jer Coady, not impressed. "And, by the lord harry, so well it might. If 'tis half as bad in reality as it was in rehearsal, it will need no epitaph from Fonsy to have it remembered forever. I've read my share of plays, from Euripides to Oscar Wilde, and I've read my own share about plays from the earliest times to the present day, but, by the snikers, there will be a new level set in play-acting this night that will endure till God gathers the nations together in the Valley of Jehosaphat. Every time I watch ye on the stage, Peter, I say to myself, 'Lord, what a poor, futile, posturing creature is man.' And I thank God that the poor author is not here to see his brain-child stuttered to death by twenty congenital idiots with potatoes in their mouths."

"Well," went on Peter, firing his broadside, "we have one professional touch about the performance anyhow. The leading lady is becoming temperamental."

"The leading lady!" echoed Jer Coady with studied calmness. "Our leading lady is turning temperamental. Julia Stapleton is contracting hysterics! Fancy that, now! The creature! And where did you pick up that important item of news?"

"She told me herself this evening," answered Peter carelessly. "I met her above at the coursing."

"Temperamental! Temperamental, no less! And who was so kind as to spell out that big word for her to use? And who gave her any right or permission to go temperamental? Isn't she only in the play on sufferance and because we could get no better? By the lord harry, Peter O'Dea, you must have sweet damnall to do if you must talk to Julia Stapleton at coursing matches in order to kill the time. Wouldn't it be fitter for you set a couple of greyhounds after her to chase her for her life and off yourself to the beer tent for a fine philosophic discussion about the future of the human race with whoever you might chance to meet at the counter?"

"Actually," declared Peter, trying to muster his dignity to

49

his own defence, "I wasn't talking to her. It was she who was talking to me. And she never used the word temperamental at all. I deduced from what she said that she was turning temperamental."

"That girl could never become temperamental," decided Jer Coady, sitting in judgement. "She couldn't even become a mental case, never mind a temperamental one. A certain amount of grey matter at the back of the face is needed to become either, and that girl has about as much brains as a goat has wool. If you shook her head you'd raise a rattle could be heard in Waterford."

"Be that as it may," persisted Peter, "she's our leading lady; and the fact remains that she's not satisfied to have the play finish as it does in our version. She maintains there's no sense in holding a play at all if it's not played out to its artistic climax. And she says, too, that when there's no artistic climax, she won't be able to do her artistic best."

Jer Coady, unruffled, whistled a slow bar of *The Foxhunters' Jig*. "I see! Oh, I see! Yerrah, the poor little girl! Begor, but 'tis a great pity to deprive her of her artistic climax." He reached up, took a pipe off the mantel-shelf, had half-filled it when on a sudden his anger boiled over. "By the god of Carrick, that squint-eyed little trollop is safe enough if I don't make an artistic climax out of herself and her temperament! And what does she know, is it any harm to ask, about artistic climaxes?"

Peter kept the smile from his lips, replied with due solemnity. "She says they taught her a lot about the drama when she was at school in the convent. She says she was very fond of the drama always. She made reference to Shakespeare."

"Holy Father in Heaven tonight," prayed Jer Coady with great fervour, "and what harm did Shakespeare ever do to her? And what reference did she make to him?"

"Well, she mentioned his name."

"I see. I see, begor. Oh, that's today's great thought. The name of Will Shakespeare in the mouth of Moll Malone's Julia! Ah, there never was such times. Oh, begor, I'm sure that sent the poor Bard of Avon threshing round in his grave." He considered a moment, then gestured gravely with his pipe. "Peter boy, you're in dire peril from that woman, and you'll be very well advised to leave your defence absolutely and entirely in my hands. First of all, we must get safely through this night. Let you tell her, if you like, that she can have twenty-four dozen artistic climaxes, but I promise you I'll spend every minutes of that play with my hand on the slip-knot of the curtain rope. And the very first move Julia Stapleton makes towards staging an artistic climax, I'll stage the last artistic curtain and to hell with the audience."

Row on row the massed critics of Carriglea sat facing the stage—Canon Costigan enthroned in the very front line, flanked on his left by Mrs. Molly Stapleton, flanked on his right by old Ned Gorman from Ballyvarna. Beyond them, on either side, the front bench was filled by relatives of the other leading players and by the remaining plutocrats of the district, some excited, some bored, some laughter-racked, their state of mind depending on whether they had come to see their children win glory, or had turned up because they felt that duty demanded their presence, or had merely rambled in to be vastly and uproariously amused by the sight of sensible work-aday neighbours making of themselves a public spectacle.

Behind, half the district sat, crowded together on benches that went back and back until the prime boys, who preferred to form the rearguard of the audience, found themselves hemmed in between the last packed bench and the end wall. But, even in their cramped quarters, these boisterous gentlemen had found much to amuse them this night. The sight of so many old friends posing in such unaccustomed attitudes and mouthing such unusual sentiments had held them spellbound for a while. Even the dignified entry of Andy Gorman, in a frayed dinner jacket, to announce, "Ladies and gentlemen, lunch is served," had nonplussed their first titter into silence. But he had soon reduced them to tears of merriment when, in attempting to walk backwards off the stage with all a butler's innate pomposity, he collided with a side-scene and fell, bringing down a whole wall of a ducal dining room in his fall. To free himself he kicked out wildly and went crashing back over the edge of the stage, leaving a great gap where the side-scene had been, through which the astounded audience secured an intimate view of Julia Stapleton arranging her hair. And, as if to shake the solemnity even of Canon Costigan, there came a bull-roar from the anguished Andy, prone in some dark beyond: "Ah, Janey mackerel, me back is broke."

That the play survived at all after such early disaster was due in equal measure to Jer Coady and to Peter O'Dea. Jer bullied the scared players behind the scenes till they charged out on the stage to escape the fury of his tongue, being more afraid of his blistering sarcasm than they were of the audience which howled beyond the footlights. Meanwhile on the stage Peter strove so effectively that time and time again he won back even those who gibed loudest to a silence which they maintained only until the reappearance of the humbled Andy Gorman renewed the howls and whistles and ribald comment.

However, despite the growing good humour of the house, the first and second acts were, at last, safely over, and the third was well on its way. Jer Coady, wet with perspiration, stood just off stage, thanking his stars that further calamity had been avoided. Then, behind the drop-scene, he heard the rascally Packey Regan hiss a few words of advice to the temperamental Julia Stapleton.

"If you're goin' to kiss Peter," Packey warned, "your one hope is to do it this minute, at the beginning of this last part, and not wait till the very end at all. Coady will have his two eyes glued on you towards the finish. He'll be watching you like a hawk. If you do it now, Coady will be took by surprise and the people lookin' on won't know the differ. Off with you now, and good luck to your venture." And onto the stage she went before Jer Coady could make move to stop her.

Graciously, as befitted a duke's daughter, she flounced across to where Peter was giving some order or other to Andy Gorman. Whether she meant to obey Packey or not must remain a matter for conjecture to the end of time, for, just as she reached them, Andy, in turning to march off, collided with her and sent her flying straight into Peter's arms. Julia, toppling, draped her arms around Peter's neck; and Jer Coady, prompt to his word, let the curtain fall. The audience, or that portion of it which was not standing already, rose to its feet, and the whole hall cheered itself hoarse, there being but three people present who did not loudly hail such a dramatic and artistic climax—Canon Kieran Costigan, Mr. Edward Gorman, Senior, and Mrs. Molly Stapleton.

Jer Coady shook a slow head above the supper table. "By the lord harry, Peter, but you had a narrow shave! If that woman had brought her scheme to perfection this night, you'd be as good as married to her by now, and that would mean, in plain language, you'd be condemned to death for the rest of your mortal life."

Peter rubbed his face tenderly. "Even so, she needn't have given me such a slap across the mouth when the curtain came down. If she wanted to strike anyone, she should have belted the man who pulled the rope."

"Aha, and doesn't that demonstrate the breed of the vixen in her?" announced Jer comfortably. " 'Tis a great wonder to me she didn't spit in your eye."

"Still," said Peter, turning dour, "the girl got provocation enough, being made a show of before the whole parish, her mother and Canon Costigan and all. Her acting spoiled and herself publicly disgraced. She'll be the laughing-stock of the country for ten years to come."

"My own poor opinion," chimed in Fonsy Farrell, silent till now, "is that to be laughed at never done anyone harm. An', while what happened tonight might prove the daunting of many a woman twice her years, bedamn but it knocked very few feathers out of Julia Stapleton. When I was coming along just now, didn't I see her stepping off for home with a man under her wing!"

"By the lord, Peter," cried Jer, winking at Fonsy, "it didn't take that lassie very long to forage out fresh woods and pastures new! You didn't, by any chance, Fonsy, see who it was?"

"I did indeed," assured Fonsy, puffing at his pipe. " 'Twas none other than my great gom of a stage actor who spent this

53

night failing to come to any reasonable agreement with his own two feet. No one else but the brave Andy Gorman, an' he lookin' so pleased with himself as if he was after winning the first prize in a raffle."

Jer Coady jumped up from the table, raised his right hand solemnly. "Peter! Peter! Let this night be a warning to you, boy, now and forever more. Place not thy trust in woman, Peter O'Dea, for they are fickle cattle that desert their leading man, at one moment's notice, begor, for a glinkeen whose only contribution to the dramatic art was to fall off the stage on his bottom!" He slapped his thigh, gave a great guffaw. "By the lord harry, Fonsy, maybe that's her idea of an artistic climax!"

Chapter Four

DESPITE the occasional attentions of amorous females anxious to succeed where the ambitious Julia Stapleton had failed, Peter O'Dea and Jer Coady lived out many a happy year there in that box of a house below the straggling street of Carriglea. There they grumbled through many a soft, wet spring while the blue skies won an annual battle with February's fogs ere the harshness of March came to dry the land in readiness for April's showers. There they drowsed away many a summer, with every May a flower unfolding, and every leafy June a green-robed memory of beauty, and every warm July a sun-filled prelude to the promise of autumn's plenty. There August spilled her riches on the orchards and the cornfields; thither, to every hedge, September brought red haw and clustered blackberry; there October piled the haggards high with garnered oats and white wheat and long-bearded sheaves of whispering barley. There the village ramblers came gathering round Jer Coady's fire when the long, long nights of Christmas came dragging from the black depths of winter; and there, as the pair munched through their early breakfast, they would watch the blind on the east window for the first greying of the reluctant January dawn.

To both of them there must have come a time when it seemed impossible that their happy round of life could ever change. Curates came and went, inspectors flared and faded; but still, resplendent in their long white petticoats, the infants came whimpering into Peter O'Dea's classroom year after year, an endless line. Year after year their eldest brothers and their older brothers and, finally, they themselves sent word to Jer Coady some summer morning that they were "out of all books"—their schooldays done. And many a morning after, the teachers, marching up to school, would meet their one-time pupils perched high on some rattling creamery cart, peaked cap pulled mannishly down over one eye, grinning self-consciously at their former masters or else insolently turning their heads away from all reminders of the slavery they had left behind.

Never a summer vacation came but one or two of the more brilliant pupils, and an occasional specimen who was not so brilliant, vanished from all human ken to appear thereafter only at those well-spaced times when, from the grey seminary in Kilkenny, the students came joyous home on their hard-earned holidays.

It was a custom in Carriglea that before they returned again to Kilkenny the collegians should pay a state visit, singly or en masse, to their former teachers. At night they came and because the students' presence always scared away the regular visitors, Peter O'Dea found the nights of these visits the most uncomfortable of all nights in the year. The visitors, when young, were ever too tongue-tied to speak unless spoken to; and as they grew older and grew learned in many things they sometimes shrouded themselves in superior silence, convinced that the earth-bound National Teachers had become their intellectual and social inferiors.

No matter whom boredom claimed for victim at such times, Jer Coady always remained immune. Nor, if he suspected that one of his pupils had fallen into intellectual pride, did he ever spare the culprit. A snobbish answer would light a spark in Jer's eye, making him ask meekly:

"And what class are you in now?"

"I'm in the Senior Grade," rather proudly.

"Ah! I see! And what Greek books are ye doing?"

"We're reading the Peloponnesian War."

"And what part of the Peloponnesian War are ye reading?"

"The Siege of Syracuse," getting a little impatient now.

"I see! And what poor fool of a man set brainless gomerils like ye to read the Siege of Syracuse? Ye that could no more understand its implications nor profit from its instructions than could this pipe I'm holding in my hand! Will you speak

56

up now, boy, and expound to me the lessons you learnt from what Thucydides had to say about the Siege of Syracuse?"

"I learnt Greek from it," with a fine air of defiance.

"Aye, begor! You learnt Greek from it! And did you learn from it that a city or an empire or a people that grasps and greeds too much must surely meet disaster? An' did you learn from it that the men who were left to toil and moil and bake and shiver as soulless slaves in the stone quarries of Syracuse were the proud citizens of Athens? The men who, up till then, thought themselves the salt of the earth and the light of the world? And did you ever think how it was arrogance and avarice brought them down? And did it ever enter into your head that, from what old Thucydides had to say, you could spell out for yourself a nice little parable much nearer to us both in time and place? Ah, but sure you'd never dream of the like. How would you have the time to think so deep, my poor boy, and you so busy learning your Greek?"

Or to some neophyte theologian he would say in all the deception of his mildest voice, "Ah, and what English author are ye tearing to pieces above in the College these days?"

"We do study Thackeray."

"Ah! I see! So ye do study Thackeray. *Pendennis,* I suppose, and *Vanity Fair* and *The English Humorists* and *The Four Georges*? And what's your own opinion about our friend Mr. Thackeray?"

"I do rather him to Dickens, sir."

"My God, Peter," Jer Coady would cry, rising from his chair. "Eight years I wasted! Eight good years of my life gone for nothing that I spent trying to enlighten this addle-brain! To read and to write I taught him, to reel off his catechism and to do sums in his head; and, lookit, at the latter end of it all he walks in here to my own house, as bold as a billy-goat, and tells me out to my face that he prefers Thackeray to Dickens!"

But while Jer Coady could be ruthless in warring down any ex-pupil who tried to air before him a fancied intellectual superiority, only Peter O'Dea knew the time and trouble he took in helping the lame dogs among them over their stiles.

There was, for instance, the case of Mina Mullalley's son, long noted for being the dullest lad in Carriglea school and who was packed off to the College to fulfil a dead uncle's dying wish. Every time thereafter that Jer Coady heard the boy's name mentioned, he would mutter into his beard wise saws about silk purses and sows' ears and swear that the Grace of God must be very plentiful up around Mullalley's if they hoped to make a priest out of that fellow. When Neddy Mullalley's first holidays came round he incurred Coady's further displeasure by failing to appear at any of the seances between Jer and his former pupils.

Not till the very last night of the Christmas vacation was there a timid knock on the teachers' door and a small, scared Neddy Mullalley edged himself into the kitchen and sat himself down on the uttermost edge of the chair nearest the door.

Jer Coady glared round at him. "Aha," he cried, "and who have we here? Is it yourself that's in it, Neddy Mullalley? Well, a happy New Year to you, Neddy, long though it took you to come and see us. You were too busy, I suppose, transforming yourself into a gentleman and a scholar. I'll wager that ye do have the life of Riley above in the College, Neddy Mullalley, running and racing and kicking football and hurling and playing handball."

"We do," admitted Neddy Mullalley with a watery, wintery smile, scuffing his shoes nervously on the tiles and busily seeking to recall past joys that they might tide him over present sadness.

"And tell me now, Neddy Mullalley, what do they teach ye up there in the odd intervals between all the ball-playing?"

Neddy stopped his shoe-scuffing, rhymed off a list with the air of a man who wished to speed through an unpleasant task with the least possible delay. "Greek an' Latin an' English an' history an' geography an' mathematics an' Celtic—that's Irish —an' Christian Doctrine." His feet swung a little, stopped again. "An' we do have science," he added, after a pause.

"Indeed!" Jer Coady puffed leisurely at his pipe. "And how much Irish did they teach you? Would you put Irish on this sentence for me: 'The schoolmaster is smoking his pipe'?"

There was no reply.

"Aha! I suppose that's altogether too simple for you, Mr. Mullalley. Oh, you must be striding through the fields of learning like Cuchullain swept through the Connaughtmen. But I hear that they hold an examination every month up in the College. I hope you're a credit to us all in the examinations, Neddy Mullalley."

Still was Neddy silent, and his silence only irritated Jer the more.

"By the lord harry, seeing how you're getting on so well above in the College, Neddy Mullalley, I suppose we needn't be surprised if we hear of them ordaining you within the next year or two."

A loud, whimpering wail silenced Jer and brought the tender-hearted Peter striding across the kitchen to comfort the afflicted one. "Sure, there's nothing to cry about, Neddy boy. Sure, Mr. Coady was only codding you for the sake of a bit of fun."

Neddy, unconsoled, only howled the louder. "I hates the oul' College!" yelled Neddy Mullalley, desperate now. "The teachers do be at me because I can't learn anything, an' all the boys do be laughin' at me too, an' sayin' I'm a f-fool. An' I'm afraid to go back! An' I'm in dread to tell me mother."

"Bring him over here to the fire, Peter!" Jer ordered.

Peter enthroned the weeping Neddy in his own chair by the hearth. "I think, Jer," he said, "we have a bottle of lemonade outside in the pantry."

"There's some brand of fizzy poison there." Jer Coady spat out at the thought. "I drank a mouthful of it by mistake one night lately, and the taste is on my tongue yet. But since the boy is used to no saner nourishment in the drinking line, 'twill hardly do him much harm."

Coady did not speak again until Neddy had dried the tears and gulped down half the bottle of lemonade. Then he said, kindly enough, "If you don't feel like going back, boy, and if you're afraid to tell your mother, you needn't let such things trouble your head for one minute longer. I'll tell your mother for you, Neddy Mullalley, and the telling won't knock a feather out of me. Did you ever hear, Peter, of the time I had to go down to Ballyvarna and inform Mrs. Hope-Jones, who used to live in the Big House, that her only son was after running away with a streel of a tinker girl? Begor, it took a whole decanter of brandy to recover the poor woman from the shock —that's, of course, counting in a small nip or two she forced on myself to help me through the ordeal."

"You've set him crying again on us," Peter warned. "What ails you now, Neddy? What have you to cry about now? Mr. Coady here will speak to your mother and then you need go back to college no more."

But Neddy, hopeless and helpless, still blubbered.

"Ah, cheer up boy!" encouraged Peter. "Wait till I get the fiddle and play you a few tunes."

"But 'tisn't how I don't want to go back to the College," exploded Neddy, all tears.

"'Tisn't what?" demanded Jer Coady. "Ah, sure it isn't. 'Tis only, I suppose, that you're like the rest of us and don't know your own mind betwixt one minute and the next. And who could blame you for such a small failing, Neddy Mullalley, when it's a like story with the rest of mankind?"

"I do so know me own mind," contradicted Neddy, suddenly grown resolute. "I wants to be a priest, an' that's why I wants to go back to the College. An' what I'm mostly in dread of is that they won't keep me because I'm so slow to learn. An' how can I learn when all the teachers do be at me, an' all the rest of them do be jeerin' me for bein' so slow? Will you tell me that?" turning fiercely on old Jer.

Jerry Coady stretched out, grasped the youngster's shoulder in one huge hand, swung him round so that the lamplight fell full on the boy's face. "By the lord harry, your father left you his fighting eyes; and, though I never saw it before in you, you have your own share of the Mullalley fighting heart. Dry up those eyes, Neddy, and back with you to your College to-morrow morning. And the first young hooligan that calls you a fool, give him a slap in the puss for himself to show him his mistake. And the first teacher that gives out to you because you're slow to learn, let you stand straight up to him. 'Slow

60

I may be,' says you to him, 'but willing I am, and, by the lord harry,' says you, 'I'll have ye all to know that 'tis the sworn opinion of Jer Coady from Carriglea that I'll make as good a priest as ever wore black in this diocese or any other.' "

"If I had my way," Jer Coady informed Peter O'Dea, "I'd build neither school nor college in any city or town. Out in the lone heart of the country I'd build my college, with the green grass all around it, and the singing birds above it, and the blue skies its only wall. And instead of that, what do they do? They coop young, eager fellows up behind stone and mortar to try and make them clever or to teach them to be holy. And what is all their carry-on but the height of nonsense, Peter, the very essence of tomfoolery? If a man is minded to be holy, his surroundings are odds a differ to him. A man can be as saintly walking down Sackville Street in Dublin as he could be perched on the top of Slievenamon Mountain, and vice-versa. To my way of thinking, it should be just as easy for a man to feel pious when he's dancing a waltz as to feel pious when he's saying a litany. But then, Peter, as you know yourself, the deadliest sin of both church and state is that neither is broadminded enough to follow in any matter, spiritual or temporal, the simple principles laid down by Jer Coady."

For the second time he raised his umbrella and stabbed the ferrule against the front-door bell-button of Saint Kieran's College. The door opened promptly; and Jer, beard first, umbrella martially aslant over one shoulder, marched boldly past an astounded manservant into the entrance hall.

"Whom do you wish to see, please?" asked the dazed porter.

"My good man," said Jer, "will you trot along now and tell the President that Jer Coady from Carriglea would be glad to have a few words with him."

"I'm afraid, sir, that the President is engaged just now."

"Well, you needn't be one bit afraid that the President won't disengage himself when you tell him I'm here. Run along now and don't cause me to complain about you to His Reverence."

Puzzled, the man departed, leaving Jer chuckling in his

61

beard, nudging Peter with his elbow. "That's the way, boy! That's the way to get things done! Always carry yourself with an air of authority, Peter, and before you know where you are people will be loading authority upon you." He paused, frowned. "Yerrah, 'tis no use giving such advice to you, Peter O'Dea. You're too good-natured to hoosh crows away from a field of wheat."

The door of the waiting hall swung open, and the President of Saint Kieran's, the sharp lines of his biretta a fitting match for his clean-cut features, was at their service.

"I think I have the honour," he said pleasantly, "of addressing, for the first time in my life, the mentor of some of our most brilliant students. I am extremely glad to meet you, Mr. Coady."

"The pleasure is reciprocated, heartily reciprocated, my dear and reverend sir. And this, Father, is a boy I have working for me, my assistant, Peter O'Dea."

The President bowed slightly to Peter O'Dea, and Peter O'Dea bowed slightly to the President.

"Yes," said the President, "when I was a young professor here, in those happy days when I was a young professor here, I flattered myself that I could always know a Carriglea boy. When I came in to face a big class of new boys each September, and when I saw a lad, a bright intelligent lad, well able to stand up for himself and to speak up for himself, a mine of information on every subject under the sun, 'Aha,' I used to say to myself, 'here's another product of Carriglea, here's another of Mr. Coady's geniuses.' Oh, you left your mark on them, Mr. Coady. You left your stamp on them, sir. You left your personal stamp on them, sir."

"All but the beard, Father," ventured Peter, daring to jest. "No one can imitate or emulate that. That's his own personal copyright."

"Jealousy! Pure jealousy," cried Jer in a stern effort to conceal his pleasure. "This lad here knows well that he's easily my equal now in the craft of teaching. He knows the beard is the only advantage I have over him now. Ah, by the lord harry, I have to keep a sharp eye on this assistant of mine. Jack is as good as his master now, Father, and there's a throne shaky beneath the King of Carriglea. Still, there's more to be done for any pupil than merely to teach him how to read and write and add up figures. So, when I was coming up here today, I said to myself. 'Jer, my boy,' says I, 'bring the bold Peter along with you to the College and show him that he can't go through life acknowledging all the geniuses among his scholars and at the same time let the dumb-witted gossoons muddle out their own damnation.'"

"That's a very noble thought. A very noble thought," agreed the priest, although it seemed to Peter that the good man was more than mystified as to the purpose of Coady's visitation.

"I wouldn't call it a noble thought, Father." Jer was positive but not rude. "Jer Coady, in all the years he taught school and trained scholars, never believed in setting anyone a task beyond their powers. I never let any but the cream of my pupils advance to the College, and perhaps that's why you have come to form so flattering an opinion of me. But the Lord lays snares for all our petty prides, and He caught me out as neat as you like." Jer Coady sighed. "You have a boy lately started here, Father, by the name of Neddy Mullalley, Edmund Mullalley from Tubbernalaca."

"Mullalley, Mullalley," repeated the priest, wrinkling his forehead, dragging up the names of two hundred pupils from the files of his brain. "Oh, yes. We have a young Mullalley."

"You wouldn't count him up to the usual Carriglea standard, Father?"

"Well, of course, Mr. Coady, I have very little to do with him directly. If we're both thinking of the same boy, I do recall someone saying that he is, how shall I put it, a trifle backward? He may improve in time. Many people's brains and genius don't flower until comparatively late in life."

"Neddy Mullalley's genius won't flower even if he lives to be the age of Methuselah's cat. You can't squeeze whey from a stone, Father," declared Jer Coady. "Yet, while I never came to see president or professor about the clever boys that went through my hands, I'm up here today to put in a good word for the dullest dunce that ever sat on a bench in Carriglea School."

"And a word from you is not to be lightly treated, Mr. Coady." The President smiled on his callers. "I can assure you that I, personally, will look after his interests. Our friend Neddy may not be as backward as you seem to think he is."

"Backward!" cried Jer Coady. "He's thicker in the skull than that stone!" striking the blackstone wall with his umbrella. "But, if he is dull, he's the makings of a better priest than many a lad who has more brains in his little toe than Mullalley has in his whole carcase. He has the determination, Father, and he has the vocation; and a priest he'll be even though he has to eat the books in order to learn them.

"In that case, you need have no fear for him," assured the President, jovial now. "If he has the Call from Above, God will give him the Grace to overcome his slowness."

"He will no doubt." Satisfied, Jer Coady stroked his beard. "But the word of encouragement, once in a way, might prove a great help to the same Neddy Mullalley. Along with that thick skull, he's unfortunate enough to have a very thin skin; and, as I'm sure you've often noted yourself, Father, the two together can be a very poor combination."

"I understand perfectly," said the priest.

"But no coddling, of course. That's no line to take with one of the Tubbernalaca Mullalleys."

"I understand perfectly," repeated the priest, a trifle impatiently. "We have a certain amount of experience with boys ourselves, Mr. Coady. Now, after such a long journey I'm sure your assistant and yourself wouldn't say no to, at least, a cup of tea." And he led them in through a stone corridor to the panelled parlour beyond.

It was in February that they had descended on the College to attend to the welfare, spiritual, temporal, and eternal, of Master Edmund Mullalley; and it was on a moist April evening, with a soft mist dripping from the first of the leaves, that Jer Coady sprang his big surprise on the quiet Peter.

They had, in their haphazard fashion, washed up the dinner-delf. Peter, on the settle, sat reading the *Freeman's Journal* and idly speculating as to the length of Kaiser Wilhelm's moustaches. Jer stood by the window, staring out at the grey veils of rain which had obliterated the peaks of Mount Leinster and far Slieve Coillte.

"How long are you with me now, Peter?" he asked suddenly shaking the water from his hooked pipestem.

"Ten years," answered Peter carelessly, without raising his head. "Ten years on the third of next July."

"Begor," said Jer Coady, "but 'tis short it took them to go for ten years. Well, I remember the first night you came and the meek, mild face of you, standing there at the door after some sly-tongued Waterford jarvey had put the heart across in you by his yarns about the cracked madman of a Jerry Coady you were coming to live with. 'Tis wonder to me still that you didn't faint away when I opened the door to you, black beard and all. And then Fonsy to come in half-jarred, hard on your heels, with his muse in full bloom."

Peter looked up from his paper, laughed. "A job in a madhouse was better than no job at all. I decided to stand my ground, no matter what, for the sake of the few pounds at the end of every month. And you can't say, Jer, but that I've stuck on well."

"You throve on it! What age are you now, Peter?"

Peter O'Dea put the paper down, stared at his principal's uninformative back. "I'm on my way to thirty-seven."

"And I'm sixty today. There's a long gap between us yet, boy." Jer Coady came to the end of his thinking. He put his pipe in his pocket, turned back to his chair by the fire. " 'Tis damn well time for you at thirty-seven, Peter, to have a school of your own," he said as he sat down. "I was principal here in Carriglea before ever I turned thirty, and I was a better principal then than I am now."

"That's only your own opinion, shared by nobody else," Peter told him. "For myself, I'd rather be assistant here with you than head man above in the Board of Education. The night that jarveyman brought me here he told me I'd never be short of a laugh in Jer Coady's company. But he didn't tell me a more important fact—that I'd never go short of kindness or friendship either."

Jer leaned back in his chair, "Eeyah, but I'll have to set Fonsy on you, Peter. If ever I hear you talking in that strain again, I'll call in Fonsy to write a song against you. 'The Model Assistant,' I'll have him name it, and 'twill make you long regret that ever you mentioned the word gratitude to me. It's a word should never be mentioned between friends, Peter; and if the word were to be used at all it's not on your side the gratitude would be." He straightened himself up where he sat, spat into the fire. "Now, Peter, I want you to do me a personal favour. I want you to get out your best pen and your best paper. Then I want you to write out, in your best handwriting, a tidy, tasteful application to Canon Costigan above for the position of Principal Teacher in the Male National School, Carriglea."

"You want me to what?" cried Peter amazed.

"And, while you're doing that little job, I'll be writing out, in my own royal scrawl, a decent letter announcing my decision to retire as and from the thirtieth of June next."

"Ah, but listen, Jer," interrupted Peter. "This is all pure madness. By law you haven't to retire for another five years."

Coady's laugh came sweeping through his beard. "Yerrah, wasn't I always 'agin the law,' and isn't madness always linked up with the name of Jerry Coady? Oh, if I stay here much longer, I'll be patting the heads and putting pennies in the pockets of cheeky little brats whose fathers would have run a mile in fear and dread from one waggle of Jer Coady's beard." He fished out his pipe from his pocket. "A man needn't live to be a hundred in order to outlast his time. I'm a legend here now, Peter. If I go from here now, I go while I'm still a name that can frighten infants in the cradle. 'Twould never do to have the tradition of wild Jer Coady, the King of Carriglea, blotted out in people's minds by the sight of a spent old man doddering around the Kingdom he used to rule."

"You're no spent old man," said Peter firmly, "and never will be."

"Anyway," said Jer, "I'm growing tired of this teaching busi-

66

ness. It's all very fine, Peter boy, for people to preach about a teacher's God-given vocation; but when you come to look back on thirty-five years of that same teaching, you'll find you only wasted your time and theirs trying to instill into the heads of Mickey Tom Billy and Neddy John Maggie Joe the great basic principles of reading and writing." He set about filling his pipe. "Oh, the bloom begins to wear off this pedagoguery when you find yourself teaching the second generation to sign and cipher. It all begins to pall, boy, when you discover yourself wearing out brain and muscle in an effort to hammer the self-same things into the heads of the sons that you had to hammer into the heads of their fathers before them."

He lit his pipe slowly. Peter O'Dea, his own pipe alight, brought his chair over, sat before the fire, made no attempt to speak.

"And there's yet another reason, Peter, why I think 'tis high time for me to move. Canon Costigan above, you know yourself, is failing fast. He's an old man now, with the hand of death heavy on him. When he's gone, the Lord only knows what brand of parish priest the bishop might choose in his place. Any change is a change for the worse as far as I'm concerned. It took me many a year to teach poor old Canon Costigan who was boss in Carriglea School, and I'm too old now to train in a new manager when that training would benefit whoever comes after me far more than it could benefit myself. And if that man be you, Peter, I know damn well you'd rather deal with your own manager in your own quiet, cautious way."

"Canon Costigan," stated Peter severely, "was talking to me yesterday below near Killrone. He mentioned the fact that he never felt healthier in his life."

"Moreover," continued Jer, unshaken, "I'm sick and tired of this flat, fat country, with nothing but heavy-bellied cattle knee-deep in the grass, land where you have only to fling a fistful of corn from you in the spring of the year and then, when the autumn comes, without another trouble, you walk out and find your fine field of wheat standing there the height of your shoulder." He puffed at his pipe. "Ah, Peter, when the years

67

begin to gather down around him, a man grows lonely even in the path of plenty for the far fields that reared him."

"Do you tell me so?" queried Peter sarcastically.

"I'm afraid, Peter," said the placid Jer, "that you're not very strong in your knowledge of the County Wicklow. Were you ever there at all?"

"I passed through it once, in a train."

" 'In a train,' says he! And would you sit content and look at the county Wicklow through the smoky windows of a train? Listen here now to me. One of these fine summers, if ever again there's a fine summer in Ireland, you'll leave the black town of Dublin behind you some sunny morning. Out through Dundrum you'll march on your own two feet, away through the gash of the Scalp and on down the hill into Enniskerry. There, since you have put ten good Irish miles behind you, you'll have a cool pint of ale in some quiet pub and your dinner to follow, for the rise of ground is all before you. Off with you, then, along the swinging road till you reach the biggest pub in Newtown and there we'll let you have another jorum or two and maybe, if the sun is strong, a basin of tea. Up stick with you again and away up the hills and down the hills and round the hills until you swing down with the fall of ground into the neat village of Ashford, with the Devil's Glen to your right and before you the sea and the fair town of Wicklow. But you'll cry halt for none of them. You'll tighten the pack on your weary back, and you'll get an easier grasp on your travelling-man's stick; you'll curse the blisters under your toes and you'll face the hills again, with the sea to your left hand. You'll trudge along a winding road, watching the red hand of the sunset gild all the mountains of Wicklow, and then you'll amble down a little slope into a sleepy village that straggles along a stream. And there you'll say to the first man you meet, 'Good evening, friend,' says you, 'would this be Glenealy?' 'Glenealy to be sure,' he'll answer you back. 'The gate-lodge of Paradise.' And next you'll ask him, 'Is there an old schoolmaster named Coady living hereabouts?' And he'll wrinkle his forehead and say, 'Of a schoolmaster named Coady I never heard tell in these parts; but there's a Fenian man called Jerry

68

Coady come lately to live in that little ivied cottage by the bridge. Although,' he'll say, "you'll need luck to find him there on so fine an evening. He's more like to be away luring the shy trout from some pool of the river, or tramping the hills to sweep the cobwebs from his brain, or arguing a nice point of politics with any mountainy farmer he might chance to meet betwixt here and Rathnew.' Then, Peter, you can say your thanks to the decent man and head down by the bridge and set yourself down at the cottage door to wait for me if I've rambled. Because 'tis there I'm going back to see life's candle out in the spot that saw my birth. In Glenealy, Peter, the gate-lodge to Paradise."

"Very touching indeed," said Peter a trifle sourly, "this sudden *gradh* we've got for Glenealy. Ten years I've lived with you and never before did I hear you fret about high fields that reared you or ivied cottages wherein to husband out life's taper at the close. And where would you find a trout to lure that wouldn't skeddaddle for his life from the first rustle of your beard? I don't know, Jer, whether you've convinced yourself with all your sudden notions and plausible excuses. I do know that you haven't convinced me."

"My dear Peter, I'll tell you the blunt truth so." Jer, eyes atwinkle, puffed steadily at his pipe. "I have no option but to go, and go quickly, if I'm ever to find the future I laid out for myself long ago. For many a day past, Peter O'Dea, I myself have been the most maligned man in Ireland. Far and near they believed that I, Jeremiah Coady, was the complete master, body and soul, of you, Peter O'Dea, my assistant. Isn't that so?"

"Let them say and think what they like," put in Peter quickly. "It makes no button of difference to us what they think or say."

"Ah, but that's not the point, Peter." Jer Coady wagged a sad head. "I never cared a hair for what anyone said or thought about me, lies or truth. But the hard fact of the matter is that Jer Coady is no more master in his own house today than he is King of America. Oh, now, Peter boy, no excuses!" as Peter strove to speak. "Ten years ago, when you first came here, you were a quiet young man and I was a blustering old crank, a black-hearted, black-bearded old consequence, bullying and bossing and besting all before me, lording it as lightly over Din Lalor and the law as I did over Canon Costigan and the church. I was Jer Coady, the King of Carriglea, above criticism and beyond correction."

"Fire ahead," encouraged Peter. "I can see that you're enjoying yourself."

Jer spat into the fire. "Now look at what happened in ten years! Today you're still a quiet young man, unchanged and unchangeable. But, by the lord harry, was anything like the collapse of Jer Coady ever known to mortal man? Sober! Sane! Sensible! Industrious! Never haring off now to drink black porter above in the pub with Fonsy Farrell. Never coming home at ungodly hours, roaring out disgraceful songs, a cause of scandal to three parishes. Never a wild prank out of Coady now—not like the old days when half Munster and the whole province of Leinster would be watching and waiting to see what trick he'd be up to next."

Jer paused, eyes aglint, to review his memories. "I never told you, Peter, about the time the peelers and the bailiffs and the crowbar brigade came to level the cottage of poor Mary Kate the Ducks, Packey Regan's mother?"

Peter shook his head, refilled his pipe.

"Well, I was standing there by the window when I saw the caravan passing by and noted that there wasn't one local man in the lot. Even the peelers were a special draft, just down from Dublin. So up the stairs with me and spruced out the beard. Put on my big gold watch-chain and fetched down from the top of the wardrobe a silk hat I bought for my uncle the Monsignor's funeral back in 1884." Jer drew hard on his moribund pipe. "Out I went then and up the lane to the cabin as fast as my legs could carry me. 'Twas the first time the crowbar brigade had ever come to these parts. The process server and the bailiffs were strangers too, and damn the one else was there save the Regans barricaded in their cabin, for the neighbours had not yet time to gather." He drew again at his pipe.

"You'll have to give me a fill, Peter. This damn thing is burnt out on me."

The dutiful Peter handed over his pouch.

"Up I came," Jer went on, "stepping through the puddles, daintier than the Queen herself. The process server was just for beginning the fun when I minced up to him. 'My good man,' says I very loftily, 'would you inform me what the deuce is going on here.' 'We have to evict these persons,' he says, very civil, 'for grievous arrears of rent.' 'On whose orders?' I demand. 'On the orders of Mr. Tallman, Lord Kilkieran's agent.' 'Indeed,' says I, 'and does Lord Kilkieran know about this?' 'That I don't know, sir,' says the process server. ' 'Tis Mr. Tallman gives me my orders, an' 'tis his orders I must carry out.' 'Do you know me, sir?' I asked him, very dignified. 'I'm afraid I do not, sir,' ' 'Tis no wonder,' I told him, flying into a passion, moryah, 'that this kind of bungling goes on, when even the men who are supposed to be in my service don't know me. I,' says I, making the most of the beard and the silk hat, swelling myself up like a toad, 'am Valentine George Edward Arthur Consonby, Fifth Lord Kilkieran, Baron Carriglea and Viscount Ballyvarna. And I command you to take yourself and your police back to wherever the hell you came from. And, when next you see Tallman, tell him I shall be waiting, up in Kilkieran House, for his explanation as to what the devil he means by evicting my tenants without my consent and in my absence. Good day to you, my man!' said I, pointing back with my stick. And you can believe it or disbelieve it, Peter, but off the whole procession went, docile as a flock of autumn sheep."

"Don't tell me you got away with that!" said Peter.

Jer crowed with delight. "The very next morning Din Lalor, old Din, was in the door to me. He was living above in Killrone at the time, near where the barrack is now. 'Good morning, Mr. Coady,' says he. 'Good morning, Inspector,' says I. 'Fresh and well you're looking and bright and early you're out.' 'I have to be,' says he, eyeing me hard. 'We have some very important visitors in the district.' 'Begor, but we're honoured,' says I. 'We are,' says he, still keeping a close eye on me. 'Lord

Kilkieran is home.' 'After all these years,' says I. 'Ah, by the lord harry, wonders will never cease.' 'They never will, Mr. Coady,' says he nastily. 'For instance, a very wonderful thing happened yesterday morning. At nine o'clock yesterday morning Lord Kilkieran was frightening the life out of a few bailiffs below outside Regan's, and at the identical same moment, according to what Tallman can learn over the electric telegraph, Lord Kilkieran was also having his breakfast in a Paris hotel.' 'Fancy that now,' says I. 'A man to be in two places at the one time! I'd imagine that was a sign, Inspector.' 'So would I, Mr. Coady,' says Lalor sourly, 'a sign of roguery. Anyway, the trouble is over now; for someone, whether 'twas Lord Kilkieran or the lord harry, saw to it that Mrs. Regan raised the money to meet her arrears.' 'Well, begor, Inspector,' says I, 'that's the most amazing story ever I heard. I have a strong notion to write to the London *Times* about it to see could it be explained.' 'Do. Oh, do, Mr. Coady. Let you write the letter,' says he, turning to go, 'and maybe then I'd become inspired and provide the explanation. And, by the way,' says he, from the door, 'I nearly forgot what I came in to ask you. Would you have such a thing in the house, Mr. Coady, as a tall silk hat?' 'I have indeed,' says I, 'and I find it a dam' useful article. 'Tis out there in the back kitchen,' says I. 'I have a hen on top of it at the moment hatching a clutch of eggs.' 'Ah,' says he, 'is it hen-eggs or duck-eggs she's hatching?' 'Hen-eggs,' says I. 'Begor,' says he, 'I was sure 'twould be duck-eggs. 'Twas very slack of Mary Kate not to send you up a few.' "

Peter laughed, then said, "That's all very fine, Jer, but—"

"But me no buts," roared Jer Coady. "I've said a long say, Peter, and you may as well hear even the dregs of it before you commit yourself. You know, Peter, when people saw you agreeing with me in everything, when they saw the two of us got on so well together, they thought you were under my thumb from the time you rose up in the morning until you went back to bed at night. There were times when I thought so myself, when I used to scold myself for keeping you down too much. Ah, but I can see now what I never had the sense to see then—that the boot was always on the other foot. You

72

know, Peter, I completely forgot how deep still waters run, forgot that it is the quiet men who rule the world."

He handed back the tobacco pouch to its silent owner.

"A man like me, Peter, when all is said and done, is full of sound and fury and signifies sweet damnall. I'm always shouting and spouting and talking and threatening and fighting. If there were a rising or a revolution or a rebellion in the morning, the men like me would be off, singing, at the head of it. And maybe we'd stop a bullet in the first scuffle, or maybe we'd finish up as kings of Ireland. But the quiet men like you, Peter, would stay on at home, teaching in the schools and tending the shops and tilling the farms, keeping the whole country in existence so that the loud mouths like me would have something to fight for and something to fight about." Jer paused a second. "And that might be another reason for my going, Peter. You're such a kindly, easy-going, quiet sort of a man that you could very easily make the same sort of person out of Jerry Coady, old though he is. But my heart is set, boy, on that cottage in Glenealy, and my mind set on talking treason among the mountainy men. And, lest you turn me to a quieter way of life, it might be best that I leave before I grow kind-hearted too."

Peter O'Dea put pipe and pouch in his pocket, his face shadowed by the fallen dusk as he rose from his chair. "You had been spouting out of you for over an hour, Jer, at the time it got too dark for me to see the clock. But if you talked for as long more, you'd still be wasting your breath. You've blathered so much nonsense of one kind or another that 'twould take Solomon himself to answer all your riddles. The only answer I can make is very straight and simple. It's merely this, that you'll hear Gabriel's trumpet blow before you'll see a letter from me to Canon Costigan asking him for your job."

"Indeed!" said Jer Coady, tapping the dottle of his pipe ever so gently against the sole of his boot. "I kind of foresaw, boyeen, that you'd prove both stubborn, pig-headed, and generally carnaptious about the whole idea. And so, a week ago, I took two simple precautions at one and the same time. I wrote a strong letter to Canon Costigan, tendering my resignation and nominating you for the post of head teacher here in my stead; and the self-same evening I gave strict orders to Fonsy Farrell to write a rousing, rollicking song praising the new principal teacher of Carriglea. I think, Peter, 'twill be as hard for you recall the one as to suppress the other."

> *Ye gentle Muses, assist my genius*
> *While I endeavour for to set down,*
> *The praises of the famed Jer Coady,*
> *A noted scholar of high renoun.*

That was the first verse of the song Fonsy Farrell made about the departure of Jer Coady out of Carriglea. *The Sorrowful Lamentation of Alphonsus Farrell* or *the Heart-Sadness of Carriglea*, that was the title he gave to his song; and, indeed, he had material enough for lamentation and sadness the day when Jerry Coady, to quote himself in his farewell speech, "bade fond good-bye to the low hill above the river on thence returning to sweet Glenealy and my native heath, there to live forever after, like the man in the fairy story, peaceful, healthy, and happy on His Britannic Majesty's munificent pension of one pound per month."

It was on a rainy Saturday in June that Jerry Coady gave his last farewell to Carriglea, that kingdom where he had ruled so long. There were thunder showers sweeping down in wrathful torrents from beyond the Comeraghs as his bed and his books and his butter-boxes and his beard and himself were hoisted up, in an ever-increasing pyramid of importance, atop of a dray which Packey Regan had borrowed off the publican.

From his perch high above those embattled belongings, Jer delivered his last oration, hugging in a drowning man's clutch the chiming clock which, along with a purse of sovereigns, the grateful parish had awarded him as a reward for his efficiency in beating the A.B.C. into the heads of two stolid generations of its sons. And a remarkable speech it was, even though Jer, in all the misery and excitement of parting, had taken a glass or two more than even his hard head could comfortably conquer.

74

It was a fitting speech, nevertheless, garnished with many an apt quotation from Shakespeare and from Rabelais, embellished by poetic gems borrowed from the lays of Alphonsus Farrell and set off, for some not very obvious reason, by long installments of Robert Emmet's speech from the Dock. Yet, through all these verbal trimmings, the subtle mind of Jer Coady flashed forth here and there, as when he exhorted his hearers to have no qualms in suppressing the female of the species, to whom he attributed all the evils to which flesh is heir, from the Fall of Our First Parents to the rising cost of Guinness' Stout.

Inspired, or perhaps betrayed, by the great occasion, he was in the very act of revealing to an eager world the long-kept secret of his wash-tub wizardry and had actually begun to recite his copyright formula for whiter shirts, when Sullivan's mare, perhaps unused to the wide dray-car, perhaps maddened by Jer's continued insults to her sex, made an entirely unexpected start at full gallop and bore away with her Packey and dray-car and Jer and speech and all.

So the last Carriglea ever saw of Jerry Coady was the sight of him sprawled all over his own old mattress, his chiming clock still clutched safe under his arm, managing somehow to appear both dignified and solemn behind the bush of his beard as the mare, the dray, the driver, the massed pile of Coady belongings, and the distinguished passenger himself swept away around the first turn of the road that led on to Waterford and to the railway station and to distant County Wicklow and to that ivied cottage by the bridge in sleepy Glenealy. . . . And there were those who swore thereafter that the salt tears were wet on Jer Coady's cheeks at his going.

Of a certainty salt tears were brimming in the eyes of Peter O'Dea as he turned back towards that silent house where old Jer had lorded it for so long. With every step, at the sight of every stick and stone, hosts of memories crowded round, dragging him back and back across the happy years, across the carefree years, across the laughing, singing, crowded years, back to that night long ago, when, lonely and a stranger, Peter had knocked on the door that now yawned open before him and had been greeted by those friendly eyes above the great spade beard, had sensed the warm wave of friendliness that pulsed no longer through the tall house now full of emptiness for Jerry Coady.

And even as Peter O'Dea stepped across the threshold the last verse of Fonsy Farrell's elegy on the fallen King of Carriglea echoed and doubled round and through his mind.

> To bring termination to lamentation,
>   Now, once again, I must truly say,
> That, like the chill of some winter twilight
>   When the sad sun sickens at close of day;
> Or like the sigh of the mournful breezes
>   When summer moonlight sleeps on the sea,
> Such to us has your going been, Jer,
>   For it brought heart-sadness on Carriglea.

BOOK THE SECOND

"Good Queen Tess"

My heart's Desire, my Treasure, our wooing time was brief,
From the misty dawns of April till the fading of the leaf,
From the first clear cuckoo calling
  Till the harvest gold was falling,
And my store of joy was garnered at the binding of the sheaf.

—Ethna Carbery

BOOK THE SECOND.

"Good Queen Bess"

Chapter Five

BECAUSE he was lonely and, despite all the assurances that his seven and thirty years should have given him, more than a little afraid on this his first morning as principal teacher in Carriglea, Peter O'Dea held his head high while he walked up the road towards his school.

Never before, in all the years of his teaching, had he faced a major problem without the bulk of Jer Coady beside him, a bearded guardian angel to light and guard and rule and guide his judgement. But today Jer Coady was nesting in far Glenealy, and today Peter O'Dea was confronted with a situation that might well have daunted even the spade-bearded sage himself.

Greedy for human companionship, craving the balm of friendship, Peter rejoiced to find Packey Regan, lately recruited into the ranks of the County Council's workers, already zealously mowing down the long grass wherever it flaunted tall spearheads in the roadside channels.

"God bless the work, Packey," greeted the teacher briskly. "Begor, but you have a fine day for it."

"An' that," countered the talkative Packey, "is what my father, God rest him, said to the Canon above one Sunday long ago. The big collection for the priests of the parish was on, an' the Canon was marchin' up an' down outside the Chapel gate when he spied my father tryin' to sneak in by him unbeknownst. 'Morrow, Matt,' says the Canon, all smiles. 'My collection is on today, Matt,' by way of a bit of reminder to my father, who was long noted as being a trifle shy when asked for any class of subscription. But even the cute Canon took no shake out of my father. 'Bedad, Canon,' says my father,

79

cool an' cunning, 'you have a gran' day for it, thanks be to God,' and off into Mass he went without turnin' a hair."

Peter laughed, although the story was no more new to him that it was to Packey. "I'm sure the Canon steered well clear of your father from that day out, Packey."

"Bedad, he did!" Regan agreed. "Ah, but my father was always a famous man on the tongue. There was a right lawyer lost in him. An' I was just thinkin' there to myself last Satherday that it must be a great heart-ease to the Canon, a decent man, as I an' mine know well, to have my father and Jer Coady both cleared out of his sight, one way or another, within the same twelve-month."

Packey Regan paused, waiting for the schoolmaster's comment. When none came he plunged ahead. "An', by the snikers, you, sir, the same Canon didn't wait long after Coady's going for to show his independence. Begor, 'tis pity, in one way, that Jer Coady isn't dead, till we hear how the world would ring to the sound of him rowlin' in his grave. Ah, bejaney, he'd have clawed his black beard out clean from the roots at the thought of a woman comin' to teach above in Carriglea Boys School."

Still, despite Regan's promptings, Peter did not speak.

"Aye, an' you'll find it a big change too, masther, a hell of a big change. Roses you'll have to grow in the schoolground to suit her, I suppose. Roses an' geraniums an' daffydowndillies, instead of the fine fat floury spuds that poor oul' Jer Coady grew there all his life long. Still, they do say that a change is better nor a rest," squinting up in sly speculation, "an', indeed, this could be a change for the best in every way. It mightn't be so long at all, you know," cheerfully impertinent, "till you find her every bit as much to your liking as Jer Coady was. An' maybe more so, masther. An' maybe more so."

Peter O'Dea avoided the implication, wrinkled his brow, said testily, "I don't even know the girl. I know her name. I know she comes from the far side of the hills. Otherwise I know no more about her than I know of Jer Coady's mother, if ever he had one."

Packey Regan, who, in the bloom of his twenty-fifth year

80

had two main topics of conversation, revolutionary politics and eligible maidens, laid down his scythe happily. "For a young, eligible, well-set-up, good-lookin' class of a man, Peter O'Dea, fit to catch any lassie's rovin' eye, you're more backward in many a way than any block-headed young cnat walkin' in the school door to you above. But then, again, what chance had you all your life with Coady droppin' the beard in front of you the minute you'd come within strikin' distance of a woman, just like he draped the curtain in front of Julia Stapleton an' yourself the famous night of the play long ago?"

Packey, a very wise young man for his years, eyed the uneasy schoolmaster shrewdly. "I wonder was it bein' made such a public show of that led her to take up so quickly with Andy Gorman? Between the way Coady shamed her on the stage an' the way Gorman's father belled him through the parish for trying to marry that servant girl they had, Andy an' Julia took to one another in their misery like a duck takes to a pond. Ah, begor, you, sir, you were seven kinds of a lucky man that the same Julia didn't get you tight into her clutches. Oh, you should be makin' your act of thanksgivin' to Jer Coady night, noon, an' mornin' that she didn't snare you. If she had to find a teacher in her mesh when she drew in the net she spread so far an' wide, she'd have soared to heights of grandeur never known before. Lalor's wife above in Moonbawn would only look like Biddy the Rags compared to her. Aha, but Jer Coady was the right man for her, an' 'twas quick he halted her gallop. He put a full stop to her play-actin', whether off the stage or on it."

"That's all very ancient history, Packey," said Peter O'Dea quietly, "and even what little of it might be true has no bearing at all on the present problem. I want some description of this particular female whom Canon Costigan, in all his wisdom, is dumping into my fine school. I'm looking for a few facts about Miss Teresa Fogarty and not a rigmarole of rambling fancies about the former Miss Julia Stapleton."

"Well, then," answered Packey, "my best advice is for you to make an end of your dillyin' an' your dallyin' an' be off up to your school in case she's there already before you. But, if so be you want information, I'll tell you what I know about her. She's youngest daughter to oul' Flann Fogarty above from Clashmairead in the parish of Tigbawn. 'Tis her brother Fintan that hurls with Mooncoin an', if you want to thresh the matter further still, she's the last of Flann's nine children, an' she has five good-lookin' sisters, but they're all in the penny place compared to herself."

"It seems, Packey," the schoolmaster complained, "that you'll give me her pedigree and her paternity and all her family history; in fact, you'll give me anything except an account of this girl herself."

"Ah, 'tisn't the like of me you'd want describin' Tessie Fogarty to you at all, but someone such as Fonsy Farrell with words at will an' a certain amount of control over them." Packey produced his pipe. "Well, to make a start. In the matter of money—"

"What the deuce has money got to do with it?"

"Will you take your time an' let me tell the thing in my own way?"

Peter glanced at his watch. "Oh, all right. I may as well be late the first morning as any other."

"In the matter of money," continued Packey without triumph, "I doubt if the girl has a silver sixpence to her name, seein' she only finished for a teacher a few months ago an' that the Fogartys are barely dodgin' the hard day all their lives. Although, if it comes to that again, they have an uncle Dick in America, without chick nor child, who owns half Boston or New York or some such place an' is bound to leave them a pound or two when his turn comes." Packey paused for effect. "Tessie herself is a middlin' tall class of a girl with reddish hair an' a gay kind of a way with her. I do often see her up at the dance-board near Three Elms. 'Tis certain that she need never teach a day if she didn't want to, for there's not a marriageable man, rich or poor, in them parts who wouldn't take a fair chance on murder if he thought he'd get Tessie Fogarty as a prize for his trouble. But she shows neither fear nor favour to anyone that she doesn't show to everyone else as well. She'll laugh an' joke with them all, an' she'll cod round

82

with them all, an', in the latter end, 'tis only then they finds out she's playin' every man of them off, one against the other."

"Seemingly a flighty damsel," commented Peter severely.

"The meanin' you an' I might take out of the same word, masther, could be very different. When I say a girl is flighty I mean she's like what Julia Stapleton used to be. An' when I say a girl is gay I mean she's like what Tessie Fogarty is. An' what the difference may be I'll leave you to find out for yourself."

"I'd better," agreed Peter, moving off. "You've kept me well late for my school already."

"A minute more to tell you about her five sisters," implored Regan, pocketing his pipe. "A brother an' a sister died young; there's a weak strain in them Clashmairead Fogartys. The second and third eldest girls are gone off in the nuns. The next one, Judy, was married last Shrove to big Maher from Walsh-hill. The second youngest, Nan, is away somewhere. England it could be. While Kitty, the eldest of them all, is courtin' strong this many a day with Patsy Mullins beyond from Barnarue."

Peter O'Dea glanced again at his watch, slid it back into his waistcoat pocket. "Ten past nine, Packey Regan! Ten minutes of the King's time wasted already. I'll not be in school till a quarter-past, a poor headline for my first day as principal and a very bad example for me to give this gay, or this flighty, Miss Tessie Fogarty."

He went swinging up the road while Regan called after him, "Mind yourself now, masther! Take good care of yourself now! You haven't Jer Coady to drop a screen on her like he dropped it on Julia Stapleton. Take damn good care, now, that she don't take a bite out of you if she catches the scholars with their backs turned."

Peter O'Dea drew a deep breath on hearing the light, quick, firm step come up the gravelled path which led to the school door. He scowled at the five early pupils who fidgeted before him in the front desk. In response to a knock on the door he strove to make his "Come in" deep and ungracious, reminiscent of Jer Coady growling through his beard. Mindful of his manners, he stood up when he saw the first pleat of the black skirt come flouncing through the doorway. Then he turned, solemn and serious, to meet the fate which Canon Costigan had sent him.

Grown accustomed as he was to Jer Coady's bearded visage, to Packey Regan's moon face, to Fonsy Farrell's beer-bright countenance; long reconciled to such as Julia Stapleton's pert prettiness, the entrance of Flann Fogarty's fairest daughter stunned for the instant Peter O'Dea's powers of speech.

Tall she was, and walked with a light, graceful dignity that well suited the frank face, crowned by the high-piled glory of auburn hair. She smiled on him very graciously indeed, came quickly over to his table.

"It makes me most embarrassed," she began, "when I find that my first duty in Carriglea School is to make myself known to the principal. I am Tessie Fogarty."

"I'm very glad to meet you!" Peter shook hands, too confused to return the compliment by introducing himself.

"And my second duty is to apologise. I know it was very incompetent and unprofessional of me not to have called on you beforehand, but really, Canon Costigan gave me very short notice, and I was coming to see you yesterday if the day hadn't turned out so wet. Besides, my bicycle was out of action till Fintan came home."

"Oh, do you cycle, Miss Fogarty?" asked Peter glad to grasp at any conversational straw.

"Not at all," she answered. "I keep the bike in a glass case and throw lump sugar at it every second Wednesday." Then she laughed so easily that Peter, for the charm of that laughter, forgave the snub. "You know, I'm very disappointed at finding you so normal. I was patting myself on the back all the way up the road, full of pride at my own bravery, at dreaming to face in here at all. The shadow of old Jer Coady is so much over this district still that I thought, since you were such a friend of his, you would be very hostile towards any woman who might insult Coady's memory by setting foot inside your school door. Besides, I gathered from the Canon that he never

84

consulted you when he was appointing me as assistant, and I felt you were bound to consider yourself slighted, and justifiably so."

"Not at all! Not at all!" said Peter, anxious to please but uncertain whether he should demolish her fears in bulk or one by one. "Indeed, it is I myself who have been very lax in not seeing to it that we gave you a more fitting welcome to Carriglea, Miss Fogarty. I fear that Jer Coady's long reign corrupted our good manners. But I do hope that, despite our failings, you will like it here and that our association together will prove to be both long and happy."

Not until lunchtime did he speak to her again. As a signal that the daily recess was beginning he had rung the bicycle bell which Jer Coady, in an ingenious moment, had attached to the master's desk in the larger classroom. He was watching the last laggard scholars depart towards the playground when she came, seeking him, smiling but troubled.

"I have to confess that I'm the greatest ninny-head in Ireland," she announced. "I sailed away from home this morning and forgot my lunch basket despite all the times my mother warned me to remember it. So I'll have to depend on you to inform me where in this thriving village, such as it is and what there is of it, I can procure a good cup of tea."

Peter considered sagely. "You could try Doran's," he ventured, "but then the woman of the house hasn't been too well, and I think the father is gone fishing. Or Judy Tom Peg would be only too glad to do anyone a hand's turn, only, in my humble opinion, Judy herself is no cleaner than her house, and when you see the house you'll hardly fancy the tea you'd get in it. You could go down to Sullivan's pub, of course. That's where the lady teacher used to stay I believe, when one was here years ago. But Mrs. Sullivan is seldom at home on a Monday. The son and herself usually head off to town on Monday mornings to replenish their stocks after a thirsty week end." He hesitated, conquered his shyness. "If you don't mind being restricted to bread and tea, you can share with me. I always lunch here."

85

She had been moving away. Now she turned, came lightly back. "I'd love to, if you're sure you won't be stinting yourself. You're sure it won't be too much trouble? Oh, I feel terribly mean to be trespassing on your generosity like this."

"What stint?" Peter's eagerness surprised himself. "There's plenty tea and sugar here. And tinned milk too. Jer Coady had a mania for the tinned milk. A loaf fresh from the shop, a wedge of butter, and your lunch is as good as ready, especially since Jer Coady bequeathed me his oil stove, the most prized possession he had, barring his beard." He stepped out the door, hailed one of the children. "Here! Paddy Joe! Down with you to Bessie the Shop and get me a fresh loaf and a quarter of butter! And here's a penny all for yourself."

They did not get back to a full flow of talk again until the lunch had been prepared and eaten, until Peter, filling his pipe, took the conversational lead for the first time.

"Surely you're not going to cycle up and down to Clashmairead every day? That's a killing journey. Six or seven miles each way! It's bad enough now, but 'twould be a martyrdom in the wintertime. And the roads are terrible."

She laughed, a gay little jingling laugh. "Do I really look as frail as all that? Oh, I'm far and away hardier than you seem to think, Mr. O'Dea. That distance is nothing to me on a bicycle. I've done twenty miles in a day and felt no worse after it. Anyway, I'll only be doing the trip from Clashmairead until the summer holidays come. That will be the end of the month, I suppose?" Peter nodded assent. "After that I'm going to stay with the Maddens of Clashbawn. They're second cousins of my mother, and Clashbawn, sure, is very near."

"Less than a mile down the Ballyvarna Road." Peter, too polite to strike a match while she was speaking, lit his pipe. Tessie Fogarty stood up, began to collect the cups and knives and plates, further legacies from Jer Coady's regime. Peter stared at her, astounded. "What the deuce are you doing? Will you let those few things be? I'm well used to washing them this ten years."

"It's high time you had a rest then." She smiled at him. "A match, please! I want to light the stove. There's just time to heat a drop of water before the children are due in again."

He gave her the matches, watched her set to work. When he spoke, he spoke very slowly. "I suppose, when you hear this, you will say we were two right savages; but it never crossed the heads of Jer or myself to rinse the cups in hot water after our lunch. If we hadn't any spring-water handy to douse them with, we never minded using the rainwater from the barrel outside."

She threw back her head to laugh that silvery laugh again, making smooth muscles dimple in her white throat. "It's a miracle ye weren't poisoned years ago. Or were ye? Maybe 'twas the slap-dash washing-up that made ye the noted pair ye were."

Peter O'Dea looked guilelessly up to where she stood beside the smoky stove. "I never thought Jer Coady and myself were famous enough to draw comment from ye above around Clashmairead."

The laughter had forsaken her lips, had chosen, instead, to sparkle in her eyes. "Famous mightn't be the correct word. Why, when I was a youngster running wild up there, there was only one bogey-man ever threatened on us when we mis-behaved. 'If you're a bold girl,' they'd say, 'if you don't eat your dinner or come in out of the yard or go to sleep,' as the case might be, 'we'll tie you in a bag and give you to Coady, the black schoolmaster from Carriglea. Aha, my girl, you'll be quiet enough when he stuffs you away into that big beard of his.' Oh, and the fear of him lingered on, let me tell you! Until I was sixteen or seventeen I'd duck up a side street sooner than pass by him if ever I saw him coming towards me on the quay of Waterford. And that's the chief reason I didn't come to see you when I knew I was appointed to this job. I was sick, sore, and afraid of showing my nose within a mile of Carriglea while the slightest danger remained that Jer Coady and his beard had not departed elsewhere."

Peter frowned. "But did they, even in Clashmairead, link

87

my name with Coady's when they wanted to frighten their bold children?"

She pondered, a trifle more serious now. "Well, no. I wouldn't go so far as to say that. Still, for many a year you've been Coady's assistant; and, since he was so contrary and so eccentric, you were bound to be tarred with the same brush." A smile set the dimples dancing once more. "And tell me, is it true that he willed you his secret method of washing clothes? I heard that yesterday. I heard Jer Coady had a patent system of washing clothes, and that he left the whole copyright to Peter O'Dea, and that Peter O'Dea was under oath not to betray the secret to a living soul except that he must leave it to whoever succeeds him as principal in Carriglea. And I heard, too, that, if ever the secret is made known to a woman, the whole secret of it will be destroyed, and the charm will work no longer."

Peter sat straight up in his chair. "You're humbugging me now! Or is it that ye're very gullible people up in the hills? Whoever carries up the news from Carriglea brings ye more lies than truth.That joker, Packey Regan, must be wearing his brains out telling ye of all the great wonders that happens hereabouts. Ah, there never was much of a secret attached to Jer Coady's washing. How could it be kept secret after Fonsy Farrell immortalised it in a song?"

"Fonsy Farrell!" she repeated. "Oh, up in the hills we may live far back from the road, but we can hear of Fonsy Farrell too. To mention Fonsy as an alibi for Jer Coady reminds me of a rhyme and a game we used to play long ago. *Shake hands, shake hands, shake hands, brother. You're a rogue and I'm another.*"

"Well," confessed Peter, honest man, "I can't in conscience hold Fonsy up as a model of perfection. He has his little failings like all the rest of us. But whether he is a rogue or whether he's not a rogue, the fact remains that he did write a song about Jer Coady's laundry work. And the whole process, which you claim to be such a secret, was plainly described in it for all the world to learn."

88

"Would the charm break if you recited the song for me? Would the luck be gone then?"

"It would not, because it could not, because there was neither luck nor charm about the thing at all. Here is Fonsy's description of the Coady cleansing method:

"First the pot he filled and with fingers skilled
On the fire did place.
Then a stick he took and with stern look
He began his toil.
As with learned nods and judicious prods
Jer his wash did boil,
Every female maid, fled away dismayed
Shamed to show her face.

"There's the whole secret for you now. The whole technique is there."

Tessie Fogarty frowned a little, blinked, said, "I know I'm not very bright today, but, even so, I must admit that Fonsy hasn't succeeded in making me any the wiser."

Peter blew out a puff of smoke. "You must concentrate on two words. Only two words, mind, 'judicious prods.' Jer contended that thorough prodding was the first essential. Next, he never wrung out even a single sock, but left his washing to drip itself dry. Whether his method was an improvement on the normal procedure I'm not competent to state, but I do maintain that the clothes he washed turned out at least as clean as laundry that got a more orthodox treatment."

He drew at his pipe, found to his amazement that it had gone out. He took it from his mouth to probe the bowl. Tessie Fogarty turned to the stove, cried out in mock dismay, "Look! I'll never live this day down! All the water is boiled away!" She began fussing around the saucepan and the teacups. "Oh, and didn't you inform me this morning, Mr. O'Dea, that our lunch interval lasted from half-past twelve until one o'clock?"

"I did," answered Peter, puzzled.

"Well, I don't want to drag you back to life's harsh realities, but the school clock seems to think that the time is now eighteen minutes past the hour." And, laughing at his confusion, she turned the oil stove low, blew out the ebbing flame.

The shadows were lengthening from the sparse, hardy trees that had reared their heads high above the stone fences of Clashmairead. The dead drowse of spent heat was heavy over the farmyard as Tessie Fogarty wheeled her bicycle up the last stretch of hill to her father's door. From the cowsheds she could hear the muted hiss of milk squirting into the foam of near-laden pails, reminding her of the old Gaelic triad that named the three sweetest sounds in all creation: the first cry of the babe new-born, the song of the lark in the clear air, the thin streaming of milk into the pail ere twilight falls. She listened a moment to her brother Fintan singing while he milked:

> "I know my love by his way of walking,
> And I know my love by his way of talking
> And I know my love dressed in navy blue,
> But, if my love leaves me,
> What can I do?"

Tessie Fogarty heard the verse out to its close, came sauntering lazily across to the dwelling house, smiling to herself. Through the open door she saw her sister Kitty busied around the fire, her mother knitting where she sat on the settle beneath the far window. She swung into the kitchen, set her bundle of books on the window sill, sat down heavily on the nearest chair.

"Thanks be to the great God in Heaven that I have this day over me," said Tessie Fogarty.

"And thank God again," echoed Kitty, sharp-voiced. "And when you're done bein' thankful, I'd be very glad to know what meal your ladyship expects me to serve up to you at this hour of the day? Dinner, or tea, or supper? I have your dinner there by the fire since four o'clock, but I doubt if even the pigs would face it now. 'Tis dried up into dust."

"Not one thing can I do right this day," lamented Tessie.

"I had my dinner, but that push up the hill took the good of it from me, and I could have tackled another."

"You were at Madden's so," her mother decided. "How are they all? How's Michael? Are the pains crippling him yet? Had they any letter lately from Father Tim?"

"Madden's how are you! Indeed I was not at Madden's nor near Madden's. I had my dinner where I had my lunch, with the best of high society. I dined with my new boss, Mr. Peter O'Dea."

Kitty, hands on hips, turned round from the fire. Mrs. Fogarty put down her knitting.

"Well?" demanded Tessie, defiant. "What have ye to stare at? He didn't take a bite out of me. He's a grand, shy, quiet-spoken young man. He's the most belied person in this country. He has no more of Jerry Coady's nature in him than has Shep, the dog, asleep there on the doorstep. He didn't know that I was going to go on down to Madden's. He thought I was coming straight home, so when he asked me in to have a cup of tea that would help me face the hills, I didn't like to refuse him."

Kitty laughed in scorn. "Refuse him! Oh, it would be just like you to refuse him! I suppose you put the words into his mouth an' the poor man had no option left but to ask you."

"I couldn't insult my principal, could I?"

"Oh, it didn't take you long to set your cap at him," Kitty jeered. "Begor, noted an' all as they are for talkin' down around Carriglea, you were quick to give them the chance of bandyin' your name. You'll have us the laughin'-stock of the world. You can never see anything in a trousers but you must start to run after it."

"If so, I'm not the only laughing-stock among the Fogarty's," snapped back Tessie, rising up from her chair. "And, what's more, I'd never let it be said that I was ten years walking out with any man and was no nearer to a wedding ring at the end of them."

"Tess! Tess!" reproved her mother. "That's not a kind thing to say to your sister!"

"It wasn't a kind thing she said to me."

"You'll say no word to Kitty! The lot of ye are long in her debt. There she is all the evening, roasting herself to keep the dinner hot for you, and the first thing you do is to turn on her when she tries to joke you."

Quick in repentance, Tessie crossed the kitchen, put an arm round Kitty, who had stooped over the fire to hide her tears. "I'm sorry, Kitt. I said what I shouldn't."

"My own tongue is too long," said Kitty quietly.

" 'Tis how I'm jaded out after this day, with my head splitting from all those young ruffians roaring in my ears. And I thought I had that temper of mine bested at last, yet there it blazes off again on the slightest provocation."

"Oh, forget all about it." Kitty was easily appeased. "What we want is a full account of O'Dea. What is the house like? Begor, you must be the first woman to enter that door since the day 'twas built."

Tessie took off her light coat. "Are you making the tea for Fintan and Dada? Put my name in the pot, like a good girl!" She went over to hang her coat on the rack behind the door. "The house? Dear God, but you should see the house! I only saw the kitchen and the hall, but they're enough to frighten anyone. Maybe it looked a bit better when Coady had his furniture there and the two of them were in full swing together, but now it's like— Oh, I don't know what it's like. I don't believe the floors were scrubbed for years. The walls are fair enough, and paint or plaster were never stinted; but there's not a curtain, nor even a picture, nor scarcely a stick of furniture." She numbered the items off on her fingers "An old settle-table, a stool, three or four chairs, an old rickety dresser, a couple of shelves of books, and not a thing else."

" 'Twas a queer place for him to ask you, then," was Mrs. Fogarty's comment. "Oh, all the furniture they had must have belonged to Coady."

"He said that he asked me in before he remembered the place looked like a barn since Coady moved out the other day. And you know, Mother, you know, Kitty, you'd have pity on him to see the way he has of looking after himself. Not a drop of milk in the house except out of a tin! Nothing for his dinner that you could make a dinner of! Rashers and eggs and a few onions and one potato sliced up and fried on the pan. Anyway, I helped him to light the fire and to get the tea, so that, in less than no time, he was telling me all his troubles. How he doesn't know what way to set about running the house now that Coady is gone. Whether to engage a housekeeper who'd live there constant or whether he should hire a woman to come a few times a week and clean down the place for him. The next thing is he was asking advice from me."

"I hope you didn't try to make a fool of him," said Kitty.

"I did not. I told him the best thing would be to have a woman come in every day to do down the house and have a dinner ready for him when he comes home from school. The kind he is, he seemed to have very little liking for the idea of bringing in a housekeeper to live there. I told him, too, that he'd need to be careful lest he get some old one that would rob him right and left. I promised to go down to Clashbawn tomorrow evening and ask Auntie Biddy could she recommend anyone."

Kitty picked up the teapot. "Come on now to your tea, Tess," she ordered. "Oh, pickin' a maid for the master will suit Auntie Biddy down to the ground. Auntie Biddy is never happy unless she can feel important, poking her nose into other people's business."

Tess, laughing, sat down to the table. "You're full of compliments this evening, Kitt. Did the butter fail on you, or what happened? Anyway, off we went then discussing furniture and making out what he'll want for the kitchen and what he'll want for the hall and what he'll want for the parlour and what he'll want for everywhere. I told him I'd get from our Judy all the old catalogues she has since the time she was married, and himself and myself are going to go through them and pick out whatever we think the most suitable. He doesn't seem to care a jot about the cost. He's not one bit worried about the money end of it."

"Why should he be?" asked Kitty. "He should be rolling in riches. Sure, they say he has the first penny he ever earned."

"Begor, Tess," chimed in shrewd old Mrs. Fogarty, "I think

poor Peter O'Dea is only after swoppin' one boss for another. You didn't leave him the running of his own house for long. Jer Coady is no sooner lifted off him than you're down on his back instead. Nor, I'd say, will you leave Aunt Biddy much scope in selecting this housekeeper."

Tessie Fogarty might have grown tired of talking, having already said so much in so short a time. Or then again her thoughts might, on a sudden, have flown far away. She sat for a long minute silent before answering slowly. "Well, I see no use in buying good furniture and watching some tinker woman scratch and batter it to pieces. Oh, I'll make sure that he gets a proper housekeeper."

Kitty, by the fire, winked solemnly at her mother; but Mrs. Fogarty, an old woman and wise, stayed sagely silent and did not deign to wink back.

94

Chapter Six

ALL the world and Carriglea had known well that Master
O'Dea would be left queer and lonely by the departure
of his friend, crony, and sponsor, Master Coady; but Old
Moore himself, for all his wisdom, could never have prophesied
either the speed or the manner in which Peter consoled himself. For inside the twelve-month Peter O'Dea was a married
man.

His marriage was a shock from which Carriglea took a long
time to recover; and even Peter himself, thinking back from
the early days of his married life on his lately lost bachelorhood
and brief courtship, found it all as hard to believe as did anybody else. That he should be a married man, and a happily
married man at that, with a span-new bride of his own installed
on the very hearth where Jer Coady had lorded it for so long,
was wonder enough, God knows; but that the bride should be
none other than Tessie Fogarty, the beautiful Tessie Fogarty,
the toast of three parishes, was greater wonder still.

From Carrigmichael's highest hill right down to where the
river lapped on three sides of Glenshea, it was a nine days'
wonder and a nine nights' marvel when Tessie Fogarty took
up with the quiet schoolmaster and was safely married to him
before ever the most rabid gossipers had chance to draw second
breath. There were many to query what Tessie could have seen
in him. It could not have been his salary, because she had
looked down her dainty nose at men who could and did make
more money at a single fair than the master could hope to earn
in the round of a year.

But, a fact to which many a woman who knew him could,
if she would, bear witness, Peter O'Dea was such a tender,
humorous, motherable kind of man, that, between his shyness

and his gentleness, he had, though he did not know it, a trick of twisting the ladies' heartstrings. And perhaps that was why he had not to ask the second time for the beauty from Clashmairead.

The way of his asking was typical of the man.

Tessie Fogarty had not been his assistant for more than a few weeks before she was as friendly with Peter O'Dea as if they had been cradled side by side or had toddled their first steps hand in hand. When Mary Kate Gannon was made hired help at the teacher's residence, it was Tessie who engaged her; it was Tessie who detailed out for her what work she must do; and it was Tessie who went round the house each evening after school, making sure that every task had been done and done properly.

It was Tessie Fogarty who went into Waterford with Peter and helped him buy every stick of furniture for the house from hall to attic. It was Tessie who chose the paper for the walls, and the curtains for the windows, and the carpets for the floors. So that, on the evening when the last item had been settled in and she stood, satisfied, in the kitchen with the lamplight glinting through her hair, she said nothing but truth when she told him, "There's your house furnished and fitted and finished for you now. No one can say, Peter, but that I've done all one woman could do to turn an empty barn into a snug nest that a king might be proud of. So I'm handing it over to you now, Peter, to have and to hold and to cherish. I can do no more."

He looked at her a moment, that shy grin playing tag with the corners of his mouth. "I wouldn't be too sure of that. I don't think you can evade your new responsibilities quite so easily. Because, look! You have betrayed me into buying a houseful of furniture and curtains and carpets which myself and poor Mary Kate Gannon will never be able to take care of. Oh, I'm afraid you owe a great service yet to myself and to the furniture and to Mary Kate. Having saddled me with all those properties and problems, the very least you might do is stay on here permanently and look after them for me."

She looked round at him quickly, her eyes sparkling, her

voice jocose but unsure. "Peter! My poor Peter! Am I to consider this as a formal proposal of marriage?"

He stood there, blushing like one of his own schoolboys. "I feared a blunt question might frighten you."

"A direct question, Peter," she answered slowly, "was often known to get a direct answer."

And that was how Peter O'Dea wooed and won his bride.

They chose Dublin for their honeymoon and were not lucky in the choice, for it was a bitter and turbulent and blood-stained Dublin which greeted them in those early August days of 1913. The Great Strike had lately begun, and already the batons of the police and the brick-bats of Jim Larkin's workers had been in action. And although James Connolly was rallying to Larkin's aid, and although the Citizen Army were yet to march into history beneath their banner of the Starry Plough, still, even in its second week, the Great Strike was becoming the Great Hunger, so that Peter O'Dea and his bride were glad to escape to the quiet sunshine of Carriglea from the black hatreds of the fear-swept city.

Around the door of Jer Coady's one-time residence a reception committee waited to welcome home the happy pair. Fintan Fogarty and Kitty were there to wish luck to their sister on her new hearth, and there were Ned Gorman and Fonsy Farrell and even Packey Regan, anxious to assure themselves that Peter had survived, thus far at least, the terrors of matrimony. The distant sound of the hired motor had drawn them all from the kitchen, for motor-cars, if oft heard of, were as yet seldom seen in Carriglea.

"By the lord, 'twas true what Columcille said hundreds of years ago," stated Fonsy, "how the time would come yet when carriages would move without horses to draw them, an' ships would sail under the sea, an' men would fly through the air easier than a bird."

"An' did he say no more?" asked Fintan Fogarty, winking at Regan, nudging Ned Gorman, making a mouth at Fonsy from behind the shelter of his sister's back.

"My soul, but there's ignorance for ye," said Fonsy. "Or am

97

I expectin' too much from a mountainy man? Didn't Columcille say that Ireland would be saved and freed yet by a man from Spain ridin' on a white horse? Didn't he say that we'd know the right time had come when there would be found in the County Louth a miller with two thumbs on one hand?"

"I'm thinkin', Fonsy," put in Ned Gorman, "that some of us can't be bothered waitin' for all the signs Columcille would like us to wait for. It might be wiser to get on with the work, an', if the signs care to show up afterwards, they'll be doubly welcome then."

"Begor, but they're dusty yokes to go travellin' in," commented Kitty Fogarty, watching the white cloud of dust come billowing up the road behind the car. "Begor, but Tessie's serge costume will be surely ruined. She'd have been a wiser girl if she sacrificed grandeur to comfort and came home, fair and easy, on Sullivan's side-car."

Yet she was the first to rush into the coarse dust and the blue petrol smoke; the first to shout, "Welcome home"; the first to ensure that Peter had the proper grip on his bride wherewith to carry her triumphantly across the threshold.

The high tea of welcome was over. In the parlour the five men sipped their whiskey in the quietness of the dusk, while down in the back kitchen, the women gossiped and laughed as they washed the tableware.

"There seems to be a share of trouble and bloodshed goin' on above in Dublin, Peter," remarked Ned Gorman, scraping the bowl of his clay pipe with a blunt penknife.

"There's dirty work going on in Dublin," Peter told him. "I never saw the like before. 'Tis the kind of savagery you'd expect to read about in the papers as taking place in some half-civilised town far away, but that you'd never think you'd see with your own two eyes in your own country."

"Baton charges, I believe," said Ned. "The soldiers out. The police tramplin' innocent people to death. Bricks flyin'. One law, as usual, for the rich, another for the poor."

"Begod, it won't be always so," promised Regan fiercely.

"The full wrongs and rights of it all are very hard to come

98

at," went on Peter, careful to take no sides. "But this much is easily seen! There's something very wrong in a city and in a country that lets women and children go hungry and lets men be beaten to death on the streets in the name of justice. Who's right or who's wrong I don't know. I suppose there's right and wrong on both sides. But I saw women crying with terror, and I saw men's blood spilt like water, and I thought it a black day for Ireland that we should live to see the like."

"An' isn't it a blacker day for Ireland," demanded Fintan Fogarty, flaring into a fury, "isn't it, I say, a blacker day for Ireland when men like us can sit here, smokin' our pipes an' drinkin' our whiskey, an' let our fellow Irishmen be trampled down in Dublin or anywhere else? I don't see our famous politicians that we elected to Parliament goin' out in the streets to stop the slaughter! Only rushin' off over to England to psalm about Home Rule an' to condemn Carson an' the wicked people in Ulster who put more faith in the bullet than in the ballot-box. Oh, begod, Ned Carson is the man with the right idea. If there was one man the like of Ned Carson in Dublin this day, an' he to be on the right side, there would soon be a quick end to the batoning and bayoneting and murdering of the poor!"

"True for you, Fintan," said Ned Gorman.

"Begod, it is true for you," agreed Packey Regan.

Fonsy, grown cautious, waited for Peter to speak.

The schoolmaster yawned, shook his head, stood up, set about lighting the lamp. " 'Tis only half true for you, Fintan," he said. "If you start bloodshed and strife, there's always someone on the opposite side of the fence thirsting to spill blood for blood. And, once a thing like that starts, whether 'tis a war or only a fist-fight, the people who begin it have no more notion than anybody else where it will end or what misfortune it will bring on many an innocent that had no hand, act, or part in the quarrel."

"What's all the row about?" demanded the new Mrs. O'Dea, coming in quickly from the kitchen, her sister at her heels. "Who's fighting and dying now?"

"Yerrah, 'tis nothin', mam! Nothin'!" soothed the plausible

Fonsy. "Just a few elegant disputations about politics and the like to pass away the time."

"I might have known 'twould end up in politics no matter what ye were discussin', whether 'twas seed-wheat or courtin' or codology." Kitty's scorn spared none of them, but she turned sharply on her brother. "Did you tell them what Wolfe Tone said to Napoleon? Did you? Did you give them Bould Robert Emmet's speech from the dock yet? Did you? Begor, Fintan Fogarty, if you can fight half as well as you can talk, we'll not have long to wait for a free Ireland."

"Ah, be quiet, Kitt!" ordered Tessie, laughing. "The men must talk about something." To ease the tension she turned her best smile on Fonsy. "Must I go out tomorrow, Fonsy Farrell, and tell the whole country you had no more manners than to come here tonight and never a song on your lip for the new mistress? Or do you think an old married woman like myself is in no further need of songs?"

"Is it a song you said?" Fonsy spluttered at the enormity of the accusation. "Is it Fonsy Farrell to be without a song? Fonsy Farrell who stood up before the King of England below in Waterford and made up a rebel song, although the whole British Army, horse, foot, an' artillery, were waitin' to sweep me off to transportation for high treason?" Fonsy drank off the last of his whiskey. "An' the song I made that day was so good a song, missus, that King Edward himself stood up and he says, 'Lay no hand on that man,' says he. 'My forefathers was friendly to the poets,' says he, 'from the time of Dick Shakespeare down. An' I'll never let it be said,' says he, 'that a King of England would let a great poet the like of Mister Farrell here,' says he, 'languish in durance vile.' An' if you don't believe the truth of what I'm tellin' you, mam, you need only ask your husband there that was standin' by my elbow at the time, himself an' poor oul' Jerry Coady."

Tessie O'Dea raised her eyebrows, looked across at her husband, who smoked his pipe steadily and pretended not to notice her questioning gaze.

Fonsy, taking no chances of having his truthfulness queried, hurried on, "Long 'go, Mrs. O'Dea, mam, did I write for Peter there a poem about yourself an' Carriglea that, if he ever feels inclined to make it public, will make the name of Fonsy Farrell immortal for many a day."

Peter O'Dea had spent a happy bachelorhood there in that ivied house below the village, but who could compare those by-gone years with the bliss of his married life when time slipped past the pair of them as softly as the slow drift of some lowland stream drifts onward through the glory of a summer day?

Aye, and by the time the roses were again in bloom, it was long rumoured round the parish that a newcomer was eagerly expected at the teacher's residence. Peter O'Dea, through those anxious days, would be proud as a man with two heads as he went pacing sedately up to the school with his wife, the glad smile of him worth crossing a mile of ground to see. And Carriglea was glad for his gladness because, from the first day the two had met, Tessie's laughter had drawn up from the quiet depths of the schoolmaster's soul a new, droll gaiety, which fitted him well; while Peter's calm steadiness had toned down the former flightiness of Miss Fogarty to the gay dignity that conferred added charm on Mrs. O'Dea.

From the day of his birth Peter and Tessie seemed to think the sun shone out through Markie O'Dea's blue eyes, and, if it did, 'twas well that on the day he came he brought sunshine to their home; for elsewhere, across the world, the skies were darkening. It was Fintan Fogarty who brought the doctor from Waterford behind a high-stepping mare to his sister's bedside; and it was Fintan, too, who brought the first news of war to Carriglea.

"Aye, begor," he told Peter, who waited, anxious, in the parlour for news from upstairs, "the Germans in their thousands are halfway through Belgium. The French are counter-marchin' against the Rhine. The Austrians swarmin' into Serbia. The Russians rollin' down from the East. England will be in it too before this day is out. Ah, by the Lord God, the whole world is goin' up in fire an' smoke an' bloodshed."

There was a prim, precise little knock on the door, and the

doctor came in, small, pompous, bustling. "Let me be the very first to congratulate you, Mr. O'Dea, on becoming the father of a fine, fat, healthy son. The nurse will give you a call in a minute or two, and then you can ascertain for yourself just how well both mother and baby are doing."

Peter smiled, a smile that began round his eyes, that spread to his lips, that soon seemed to beam forth from his very soul. He shook hands wildly with the doctor. "Thank you, doctor! Thank you! Oh, begod, that's wonderful news! Great news!" He shook hands with Fintan Fogarty. "Great news! Great news, Fintan! I have a son, Fintan! A son! I'm a father, Fintan boy. And, begod, I nearly forgot, sure, you're an uncle now! Oh, begod, this calls for a little celebration." And he fussed away to the sideboard.

"It's a great moment in a man's life," the little doctor informed Fintan.

"What is?" queried Fintan, who didn't like the doctor personally and liked the doctor's politics even less.

"When a man becomes a father, of course."

"Oh," said Fogarty easily, "I thought you meant me becomin' an uncle. I have four or five nephews already, an' hard it is to think of the right names for the lot of them, God knows, with them springin' up around me like mushrooms after an autumn shower."

"Aha," cried the doctor, jocose but still pompous, "wait till you're married yourself, my lad. Wait till you have a few of your own, and then you'll see the difference."

" 'Twill be a long wait, doctor," assured the dour Fintan.

Peter O'Dea came grinning back to them, a tumbler of whiskey in each hand. "Let ye drink the health of the new arrival," he ordered, handing them their drinks. He turned back, to reappear with a smaller measure for himself. "Oh, this time, if ever, I think I'm entitled to sip a taste of the strong stuff."

The solemn doctor raised his glass. "Well, here's to the health of the very youngest O'Dea. That he may never be less happy than he is now, and that he may have many a brother and sister to keep him company in the years to come."

"Aha, doctor! Trying to ensure future employment in case times turn hard," jested Peter. "Trying to make certain of at least one regular customer."

"Ah, well, rainy days! Rainy days! We must all keep an eye out for the rainy days." The doctor balanced his well-filled five-foot-six forward on his well-shod toes. "God knows, with red war down on top of us, 'tis a wise man could tell how soon the hard day might come."

"It's a terrible business." Peter O'Dea shook his head, made a wry face at the raw whiskey. "Ah, 'tis a brutal business, war."

" 'Tis a bloody business, sir," corrected the fat doctor, thrusting out his chest, planting his feet well apart. "War is a bloody business, but there are occasions when it cannot be avoided, when it becomes a necessary evil. We must teach Kaiser William to respect his pledged word. We must show him, sir, that even he cannot trample with impunity upon the rights of small nations. We will be quick to the aid of gallant little Belgium, and, by God, before the leaves fall on Unter den Linden you'll see our brave boys marching proudly through Berlin."

"There's more small nations than Belgium," chipped in the unappeasable Fintan, "an' it many a long day since first their rights were trampled on."

"Ah, but with those rights so munificently restored by our magnificent Home Rule Bill, we'll show the world how fine a race we Irish are." The doctor put down his glass. "My friend John Redmond will speak in the House, probably today, and from what I know of him and the grand type of man he is, I am well sure that what he will say will bring a glow of honest pride to the face of every decent Irishman and Irishwoman, will send a thrill of pleasure round the Empire, aye and round the world when the nations of the earth see how nobly Ireland has proved herself worthy of England's trust."

"Beyond in Westminster you should be, talkin' your balderdash with the rest of our famous Irish members," retorted Fintan, whose patience was not his greatest virtue. "A man would think, listenin' to some of ye this day, that John Redmond and John Bull made the world. Well, you may be a friend of John Redmond's, doctor, but I'm no friend of his. And no matter what the same John Redmond has to say in the House, or any other house, he'll not be speakin' for me or for many another like me."

"Indeed." The dapper doctor took up his glass. "And who, may I ask, has the honour of being your spokesman?"

"What speaks for me has no tongue, but it has a hell of a loud voice just the same, an' no man but knows what it means when it talks. Do you understand me, doctor?"

"I'd like to remind ye two statesmen," interrupted Peter, "that ye're not at a political meeting, but gathered in my parlour to drink the health of my son and heir."

There came a timid knock, and the door opened just enough to allow Mary Kate Gannon's head appear. "Misther O'Dea," she announced, "Nurse Cummins says that if you wants for to see the misthress an' the babby, you're to go on up straight away."

Peter O'Dea raised high his almost empty glass. "To God's gift of a son," prayed he.

"To the latest O'Dea," said the doctor.

"To the lad upstairs," said Fintan Fogarty.

Peter O'Dea sat by the range reading the *Freeman's Journal*, gently rocking the cradle by means of an outstretched foot. His wife, ironing at the corner table beneath the lamp, spoke back to him.

"Anything new on the paper, Peter?"

"Damn the thing," said Peter heartily. "Devil damn the word but war, war, war. All about what Mr. This said and what Lord That said and how soon such another fellow, safe at home in his arm chair, could win all the battles if only the soldiers would do what he tells them. Ah, they'd sicken you, theirselves and their war."

"Bad luck to it for a war!" Tessie came over to the range, put the flat-iron she had been using back on the hot-plate. She picked up another, spat on it to test its heat, brought it over to her table. "Things are gone so scarce and dear that we'll soon have to genuflect whenever we meet a grocer or a draper.

104

Could they find no better time for such carry-on except when we were trying to rear a son?"

"Maybe we should have told them about Markie," commented Peter, humorous. "Maybe, if they had known about him, they wouldn't have fought. Maybe, if he'd been born twenty-four hours sooner, his arrival would have changed the whole course of history."

"If was never in a true story," retorted Tessie, her mind active as she ironed. "What great secret had Jer Coady in the letter you got from him today? You never told me one word of it."

"I did tell you! I told you he congratulated us on the birth of a son."

"It didn't take him six or seven pages to do that."

"Oh, well!" Peter sighed, laid down his paper. "For one thing, he wanted to know what kind of a song Fonsy composed about the event."

"He might well know that Fonsy would make a poem, if necessary, every time he was asked to drink Markie's health. Anyway, where does the bold Fonsy spend his nights these times? He's a very rare visitor now. I didn't offend him, did I?"

"Eeyah," her husband assured her, "it is a great libel on the same Fonsy even to think that the man could be offended in any house that gives him free food and free porter. Oh, damn the fear of Fonsy being offended. Well I know where he spends his nights. Up there in one of Maggie Anne McMahon's fields at the back of Regan's, doing his idiot, drilling the soles off his shoes to free Ireland along with Packey and Fintan and Ned Gorman and a few more of the bright boys. Oh, Ireland was never rightly served till they took up the wooden guns. Wooden guns are all the weapons they have, Regan was telling me the other day. Packey is very serious about it all. Ready to die for Ireland any hour of the day or night, wooden gun or no wooden gun."

The child wailed in his cradle. Tessie came over to him, bent down to soothe his woes away. "Ah, what's wrong with my little man at all, at all, what?" She adjusted his bottle, she patted down the blankets. "Did he lose his bottle, did he? Did he? Did he kick off his blankies? Did he? Off to sleep now, boyeen bawn, and let your father read his paper in peace." She crooned a bar or two in lullaby, rocked the cradle ever so gently, looked up at her husband. "I'd expect no better from Packey," she said, low-voiced. "Being patriotic is one of the few luxuries a poor man can allow himself. And my brave Fonsy is after saving Ireland so often in his own mind that 'tis second nature to him to fancy himself as a conquering hero. But wouldn't you expect Ned Gorman to have more sense?"

"That he's mixed up in it is not my fault, at any rate." Peter laid aside his paper, produced his pipe. "I've done my best to reason with him, but Ned is gone every bit as mad in his politics now as ever Jer Coady was. And the dear knows but Jer was, and is still, very hot in his leather. The letter today was filled with the same old rigmarole all over again, about there being blood and brains in Ireland yet, ready and willing to strike a stroke for the old cause. You'd think 'twas written by a boy of seventeen and not by a man going on seventy. Free Ireland! The man might as well be whistling to the moon. And, if Ireland were free tomorrow, would that make a button of difference to you or to me or to the child there in the cradle?"

His wife, satisfied with her son's slumbers, got off her knees, chose a fresh iron, went back to her work. "They don't think of us, Peter. They only see green flags waving and crowds cheering and bands playing. They only envisage one side of things. It's people like us, Peter, who are left to study the other side. Ah, I don't know what has come over the people these last few years. The country is full of speech-making and politics and drilling and bravado and gun-carrying. There's scarcely a person left to have a laugh or a joke with, nor anyone to sing a song or start a bit of merriment. The few that aren't plotting or planning are in such a fuss and fury running around making money out of the war that they have no leisure left even to bid you the time of day."

Peter O'Dea hurriedly got up from his chair, stepped across to his wife, put an arm round her shoulders. "Girl dear, anyone would think to hear you that you were carrying the whole weight of the world on your lone back." He bent to kiss the soft cheek. "Hold up that head, woman, and laugh at all creation the way you always did. Let the worst come to the worst, Tess, and, even when it has come, there's no power on earth can conquer a glad heart."

" 'Tis easy to give encouragement, Peter," she told him quietly. "And advice, no matter how well meant, sounds very cheap sometimes. But, I feel that—" She got no further, for from the front door knocker a rat-rat echoed through the house. "God! Who can that be at this hour? Open it quick, Peter, before they wake the child. Maybe 'tis Fintan."

But it was not Fintan who came stamping through the hall to blink beglared eyes in the kitchen lamplight. It was Fonsy Farrell, and Fonsy had many a pint-pot's contents snug beneath his leather belt.

"Good night to you, Masther O'Dea," he announced, Old World courtesy perfuming every syllable. "An' good night to you, too, Missus O'Dea, an' may God bless your work." He teethered a step sideways, poised himself over the cradle. "And has my own boy, Markie, no word at all to say to his old Uncle Fonsy?"

"For heaven's sake, don't wake him again on me," warned Markie's mother. "If you do, you'll have more words than you want from me. If he wakes again, now, I'll get no good of him for the rest of the night."

"An' I'd be the last, mam, the very last," declared Fonsy, dignified though alcoholic, "to draw down a single minute's sorrow or wakefulness on yourself or Markeen there. For sleep, Missus, as Jack Shakespeare says, twists up the ravelled sleeve of care an' comes as a boon an' a blessin' not only to long-sufferin' humanity, but also to every single one of God's creatures, from the monstrous elephant, mam, in his caboodle amidst the steaming jungle, to the humble flea, savin' your presence, snug in the fur of the domestic cat."

"True for you, Fonsy," praised Peter.

"Everyone, sir, must have their sleep, from the Pope beyond in Rome to Markeen there in the cradle. The only animal, accordin' to Jerry Coady, that never needs to sleep is the eagle, which, rightly speakin', is not an animal at all. An' because the eagle never sleeps, he can do two things that no other livin' creature can do: He can stare the sun in the face an' never blink no more than if that same sun was but a ha'penny candle, an' he can hear the dew fallin' just as loud as any of us here might harken to the raindrops chatterin' on a tin roof in a thunder shower."

"Isn't it a shame and disgrace on you, Fonsy"—Tessie held up one of her husband's shirts as she spoke—"that a man with all your brains and your words and your flow and your knowledge should quote from Shakespeare or from anyone else on such a subject as sleep?" She gazed critically at her handiwork, laid the shirt back on the table, unironed side uppermost. "You're degrading yourself and your talents to be reciting other people's poetry when you too have the gift."

"Well, now," pondered Fonsy, "do you know, now, that notion never occurred to my head before. Yerrah, I do get so much tangled up in the things that do be happenin' around me, that I do have no time left to devote to . . . to . . ."—he wrinkled a troubled forehead—"to the eternal veracities. An' yet, mam, Fonsy Farrell has never been unsubtle to the moods an' fancies of beauteous nature." He hooked his thumbs in the armholes of his waistcoat. "One time, an' I a risin' lad, I off up to Dublin in the spring of the year to make my fortune." He spat, sour-faced at the memory. "An' do you know what I wrote a poem about? Do . . . you . . . know . . . what . . . I . . . wrote . . . a . . . poem . . . about?" Slowly, distinctly, poking an accusing finger at Peter's nose.

"I told you not to wake the child." Tessie glanced, apprehensive, at the cradle.

"There in the heart of the big city," Fonsy's voice was almost a whisper, but his earnestness compensated for all other deficiencies, "do you know what I did up there in the heart of the big city? Do you know what I wrote a song about? I wrote a song about the wind of March, an' about how, if I were at home, I'd hear it come whistlin' over the crests of the Comeragh Mountains, an' sweepin' across the plains, an' away again, scootin' up the hills. A free wind, an open-minded wind, a wind that could see no sense at all in a city the like of Dublin or in the misguided breed of people that choose to live in such a debacle. That's a French word, Peter, debacle. A great word of Jer Coady's."

"I thought myself," said Peter, "I knew off by heart every line ever you wrote, but your poem on the March wind I never heard. Give it out now, and I'll write it down for you."

"I never wrote a better poem than my poem on the March wind," replied modest Fonsy, "an' what heart-scalds me this minute is that, after all the years, damn the word of it can I call to mind at the moment, barrin' the last few lines." He cleared his throat, assumed what Peter had long ago christened "the recitation face."

"Fonsy Farrell," Tessie threatened, "'twill be a sad and sorry night for you if you wake that child."

Fonsy put his hands behind his back, bent his head forward, closed his eyes, began to recite.

> "There are swans on Anna Liffey
>   An' round College Green there's grass:
> From Stephen's Green spring daisies smile
>   To greet me as I pass.
> But the daisies of the springtime
>   Only call up tears that blind,
> For the hillsides come to haunt me
>   On the wild an' mad March wind."

"More power, Fonsy," cried Peter. "Words at will, boy! Words at will! 'Tis a nice piece of work. Oh, a very nice piece of work. And I suppose the next effort we'll have from you will be a great song about the Volunteers and the drilling up in Maggie Anne McMahon's field."

"From me," announced Fonsy, solemn and serious, "you will hear no song about the Volunteers nor about the drillin' in Maggie Anne McMahon's field or in Maggie Anne Anybodyelse's field. Fonsy Farrell was loyal to the Cause from the first day ever he loosed his grip on his mother's petticoat. When the question was asked, 'Are you ready to die for Ireland?' there was no man quicker with his answer. Fonsy Farrell was always in the vanguard of the struggle for life, liberty, an' the pursuitation of happiness. You know that, Peter!"

"I know that well, Fonsy."

"When these young Volunteers began their marchin' an' their drillin' an' their loud talkin', Fonsy Farrell never made mention of his long service to the Cause, but joined up, in all humility, as a simple soldier. An', believe you me, Peter, the simple soldier was nearly bird alone among so many generals of all ranks an' grades an' standin's. But Fonsy Farrell made no move in search of his rightful promotion. Fonsy Farrell, until this night, marched side by side an' step by step with the Volunteers, true to the Cause an' no matter what his opinion of some of them might be. But after the events of this night, after the slurs that were slung at him this night, after the aspertions cast on his character this night, Fonsy Farrell, though still true to the Cause, marches side by side an' step by step with the Volunteers no longer."

"By the lord, Fonsy"—Peter paused from his pipe-filling to wink at his wife—"they must have gone beyond the bounds when a man with your record has to take such a grave step. And how did all this happen?"

"I'll tell you the how of it." Fonsy seated himself on a chair beside the cradle. "The how of it I'll tell you an' the where of it. Above in Maggie Anne's field we were, an' I lively as the best of them, although I'm risin' sixty an' not what you could call a young man. There I was, anyway, shiverin' in the cold of the wind, but determined not to miss even one 'form fours.' Well, when Fintan above came to call us to attention, hadn't he another lad with him, a square cut of a man from the North of Ireland with a pair of spectacles on him an' as queer a method of speech as ever you heard!"

"Begor. A north of Ireland man, no less," was Peter's wily comment.

"A special organiser, accordin' to Fintan. A special organiser sent down from Dublin to organise us into an efficient fightin' force, 'because, men,' says Fintan, 'the day is not far distant now.' With that my spectacled hero starts off a long ramblin' discourse about the history an' sufferin's of poor Ireland, though some of us knew more of our history book than he did. Then he says to us, 'Let ye kneel down now,' says he, 'an' take off yeer caps till I administer to ye the Republican Oath.' He seemed so damn well certain that he was the first man ever to think of freein' Ireland, I thought I'd let him see how some of us were up an' doin' when his father was a babby."

"Fonsy," asked the master's wife, "is the child asleep?"

"Sound, mam, snug an' sound," with a sidelong glance at the cradle. "An' so, Peter, says I to him, very polite, 'Excuse me, sir,' says I, 'but will it be necessary for me to take this oath? Because,' I says, 'I took the Fenian Oath here in this self-same field, an' I not yet seventeen. An' that,' says I, hittin' a hard blow, 'was nigh on fifty year ago.' "

" 'Twas a fair comment," assured Peter.

"He had to chaw on that for a minute, an' then he says, 'I'll leave that to your own judgement, friend.' I seen at once that I had him on the run, so says I, still very polite, of course, 'What was good enough for the Fenian men fifty years ago is still good enough for Fonsy Farrell this night.' There I stood, the hat jammed well down on my head, while the rest of them went on their knees an' repeated the words after him."

"You were well within your rights, Fonsy," said Peter, pleased with his new role of Job's comforter to the harrassed poet.

Fonsy spat into the fire. "Once he had the oath administered, he started off the preachin' again. 'Now, men,' says he, 'I needn't remind ye that whenever the Irish people tried to come together to make a bid for freedom, they had, in the first place, to fight, in addition to the enemy, the spy an' the informer.' 'Fonsy Farrell,' says I, 'was never either, nor was anyone belongin' to him even if you traced back all the generations since Adam was a boy.' 'Silence in the ranks,' orders Fintan. 'An' what's more,' says I, 'there was never spy, traitor, or informer in this part of the country, which is more than can be said for some parts far away.' 'Will you close your big gob or will I have to shut it for you?' shouts Fintan. 'That's not very soldieringly kind of talk,' says I, 'from a commandin' officer.' 'Ah, shut up your mouth,' says he, 'an' listen to what the man has to say.'"

"Indeed, our Fintan must think he's boss of the country already if that's the way he speaks to ye," observed Tessie. "Begor, he'd not show such bad manners if his sister Kitty heard that brand of talk from him."

"In any case," continued the martyred Fonsy, "I left my northern bucko go ahead. 'An' now,' he says, 'intoxicatin' liquor has only too often been the ready ally of the spy an' the informer. 'Twas drink that brought us down,' says he, 'in '98, at Wexford an' New Ross an' in many another place at many another time. So,' he says, 'the next thing I want ye to do, if any of ye do touch the stuff, is to promise me ye'll never touch another intoxicatin' drink until Ireland is free.'"

"Begor, Fonsy," and Peter winked again at his wife, "but that was a tall order."

"Worse still! There were some to shout 'hear! hear!' an' all of them off with their caps at once to swear the oath against porter. 'Hold on one minute now,' says I. 'I always understood that the Volunteers was founded to fight for Ireland an' not as a recruitin' centre for any kind of a teetotallers' organisation. An' I understood, too,' says I, 'that this movement was founded to fight for freedom. Yet the very first thing that's sponsored is tyranny an' coercion, preventin' a man from doin' what, even under our present so-called laws, he's legally entitled to do, drink his bottle of stout an' give offence to no one.' My nabob could only appeal to Fintan, who turns very nasty on me again. 'Fonsy Farrell,' says he, 'you've been a constant source of trouble an' bad discipline in B Company since the first day ever you joined it. We tried to put up with your antics,' he says, 'because no man in all Ireland has a sounder national record than you have. But,' says he, 'if you can't fight for Ireland without a pint-pot of porter in your fist, you're no damn use to us an' no credit to our organisation. An' so,' says he, 'I'll give you one minute either to take the pledge with the rest or hand in your resignation.'"

Fonsy heaved a great sigh of self-pity. "And that," he said sadly, "was how Fonsy Farrell parted company with the Irish Volunteers."

Chapter Seven

EASTER came late and came very late that year, for it was the last week of April before ever Good Friday dawned, and the first flush of summer was already warm over the land, with the apple blossom thick in every orchard.

Easter came late that year and Easter came, troubled, to a troubled Ireland. For many a month the dread drums of death had raved over the red fields of Europe. On all the war fronts the flower of nations withered in the flame of battle, among the bloodied mud-pits of Flanders, around the shambles that once was Verdun, between the black swamps of the Pripet. For flags and kings, for emperors and ideals many a humble hero went nameless forth to die, on the land and in the air above the land, on the sea and in the green hells beneath the waves.

But it was an impatient Ireland which waited on that Easter dawn, which spoke with bated breath and side-long glance over lifted shoulder of what Easter might bring. And through a nervous Ireland rumour ran riot.

At times it seemed to astute Peter O'Dea, snatching words from the wind as he strode up the road to his school, that rebellion hovered in the air, a palpable substance, almost a living thing. At times it seemed to Din Lalor of the Royal Irish Constabulary, whom experience had taught to sense the pulse of the country from the mere intonation of a spoken word, that every rumour, be it ever so wild, carried a kernel of unpleasant truth. And from the rumours and the signs and the portents they drew the same conclusions, Peter O'Dea the quiet schoolmaster, sitting by his fire in Carriglea, telling his mind to no one, and District Inspector Din Lalor poring over the secret police reports above in his house at Moonbawn.

While April waned the rumours grew ever wilder. The Volunteers would rise out at Easter— The Germans had landed at Cork and Sligo— No, but they were landing from submarines at Cork— Yerrah, no, 'twas next week they would land, guarded by the guns of the High Seas Fleet, led by the Kaiser himself, at Fenit beyond Tralee— From Limerick twenty thousand Fenian men were marching northward— The West was awake— Over frothy glasses in dim public-houses Connaughtmen whispered, one to another, that the Tree of Liberty which the French General Humbert had planted in Killala, during that mad but gallant adventure of '98, had bloomed, and all the flowers were red, the red of new-spilt blood.

Aye, and even in Dublin town, murmured the whisperers, there were men ready to rise and ready to fight and ready to die under their chosen leaders—Pearse's Volunteers were ready, and James Connolly's Citizen Army, and the faithful and few of the Hibernian Rifles.

Wilder still the rumours grew. The old prophecies, 'twas said, were being fulfilled— To Louth had come a miller with two thumbs on his right hand— Long-dead heroes shouted war cries from Tara's hill— The Black Pig of old Celtic mythology was seen rooting for husks on the Ulster borders— Men spoke of a Man from Spain, fit to lead Ireland to freedom—

In city streets, at country crossroads, ballad singers plied a steady trade with old songs and new.

"Soon we'll have our own again," promised the ballad singers, and loyal citizens slept none too easy in their beds. And they sang a new song, the words of which Din Lalor wrote dutifully into his black notebook.

> Oh, God rest you, Robert Emmet,
>   And God rest you, brave Wolfe Tone,
> God rest you, Patrick Sarsfield,
>   And O'Neill from far Tyrone.
> God rest you, Hugh O'Donnell,
>   In your grave far, far away;
> God rest you and God keep you
>   To the Dawning of the Day.

114

By lonely cabins, mystery-veiled at twilight, mountainy men told how Sarsfield and his Jacobite troopers had been seen riding hard across the hills; how Wolfe Tone, with never a scar on his managled throat, was marshalling phantom hosts at midnight on the plains of Kildare; how Betsy Gray and the Hearts of Down were rising from their graves to march in ghostly battalions across the moonlit heather of the Ulster Glens. . . . And in Dublin City there were those, with little faith in ghosts or fantasy, who were not slow to say, openly and without fear, that Emmet's epitaph would soon be written and Ireland's thralldom ended.

But Dublin and Ireland had heard all those dreams before; had long ago grown tired of visions, inured to the sight of marching men. And only those who talked little and thought much, like Din Lalor among his police reports or Peter O'Dea by his quiet fireside, cared to sift through the sands of rumour and see, beneath, the embers of a nation's destiny smoulder slowly into revolution's Phoenix flame.

Sheltered from the bitter east wind by his house and by his trees, Peter O'Dea tended his garden in the mellow evening. Twenty-months-old Markie sat up in his pram to watch, all interest and solemnity. The schoolmaster raked a little rabble of stones from off the seed-beds onto the narrow path, paused, leaned on the rake to survey his labours, fumbled then in coat pockets for pipe and matches.

As the first puffs of smoke went drifting, pale-blue in the sunlight, Markie suddenly gave tongue. "Da-da!" he shouted. "Ad-ad-da."

"Now, young man," Peter warned, grown stern, "it's no use at all for you to be a-da-daing me. You can't soother your father that easily with your soft talk. No, begor, you can't put the comehither on your poor tired father that quickly. You can't twist him around your little finger. It's not your mother you have now, but a busy man with a thousand things to do and no time nor inclination to take Markie walking."

"A-da-da-a-da," repeated Markie more loudly.

"Ada-da yourself," answered Peter, strolling across to the

115

pram, bending over his son, building a smoke-cloud in the air. "Is it a pull at the pipe you want? Oh, Markie is too little yet for his da-da's pipe. No pipes yet for Markie! Oh, we'd all get our seats dusted by mama if small boy were caught smoking."

"Mama-mam-ma-ma," cried Markie, his small brain taking tight hold of the familiar word.

"Who's taking my name in vain?" Tessie O'Dea, the auburn hair piled high, the gay laugh quick to follow her question, stood behind them in the doorway.

"Mama! Dad-a! Mam-a! Dad-a!" yelled Markie in a wild outburst of eloquence.

Peter straightened up, his back stiff after his toil. "Begor, you made quick work of your visit to the chapel. Your prayers must have got a short knock or a quick answer. You're not half an hour gone."

"And amn't I a trusting woman to leave the child for half an hour in your charge, not knowing what catastrophe you might have caused him in my absence! He'd get the pipe to smoke if he were to demand it."

"But, my dear woman," argued Peter, all too solemn, "what sense would there be in giving him the pipe? His teeth aren't strong enough to hold it yet."

"Aye," answered his wife, solemn as himself, " 'twould be difficult too for him to spit out, and he without his dribbling bib. Go on now, Peter, you cod! Finish up this messing about in the garden and give me a chance to get you cleaned up and off to your evening devotions in a manner befitting the school-master of Carriglea."

"Yes, love." Experience had taught Peter O'Dea that immediate and humble submission provided the most certain hope of getting his own way in the end. "But, according to my watch, the time is only half-past five, and the devotions are not till half-past seven."

"And won't it be a full hour before I manage to stop you tearing up what few seeds are left in the ground?" demanded Tessie. "And won't it take another hour to get you shaved and washed and into your second-best suit, with your shoes shined and your hair brushed?"

"Ah, here, Tess," he appealed. "The clothes I have on will do me. Who's going to notice in the dusk? And who's going to mind even if they do notice?"

"I'm going to notice, and I'm going to mind! You'll leave this house looking a credit to me, even if I have to take the scrubbing brush and do a job on you myself."

"Yes, love," said Peter and changed the topic. "Have they no news at all from the great world in the seven thriving houses of Carriglea?"

"News?" asked Tessie. "Is it news he said, Markie? News and rumour and truth and lies—never before in my life did I hear the like. The shop was full, half the people talking in whispers, the other half roaring loud enough to be heard a mile away. And such arguments! Fonsy Farrell with a drop of drink in him—on Good Friday, mark you—fighting mad one minute and maudlin sad the next, arguing away with Andy Gorman about the war and the Germans and the Volunteers and God knows what besides. Then Fonsy would give a hiccup and Andy would point at him and shout to the crowd in the shop, 'Look at him! Look at him, let ye! Let ye all look at him! There's one of the men that's goin' to free Ireland!' Oh, such a circus was never seen in Carriglea, Peter, since the famous night Julia Stapleton was chasing round the stage after you for a kiss, and Jer Coady had to drop the curtain lest the blast of her lips might wither you."

"All lies," stated her husband comfortably. "Lies of Packey Regan's. And if they're not Regan's lies, they're Ned Gorman's lies. And if they're not Gorman's lies, they're Fonsy Farrell's lies. Sure, you couldn't believe the daylight from any of them. The woman never laid a finger on me, that night or any other night."

"And didn't she now? Well, if she didn't, the whole parish are liars, for 'tis the exact same story I hear from everyone."

"Dad-a! Mam-a! Fonsa!" cried Markie, displeased at being so long ignored. But he was to remain unattended yet awhile, for, even as he called, the house echoed to a rat-tat on the front-door knocker.

"That's a stranger!" Tess listened, puzzled. " 'Tis an out-

117

of-the-way time for anyone to call, on a Good Friday evening."

She turned away into the house, returned almost at once, a frown tight-knit between her brows. "It's Lalor, the police Inspector. He wants to see you on urgent business."

"Bring himself and his urgent business out here to me so," ordered Peter, "and you're to come out with him. I lived too long with Jer Coady not to know the wisdom of having a witness present when the majesty of the law pays me a visit."

Mrs. O'Dea stepped back into the kitchen. "This way, Mr. Lalor," she called, and then moved out into the garden to leave the way clear for his coming.

District Inspector Din Lalor was not in uniform, and the black suit and the black tie and the black bowler hat lent him the appearance of a particularly grim but prosperous undertaker. Tall man that he was, he had to stoop a little to avoid the low lintel. Peter, watching him closely as he came, knew by the glint of his eye that there was trouble ahead.

"A fine evening, Mr. O'Dea," greeted the policeman warmly enough. "I'm very glad to see, ma'am, that he's making sure ye won't go short of fruit and vegetables, whatever else may run scarce before this war is over."

Tessie laughed. "If we have nothing else to see us through the war except Peter's fruits and vegetables, I'm afraid there won't be many left in this house to greet the peace."

"There's a woman's base ingratitude for you, Inspector." Peter gestured with his pipe. "A whole gardenful of vegetables she ate on me last year and hardly gave me a smack of my lips at one of them."

"And His Nibs here!" District Inspector Lalor waggled the fingers of his right hand in front of the dubious Markie. "Growing up into a big, strong, hardy man in less than no time. Don't you think, though, ma'am," with a lift of his dark eyebrows, "that 'tis growing a trifle chilly for him out here? There's harm in that east wind, you know. Good neither for man nor beast once the sun starts to decline."

Troubled, Tessie eyed her husband.

"Let him be," said Peter easily. "He'll let us know all about

118

it, never fear, the moment the wind or anything else is not all he'd wish it to be."

Lalor continued less heartily, "I wanted to see you about a rather important, a rather urgent matter, Mr. O'Dea." He stopped. He stared rather pointedly at nothing in particular, leaving the next move to his host.

"Fire ahead!" urged Peter. Lalor remained silent. "Go on, Inspector! Anything you have to say you may as well say it before my wife. She'll bully it out of me afterwards in any case."

"You never heard a secret yet," scoffed Tessie, "but you had to share it or burst."

Lalor, uncertain, a little irritated, looked from one to the other. "Personally, I have no objection to Mrs. O'Dea's hearing what I came to say. Only, as the matter is so serious, and may prove, to her, even distressful, I wished to spare her feelings."

Peter sucked lazily at his pipe. "She claims that she thrives on serious things, Inspector. Try her with a few and test the truth of her boast."

Lalor sighed, took off his hat, peeped into its crown as if the news he brought lay concealed therein. "It's well for you people who can still afford to be gay and light-hearted, instead of being weighed down with work and worry the way I am this day, not knowing where . . . Oh," he said resignedly, replacing his hat, "there's no use putting a tooth in bad news when it must be spilled. There's a rebellion, a country-wide rebellion, planned for Sunday morning next."

Tessie gasped, moved instinctively toward the pram to place herself between Markie and all dangers. Peter straightened up, drew a deep breath, then shook his head. "Too fantastic, Inspector. You've been listening to old Fonsy Farrell. Fonsy has been announcing rebellions every third Sunday for the past twelve-month."

"Well, it's not Fonsy who's announcing this one," growled Lalor. "This is none of Fonsy's visions. Oh, no! This is going to be the real thing. The ringleaders in Dublin expect the whole country to rise when they call." The District Inspector permitted himself a thin smile. "But the country is neither bad, mad, nor traitorous, thank God. The country at large will not rise. And the few Dublin malcontents will stage no revolution if the authorities up there have gumption enough to act on my repeated warnings and lock up those madmen before they kill themselves and half Dublin as well with their crazy schemes."

"By the lord harry," said Peter, "that's a hatful of news."

"And safe enough if it's not a coffinful of news for some of us. I came here, sir, to seek your assistance in trying to ensure that, in this part of the country at least, we shall have no madness, no loss of life. The ringleaders here, you know them as well as I do, must be made to realise how senseless the whole project is."

Peter O'Dea looked away across the plain to where Slievenamon was shrouded in sunset rays. "The preservation of the peace is your duty, Inspector, not mine. Why should I go looking for trouble?"

Exasperated, Din Lalor crammed his hat farther down on his head. "At a time like the present, sir, the preservation of the peace is the bounden duty of every law-abiding citizen. These men won't listen to me, and I know it. If I set about arresting them, I'll start the exact trouble I wish to prevent. But they will listen to you. Ned Gorman is your friend. Fogarty is your brother-in-law. Regan will abide by what you say."

"If you'll pardon me butting in, Inspector," said Tessie O'Dea quietly, "I see your point and agree with it. Nobody wants war and death and bloodshed. But, to be perfectly frank, I'm rather worried as to your motive. Are you being soft-hearted, anxious to make sure the hot-heads don't run themselves and all of us into trouble? Are you trying to do your duty in a roundabout sort of way, killing the rebellion with kindness?" She paused. "Or are you trying to keep your conscience and your police record both clean by getting my husband to do your dirty work for you, so that, if there is a rising elsewhere, and it fails, you can say smugly to your superior, 'Well, there was no trouble in my district.' And if, by some miracle, the rising succeeds, you could still say to the people of Carriglea, 'Well, I didn't stop the Carriglea boys from playing their part. That was Peter O'Dea's work.'"

Din Lalor, despite the increasing chill of the breeze, took off his hat, used it vigorously as a fan. "My dear woman, here I stand, facing threats of war, murder, conspiracy, civil strife, bloodshed, and the Lord only knows what else besides; and there you stand trying to cross-examine me on my motives. Listen, ma'am, for the sake of easing your mind I'll tell you more than maybe I should. No German guns will be landed. The ship carrying them has been sunk off Queenstown. There will be no aid from Germany. Sir Roger Casement landed near Tralee this morning with that news. He's a prisoner now."

Lalor once again put on his hat, then continued, "Therefore the planned rising must fail! Now, what I want to ensure is that our fellows down here will know the full facts in time and won't, through ignorance, run their heads into the hangman's noose."

"And ensure at the same time that, no matter what way the wind blows, you won't lose your job," added Tessie.

"If you want it that way, you can have it that way, Mrs. O'Dea," said Lalor resignedly. "I'm no more anxious to forfeit my few pounds a month than anyone else is."

There was a short, sharp silence, broken only by the creak of pram springs as the neglected Markie bounced himself up and down. Then Peter said, very slowly, "In all this matter, Inspector, I'm neither for you nor against you, just as I'm neither for them nor against them. I'm for nobody, really, except for my wife and my child and myself. But I have no wish to see people suffer either on one side or the other. Therefore, if it will help to keep the peace, I promise to do this much: I'll put the full facts before the men in question. I'll make no effort whatever to influence them one way or the other. I'll leave them to make their own decision, to the satisfaction of their own ideals and their own consciences. And I'll do no more."

"Do that much, my dear sir, and you will have done a good day's work for Ireland." Lalor, satisfied, made ready to leave. "By God, Peter O'Dea, I'll never forget this day's service to

121

you, and neither, believe me, will any man, woman, or child in Carriglea forget it."

"I hope Carriglea will have no reason to say that they won't forgive it," put in Tessie.

Lalor could laugh a little now. "Come, come, Mrs. O'Dea! You shouldn't pollute official ears with such disloyal sentiments. And I'm surprised, despite your loyalty to your brother, that you, a Government servant, would even dream of breathing a rebel word."

"I'm no rebel," she replied coldly, moving round to take Markie from his pram. "But it so happens that, if some of us were Government servants a thousand times over, we'd still occasionally remember that we're Irish and the Government is not."

Lalor bowed. "I'm an Irishman myself, ma'am, but may I point out this: To be 'agin the Govermint' is every Irishman's privilege; to be against treason and murder is the birthright of every honest man."

Fonsy Farrell sat on the wall outside the teacher's residence and preached rebel doctrines at the world in general and at Andy Gorman in particular. It was a warm Sunday evening, the evening of the first Sunday in May, and there was a balm on the breeze which gave fair promise of sunny summer days to come.

"It was a great an' a glorious deed," declared Fonsy, "a deed that will be remembered forever wherever an Irishman lives or travels or settles down. In the pages of history to come the name of Easter, Nineteen an' Sixteen will never be forgotten."

"Nor forgiven either," retorted Andy. "Of all the treacherous stabs in the back ever known to man this week's work will rank as the worst. Takin' foreign gold to strike England from behind! The men who, when Ireland was at last gettin' a fair deal, would stoop so low, are no men at all. An' the fact that my own brother is still hidin' out on the hills with my shotgun under his oxter doesn't alter my opinion one iota."

Fonsy filled his pipe, did not deign to speak until, fully loaded, it sat jauntily on his lower lip. "The way it is with you now, Andy," he said comfortably, "is that you have no eye or no ear, or, I could say, no head at all for the general trend of events. You can see no farther than your nose, an' God knows but that's not far, an' you buried to your eyelashes this last ten year below on your farm in Ballyvarna."

"A man," commented Andy, with a certain sage savagery, "can see as well, if not better, through honest clay, than he can see through the moldy froth on perpetual pints of porter."

Fonsy Farrell raised a deprecatory hand. "Andy, my lad, I'm holdin' arguments with you since the first day ever you dragged on a pair of long trousers, but that thick skull of yours hasn't yet absorbed the first principle of debate. The first principle of debate, as laid down in all the great books on debatin' for debaters, is never to get personal. It only causes the introductin' of unnecessary heat into the disputations, an' makes a man less liable to be able to prosecute his arguments to their pre-destined conclusions."

"An' who started gettin' personal? Who made insultin' statements about me havin' my nose always stuck in the clay? What answer does your First Book for Public-House Debaters give to that, Mr. Parish Poet?"

"Hold on there!" cried Fonsy, indignant. "Hold on there now! The Man Above, when He made us, gave us all some little failing, an' we must regard it as a legacy from the sin of our First Parents that such little weaknesses be slapped in our faces from time to time by the malingerin' ignorant. But, when it comes to drawin' down ridicule on my God-given gift, that's a horse of another shade altogether, Andy boy. That's one insinuendo Fonsy Farrell will neither thole nor tolerate."

"One of these days," Andy warned him, "a couple of them big rocks of words are goin' to stick in your throat an' you'll be choked, begod, without even knowin' the meanin' of the words that choked you."

Fonsy, with fine restraint, throttled down his temper, lit a match, kindled his long-neglected pipe. "To get back to where we were," said he with conscious dignity. "You'll never be on the side of these rebels, Andy, or of any other rebels either. An' do you want me to tell you why?"

123

"Why should you have to tell me why when I know well the why of it myself? Because they stabbed us all in the back."

"No, Andy, them's not your reason at all."

"Don't tell me, Fonsy, that you're still trying to convert poor Andy." Peter O'Dea had come to the door behind them. "I thought you'd have learned sense after all those years."

"I was only pointin' out to him . . ."

"He was only tellin' me that I don't know my own mind. He's the only man, it seems, who knows the why of every damn thing I do."

"Lookit," said Fonsy, "I'm only statin' facts. Lookit, master! Lookit here! You're no more in agreement with the rebels than Andy is. An' because why? Because the both of ye is not able to look any farther than yer noses. Andy there can't see beyond his wife an' his farm an' his family. You can't see past your wife an' your school an' your son. Neither of ye cares a tinker's curse what happens to the rest of the country so long as ye're able to do well in yeer farms an' yeer schools, an' can keep yeer wives an' families in peace an' comfort. Amn't I right there?"

"And, if I may answer your question with another, what more does anyone want?" The schoolmaster winked at Andy. "If everyone was left in peace to do those things, you'd see neither war nor trouble in this country or in any other."

"Ah, lookit here, master," objected Fonsy, "did you never hear the word freedom? Look at the men who died fightin' above in Dublin last week! Look at all the men who died fightin' in this country since the year One! What did they die for on'y for freedom? An' 'tis many an' many of them had wives an' families an' farms an' schools."

"Freedom for whom? Freedom for what?"

"Freedom for what?" repeated Fonsy, all sarcasm. "Freedom for Ireland, of course."

"For Ireland? Or for the people of Ireland?"

Fonsy, less positive, frowned, scratched his head. "For the people of Ireland, I suppose."

"And who else are the people of Ireland only Andy and

124

myself and our farms and our schools and our wives and our families?"

"Come on now!" dared the gleeful Andy Gorman. "Answer the man! Answer up to the man now, Fonsy! Where are all your grand arguments gone now? Answer up now!"

"But sure that's not the point I was arguin' about at all. I was debatin' another matter altogether." Fonsy gave up the struggle. "Ach! Ye have me moidered between ye. I have no more time to waste with ye, arguin' around in rings. But, by the god of Carrick, if Jer Coady were here this day, he's the boy would soon argue another ring around ye for every ring ye'd try to argue around him."

"Ah, you shouldn't be too hard on poor Fonsy, master," advised Andy, winking back at Peter. " 'Tis how he's liable to get a small bit confused in an argument when he haven't his Primer for Debaters to his hand to instruct him."

"The gift of the sense of humour," announced Fonsy, climbing down painfully off the wall, "comes next, I'd say, after the gift of poetry. But when a man thinks that he's funny, an' he's not funny, there's no greater curse can be inflicted on mankind." He stared down the road. "I see your wife comin' up now, Peter, an' I'd estimate, from the hump on her back, that she's chockful of news an' burstin' to tell it."

"She was at home in Clashmairead," Peter told him, "and they always have some news, true or false, in Clashmairead."

Tessie O'Dea, still the only lady cyclist in the whole district of Carriglea, came slowly uphill towards them, dismounted, leaned over the handlebars to regain her breath. "I'm murdered from tearing up that hill," she said at last. "You'll have to buy a motor for me, Peter, the minute this war is over, and not have me breaking my back on this old push-bike. Hello, Fonsy! Hello, Andy! You're a right stranger to us now! You'd nearly need to tell us what your name is, 'tis so seldom we see you nowadays. How are all in the care? All well? Mrs. Gorman? And Tom? Begor, he's getting to be a hardy little lad. And Cissie? Well able to walk and talk now, I'm sure! Mind you, I think she's cuter than Markie, although they're only the same age." She did not wait for a reply. "How did Markie conduct himself, Peter? Was he cross? Was he crying after me? Did he go quietly off to sleep for you?"

"He did, like a lamb," Peter assured her.

"Oh, Andy, how's the new baby?"

"The new baby," said Andy Gorman, "is hardy as a sandpiper an' the quietest child that was ever born."

"Ah, the third child," stated Tessie O'Dea, readily assuming the mantle of motherly knowledge, "is always the quietest and the best. How old is he now? A couple of months? What did ye christen him? Andy, I suppose, after yourself."

"He was born, mam, on the Fifth of March," replied Andy patiently, "an' he was christened Kieran because of him being born on Saint Kieran's Day."

"Fancy that now! I'm well sure 'twas never you who thought of that. Ah, well, ye can call the next son Andy and put the ledger straight again."

Peter coughed, asked with a gravity that might have been either genuine or assumed, "Tess, did you ever kill a man?"

His wife, puzzled, smiled at him. "I never did yet, Peter. But I'll do my best, if you have anyone in particular in mind, to rectify the error. I'm a very dutiful wife, you know."

Her husband half-turned his head, spoke back to his friends. "Fonsy, I take back every word I said in favour of the married men." He turned once more to his wife. "If you never killed a man before, Tess, you're well on the way to killing one now. Poor Fonsy there will explode in precisely one minute from now if he doesn't get some news of the fighting in Dublin."

She threw back her head in that happy way of hers, tossed out the rich hair from beneath the encircling scarf, laughed her ringing laugh. "Oh, the men for it," said she. "If it was news you wanted, why couldn't you ask for it long ago and not be hemming and hawing and stuttering there like a child looking for jam?" She grew suddenly serious. "God forgive me, 'tis far from laughing I should be, and the news so tragic." She paused to gather her thoughts. "The Rising is all over. The fighting in Dublin is ended."

"God be good to the men who died," praised Fonsy.

"Amen," echoed Peter.

126

"They asked for what they got," said Andy sharply, "but they're gone before a higher judge than I am, so I'll leave them to Him."

"Dublin surrendered yesterday," Tessie went on. "Fintan, though he did no fighting himself, knows all the facts. The whole centre of the city is either burnt down or blown up. God knows how many soldiers and volunteers and civilians are dead or wounded. The very hotel we stayed in, Peter, blown to smithereens. Oh, Dublin will never recover, Fintan says. Never!"

"How about the Volunteers?" asked Fonsy.

"They're prisoners, what's left of them. Fintan had an English paper that he got from a sailor in Waterford, and it says that the leader, a man called Pearse, was badly wounded. And do you remember Connolly, Peter? The stout man we saw speaking at the big labour meeting? He's supposed to have been killed."

"I wonder what will happen to those who surrendered," said Peter.

"They knew well when they went into this what the consequences would be," stated Andy Gorman grimly. "They'll have to take them consequences now."

"What talk have you of consequences?" demanded Fonsy. "Aren't they prisoners of war, taken in fair fight an' due the same rights as any other prisoner so taken?"

"What rights have rebels an' traitors an' murderers? No right, but the right to a fair trial an' a merciful death."

"Easy, lads! Easy now, lads. This is not the time or the place for arguments," objected Peter. "Go on, Tess! Have you no more news?"

"I have plenty more if one-half of it can be believed. The Volunteers hold all County Galway yet. And there's an army of them fighting yet to the north of Dublin. They have the town of Enniscorthy also. But it's only a matter of hours anyway, Fintan says, until it ends in those places too, because the surrender in Dublin holds good for the whole country, and they'll all have to lay down their guns."

"Why should they?" cried Fonsy, "An' victory maybe within their grasp!"

"An' why shouldn't they?" cried Andy. "If they have one single atom of sense left, they'll surrender an' avoid more bloodshed."

"Shut up, the pair of ye, for God's sake," ordered Tessie sharply. "I'm hard set enough to remember what news I have without the two of ye yelping in my ears like a brace of greyhound pups. Ah, but stranger still, Peter, in the midst of the fight who comes marching in to Dublin, with a dozen men at his back and the white whiskers bristling for battle, only the bold Jer Coady!"

"Oh, true to form," was Peter's comment.

"Could it be held without him?" asked Fonsy.

"Jasper Wyse, an engine driver from Waterford, was there and saw him and told Fintan the story yesterday. The evening Jer and his men reached the outskirts of Dublin, near Inchicore, Wyse was there. Some of the people were remonstrating with Jer, trying to make him turn back when they saw him so old. "Home!" says he. "Home, is it? Jer Coady is at home wherever bullets are flying and powder burning. Jer Coady fought in '67 and he's not after living forty-nine years and walking five and thirty miles to be told to go home again without having the privilege of striking another blow for freedom." Then he took a look round the crowd and saw Jasper. 'The very man,' says he. 'I'd wish you to do me a small favour, Jasper Wyse. I want you, when you get home, to tell all the heroes of Carriglea how you saw King Coady, at the age of six and sixty, marching off to fight for Ireland,' he says, 'when they, I don't doubt, were scraubing their way into the darkest corner they could find under their mother's bed.' Off with him then into the brunt of the battle, and no sight or sound of him since. Whether he's dead or wounded or prisoner or what, no one knows."

"Aye, begor." Fonsy's voice had softened with what might have been the softness of tears. "If he's gone itself, he'd ask to go no finer way. The ould steel was always there. You can't beat the breed of the Fenian men."

128

"It could be," said Andy Gorman, without bitterness, "that there's no fool like an old fool. But, let him be wrong or right, there was never braver man born than the same Jer Coady."

In token that his muse was at work, Fonsy had raised a solemn hand. Then, without pause he spoke his lay.

> "They call out Emmet's praises,
>   And they honour Dwyer's name:
> No other one displaces
>   The pride of Wolfe Tone's fame;
> But his fight to glory raises—
>   Of Coady bold I speak—
> His death midst Dublin's blazes
>   In deathless Easter Week."

Peter O'Dea turned from them without a word, walked straight up the path and into his house, slamming the door shut behind him.

His wife, an understanding woman, made no attempt to follow. Instead she bade good night to the men on the roadway and wheeled her bicycle slowly round towards the shed behind the kitchen.

But Fonsy's muse was not the only one that raised a rebel rann ere yet the fires of shattered Dublin had burned cold. From those bloodied ashes the spirit of dead poets arose, Phoenixlike, to send a song of freedom round the world. To Francis Ledwidge on some shell-swept plain in Picardy, to Arnold Bax in his trim London office, to gay Joyce Kilmer on the distant sidewalks of New York that rebel muse spoke, loud and clear, even as it spoke to an ageing woman of loyalist blood and breed and sympathy who had done so much to kindle in the hearts of a younger Ireland the Flame of Liberty. For, among the weeping woods of Lissadell, Augusta, Lady Gregory, had written, too, her tribute to the fallen and their dream.

> "In Easter week a wisp was lit
>   Waked Dublin from her drowsy years;
> I hate the battle-anger, yet
>   What did we ever gain by tears?

129

Our ballad-singers long have cried
The hero-names from far away,
Now let them rhyme the men who died
With the three colours, yesterday."

Easter week was over, and Easter week had just begun.

Chapter Eight

PETER O'DEA lay in his brass-knobbed bed and heard outside the brave note of the blackbird pipe a reveille to the slow-rising spring. He turned his head towards the east window so that he could see the bleak, bare fields of February, then wondered at his own weakness when he tried to lift a hand to his forehead.

He looked hopefully at the little doctor who talked away busily where he stood by the side of the bed, folding up his stethoscope while he talked. Peter noted the worried furrows above the tired eyes, marvelled that, despite long weeks of ceaseless work and endless worry, the fat man's cheerful pompousness seemed more pompous and more cheerful than ever.

"This damned 'flu," the doctor was saying, "is killing off more people than the war has slaughtered. The insatiable cannon of civilisation have not left more corpses in their trail than has this Rider on the Pale Horse, this Fourth Affliction of the Apocalypse. Yes, Mr. O'Dea, even though he has been kind enough to pass you by, the Pale Horseman is riding far and fast through Ireland. And, you can take it from me, sir, that he finds Ireland a very happy hunting ground."

The little doctor squared round, turned his back to the bedroom fire, set his heels against the fender, swung his stethoscope to and fro, his every move watched, from the cot in the corner, by a fascinated Markie. "We've escaped lightly here, thank God, but in other parts the people are dying off like flies in a frost. Now, this Black 'Flu is a particularly virulent form of influenza; but the people of this country, free from the worst ravages of war, should be making a better stand against it than they are doing." He put hands and stethoscope

131

behind his back. "Mind you, Mr. O'Dea, I have a little theory of my own as to why our mortality rate is as high as that of the belligerent nations. And do you know what my theory is?"

Confident that there could be no reply, he beamed round on his listeners, stuffed the stethoscope into his black bag, clicked the clasp shut.

"Well, here is my interpretation of it," he continued, delicately warming his rear to the fire. "Many of our people are actually digging their graves with their own greed. If you doubt that, remember this: Agricultural activity has never been greater here than during the past six or eight months. Food prices are still soaring up and up. The U-boats have almost starved England to her knees, and there she is, clamouring for more eatables from Ireland. Hundreds of farmers, seeing an ever-extending vista of ever-increasing profits, are working to-day as they have not worked since the worst days of the rack-renting. Oh, I know many a man who is actually stinting himself so that there may be all the more food to fatten the priceless pigs, that there may be all the more money to buy still more cattle and still more grain and still more seed potatoes."

"But I think that censure can only apply to a very small minority," objected Peter weakly.

"A minority, maybe, but not so small a minority, sir." The doctor shrugged his chubby shoulders. "And now, like a scourge from God, this Black Death has come down on us. The Pale Horseman has no time, I fear, to pick and choose between the innocent and the guilty. He takes his victims as he finds them."

The schoolmaster stirred uneasily in his bed. The child, impressed by the gravity of his elders, began to whimper. The knuckles of Tessie O'Dea's hands were dull white where she grasped a brass-topped bedpost, the blood had drained from her cheeks so that her face held the pallor of worn ivory, yet her voice was light as ever when she spoke.

"I thought gaiety was supposed to be the best medicine, doctor? I'm afraid too much work is playing havoc with your famous bedside manner."

Before he buttoned up his coat, the doctor allowed his high

132

melancholy to hold him entranced a brief moment longer. Then his cheerfulness came flooding back. "If you're worrying about that man there, Mrs. O'Dea, I may tell you he doesn't cost me a second thought. Oh, poor Peter has many a hard road to travel yet before we can strike his name off the baker's list. You need make no arrangements for getting a new husband yet, madam. That man will top any another egg before his turn comes." He put on his hat, remembered his manners, removed it again. "The year is turning, the war is almost over. In another month, please God, this 'flu will be only a memory, and myself and yourself will be heating up a good bumper of punch, Mr. O'Dea, to celebrate the day that the khaki boys go marching through Berlin to hang the Kaiser."

Peter raised himself slightly on one elbow. "So, in your opinion, doctor, 'twill be all over soon?"

"A matter of time, sir! A mere matter of time! America's men and money and munitions are pouring on to all the battle fronts, and, though no change may be evident just yet, 'tis merely a matter of time until Germany folds up like a house of cards."

"Even with the Russians out of it?"

"Even with the Russians out of it. Oh, you can see for yourself, even by watching straws, what way the wind is blowing. Only this morning I was reading the Times and, God knows, but I had to laugh." He laughed again at the very memory. "Who do you think are talking now of sending delegates to the Peace Conference? Oh, you'd never guess! Our own hotheaded rebels, who were all down here in this county a few months ago, the time of the bye-election, telling us to put our faith in the gun and our own strong arms and our gallant allies in Europe! Gallant allies in Europe, if you don't mind! Oh, we all know who those gallant allies in Europe were! But now, faith, our famous Sinn Féiners have changed their tune. Oh, very quick they were to note the change in the wind. Delegates to the Peace Conference, no less! Staking out already Sinn Fein's claim on President Wilson's Fourteen Points. Merciful heaven, who ever heard the equal of that for brazen cheek?"

Tessie O'Dea, roused herself, laughed softly. "I suppose, doctor, with so much loud talk going on here, there and everywhere, the Sinn Féiners consider they should shout as loud as the next. Well, let them shout, say I. While they shout, and do no more, we're safe enough from harm."

"Ah, but look at the harm they're actually doing already by their prating!" objected the little doctor. "Turning the heads of thousands of young fellows. Keeping them strutting round in green uniforms with wooden guns, when they should be out where they're sorely needed, fighting for their country in the trenches of Flanders. Oh, if recruiting is retarded much further by these fools spouting about freedom at every crossroads, we'll have conscription down on top of us before we know where we are."

Tessie laughed again, though the laugh brought a knife-edge of pain to stab beneath her heart. "In this house, doctor, you're only preaching to the converted. You should go up to Clashmairead and talk some sense into that brother of mine, or into my mother, for that matter. You'd think, to listen to the two of them, that De Valera made Ireland."

"De Valera!" The doctor had been moving away, but now he paused, flaring into a fury. "De Valera! My God, it sickens me to hear people praising this man De Valera, as if the fellow were doing anything constructive for the country! A mushroom of a man whose name was never heard tell of till he came out of jail, twelve months ago, to lead honest people astray with his treachery and his treason."

"He seems to have captured the admiration of my own people back in Clare," put in Peter.

"And devil a far that admiration will bring him or them," cried the angry doctor, grasping the doorknob as fiercely as if he had the whole Sinn Fein movement by the throttle. "Ah, it makes my heart bleed to hear young fools shouting for this De Valera, who's out to make trouble for us all, and to see the same fools with nothing but contempt for my poor friend, John Redmond, who has devoted a lifetime to the good of our country and our people. My poor friend Redmond, who healed the wound of the Parnell Split, who won us Home Rule at last, who, against my friendly advice, is wearing himself to his grave above at the All-Party Convention in Dublin, trying to achieve what's best for all of us."

Peter coughed sympathetically; Markie made restless noises in his cot, was hushed to silence by his mother.

The doctor juggled with hat and umbrella, indignant still. "Yesterday, no later than yesterday, an ignorant lump of a County Council labourer, a nincompoop named Regan who has no finer calling than to scrape the roads, had the damnable cheek to inform me that, in his opinion—in his opinion, God bless the mark—John Redmond was nothing but a fat old cod." Purple-faced, the little man paused for breath. "Oh, but I matched him! I soon matched our dear friend Regan! 'Is that so?' said I, polite as you like. 'Is that what you think of Mr. Redmond? Well, Regan,' said I, 'I'm in a bit of a hurry,' opening the medicine chest. 'Here are a few pills for you,' I said. 'Take one of those every hour and you'll be right as rain in a day or two.' Oh, I quickly matched the bold Regan." The memory of his triumph seemed to shine like a halo round the doctor's bullet head. He lowered his voice lest he offend. "Strictly between ourselves, and saving all your presences, one of those pills would have colicked a draught horse. Oh, the great Regan doesn't feel like insulting John Redmond today, I warrant you!"

Still chuckling, the doctor pattered down the stairs, waited in the hall till Tessie O'Dea followed. "Oh, he's well out of danger, ma'am. Oh, the worst is over. All he needs now is plenty of rest and nourishment. A beaten-up egg several times in the day, all the milk-puddings and suchlike that you can give him, but above all plenty of rest, and he'll be himself again in a week or two." He eyed her sharply. "This is Thursday. I'll call again on Saturday, and if you're not looking any better by then, young woman, I'm going to give you a complete overhaul. Teaching and looking after Markie is wearing you down. When those beaten-up eggs are knocking around, swallow off a few yourself." He put on his hat. "I'm ordering you, here and now, to take life easy for a while. I have too many patients on my hands already, you know."

135

Peter O'Dea, a man wont to worry about his health, lay anxious in his bed and heard his wife bid the doctor farewell, heard the doctor's noisy motor-car splutter into life, heard small Markie's sigh of contentment, now that the doctor, Markie's bogey-man, was safely departed. Peter O'Dea heard the front door close, counted his wife's slow footsteps on the stairs, and noted, fear gnawing at his brain, how lifeless her footfalls were, how pale and worn her face when she re-entered the room. God, thought Peter, the news must be bad. Is it my heart? Or my lungs?

Aloud he said lightly, "Well? What did he tell you? Should I hire a harp and put in some practice lest I disgrace myself when I take my place in the eighth choir of angels?"

She laughed, but there was no mirth in her laughter. "He said he never met a greater schemer, nor a greater humbug, nor a greater impostor. He said he only wished he himself had your health, but that, since you want to be petted, we'd better leave you in bed a week or two longer and humour you into believing you were terribly bad so that you can tell everyone, in twenty years time, what a narrow shave you had the time of the big 'flu." She smiled, but the smile never reached her dulled eyes.

His anxiety was quick to take a new turn. "And did you ask him about yourself? Did you tell him you're not feeling well?"

She caught at the end of the bed as if to steady herself. She turned her face away. "I said nothing to him. You know how fussy he is. He'd only give me a pink bottle and order me straight to bed. He remarked that I was looking a bit tired and said I should take things easy for a while."

Peter frowned. "You were foolish not to tell him how quickly you tire and how badly you sleep. Even if he did order you to bed, we could easily put a substitute above in the school, and someone from Clashmairead could come down to give Mary Kate a hand in looking after ourselves and Markie."

She stood away from the bed to lean back against the dressing table. "I don't mind being tired, Peter. And I always was a poor sleeper. It's the dizziness that frightens me. And all this day I get a pain between my shoulders every time I breathe.

136

It eased a bit there when the doctor was here. But it's at me again now, Peter. It's inclined to get worse and worse." She braced herself up, her palms flat on the tabletop, her eyes grown brilliant in the grey pallor of her face. "I find it . . . a bit difficult . . . for me . . . to draw . . . my . . . breath."

Knees and arms could keep her upright no longer, so that she had crumpled into unconsciousness before Peter could throw aside the bedclothes and scramble to her aid, or before Markie could mouth his first cry of terror.

Old Mrs. Fogarty from Clashmairead came fretfully down the stairs of the teacher's residence, crossed the hall, grunted her slow way into the kitchen. " 'Twas a damn shame for them, Pether, ever to build a stair that narrow in any man's house. An' they that could have built it broad as a road if they wished when 'twas all Governmint money went into the building of it."

She sat down in a chair by the fire nor ever looked either at Peter O'Dea or at her own son Fintan whose chairs flanked the fire already. She sat silent a moment, helped herself to a pinch of snuff, sneezed heartily. "That girl abovestairs is not well, Pether," she announced at last, "an' I'd not trust that little whipsther of a doctor as far as I'd throw him. So I think I'd betther stay on here a while, Pether, an' keep an eye on her myself. Fintan there can take the child with him up to Clashmairead for them to care, an' I'll stay here with Tess until her time is due."

Peter, haggard and unshaven, hunched forward in his chair. "That's a decent offer, ma'am. You'll be a great head to us here through this sickness and trouble, but, if it's all the same to you, I'd rather not send the boy up to Clashmairead. Up there he'll only be in everybody's way, wasting everybody's time. 'Twould be different if you were there yourself to keep an eye on him, but with you down here he'd be only a trouble and a hindrance to them above. Besides, 'twould worry Tess to have him away from her. She'd only be fretting about him from dawn to dark, and, worse still, she'd keep on worrying from dark to dawn. Mary Kate Gannon is long used to looking after him, and I'll guarantee that he'll not annoy Tessie. Not while I'm around."

The old woman stared at him shrewdly. "I don't think, Pether, you'd take very kindly to parting from him yourself."

"That could be."

"It could," said she. "Ah, you see no sun in the sky only the same Markie, an' I can only pray to my God, Pether O'Dea, that you never have cause to regret your *gradh* for him."

Fintan Fogarty rose out of his chair, spat into the fire, began to button up his overcoat. "I'd better be off home. The Lord only knows what they're thinkin' at home, 'tis so long since we left an' no word gone back."

"What could your father think only one thing, the worst," declared Mrs. Fogarty comfortably. "I'd not be surprised to see him arrive outside with a hearse any minute. That's the kind of him."

"Well? What am I to tell them above?" asked her son. "They'll all be anxious about Tess."

"Tell them she's not well, that she's not in the betther of that whipsther of a doctor, but that I'll have her on her feet again, please God, in less than no time. Tell them that. And tell Kitty to send me down a few clothes to tide me over. Bring them yourself the next time you're coming."

She sat on, silent, waiting for Mary Kate Gannon to return from the well with a bucket of water, watching her son and son-in-law walk out together to where the restless pony champed on his bit, hostile to the reins hitched tight around the gatepost. In the sickroom upstairs, Markie began to cry fretfully. She heard Tessie's voice raised in weak remonstrance.

Mrs. Anastasia Fogarty from Clashmairead helped herself to another pinch of snuff, seemed to shake from herself, without effort, the weight of her seventy years. She raised her massive self upright and, stolid but resolute, went wheezing up the steep, narrow stairs to minister to her ailing daughter, to soothe her wailing grandson.

The twilight came stealing up along the river, climbing from the east, a grey veil of soft dusk that deepened into a blue

138

mantle, that thickened into a purple cloak; and, though the tiny clouds high overhead were pink in the after-glow of the sunset, and though the western heat-haze was still a collar of bronze about the mountains, yet the first star was bright now above the distant city and the satin silence of night was seeping towards the hills, creeping across the plain.

In the gloom of the gloaming Peter O'Dea sat on the coverlet of the brass-knobbed bed, speaking little, thinking long, the embers in his pipe bowl glowing ever brighter as the shadows gathered.

His wife stirred herself where she lay, wan and worn, on her pillows. "Long though the day is, Peter," she said softly, "the black night always comes at the close of it."

"Aye," said Peter.

"And the longest night ends in the dawn and the sunrise."

Puffing away at his pipe, he made her no answer.

For another brief while she lay silent, then the laughter that was her life came bubbling to her lips. " 'Tis lucky, Peter, that yourself and my mother got Markie so quickly off to sleep. If he were to come in and find you there in the half-dark with that glum look on you and that sick frown on you, he'd never be persuaded that you weren't the boodey-man. He'd never be quietened or coaxed off to sleep again."

Peter took the pipe from his mouth, bent closer so that she might see him smile. "So that's what you're calling me now? A boodey-man! A boodey-man to frighten my own son! Will you go quietly off to sleep, Mrs. O'Dea? Or will the boodey-man have to frighten you too?"

She smiled back at him. "But I'm not afraid of boodey-men, Peter. I'm not afraid of boodey-men, and I'm not afraid of boodey-anything. There was a time, Peter, and a time not long ago, when I was afraid of some things, but nothing can frighten me now." The smile had died from her eyes, but it still lingered on her lips. "Before I got really sick, before God took back to himself the little sister that He sent to Markie, I used often be afraid of . . . of things . . . of losing you, of losing Markie, of those kind of things. But I'm not afraid now, Peter, not any longer."

"You afraid?" he scoffed. "Sure, how could you be afraid? Sure, the end of the world wouldn't take a scare out of you."

She turned her head from him, stared out the west window to where the grey pearls of twilight shone bright above the river. "There's nothing can scare me now, Peter. I've faced up to the worst . . . and I'm not frightened. No, not even frightened by the thought that I might have to leave you and Markie."

He stretched across the bed, caught her thin hands. "Ah, Tess," he said, very earnestly, "what put such a foolish notion into your head? The doctor told me today that he's delighted with the way you're coming on. Inside the next month, girl, you'll be on your feet again right as the rain, tripping up the road to school in the mornings, livelier than a cricket."

"Please God, Peter!" she put in quickly, "Say please God! Because, when everything is worded and weighed, it wasn't the doctor who gave me my life, and it's not for the doctor to say when that life might be taken from me." She twined her hands through his. "When I was very, very sick, there the time poor little Mary was born, I knew I might die any day, so every minute I was conscious I prayed that God might spare me for you and for Markie. Then, when little Mary died, I realised I was doing wrong in seeking to go against the Will of God. Ever since, Peter, it has consoled me to think, that, even if I were called away itself, I'd be with you still, oh, in a million ways, until the day you'd join me again."

She paused to husband her breath, to marshall her thoughts. Peter O'Dea stirred uneasily, but found no words which could express his feelings. In a moment she spoke again.

"I thought to myself that you'd never see the sunshine on the river but you'd remember me; that you'd never see the copper beeches, bronze in summer, but they'd mind you of the colour of my hair; that you'd never again hear the morning thrush's song but you'd hear me singing in the kitchen while I watched the kettle boil; that you could never listen to the curlew's night-time call but that you'd pray, as I taught you to pray, for all poor souls in Purgatory." She paused again. "After all, Peter, Eternity is only beyond the next turn of the road. Heaven is just across the hill. Even if one of us has to go on before, and even if another of us has to linger on behind, 'tis short the few years take in slipping by. And then we'll meet again. Then Mary and I will be waiting to welcome you and Markie."

Peter O'Dea rose up abruptly from off the bed. "You've been reading too many prayerbooks, Tess girl," he stated brusquely. "Too much piety, concentrating too long on the next world—that's what is the matter with you. Well, you can put all those fine, theological, philosophical thoughts out of your head, girl, for another thirty years at least, because you'll make no bow to Saint Peter for many a day to come." He waved his empty pipe, he gestured with an air of finality. "Oh, no, indeed, girl dear. You can't evade your duties to your son and to your husband quite so easily. You'll have to make many a strong cup of tea for us yet before we'll allow you transfer your allegiance to Saint Michael and all the angels."

She strove to smile. But she was glad within herself because he could not, in the dimness of the fallen dusk, see the tears that came so swiftly to her eyes.

Peter O'Dea stood on the flagged hearth of his tiled kitchen and tried to prevent himself from thinking of the woman with the auburn hair and the white throat, the laughing woman whom he had married, who lay tonight in the quiet bedroom above his head fighting her last fight for the life that was ebbing slowly from her.

First the cursed influenza had brought her down, then pleurisy had come with short-lived baby Mary. Pneumonia had followed fast in the trail of the evils gone before; and finally, long after the crisis of penumonia should have been past and forgotten, and she had still lain there, battling for breath, while the little doctor's worried frown cut deeper and deeper into his forehead as he listened to her labouring lungs, as her temperature refused to fall, as he went home to pore again over his textbooks and scowl at what they told him about galloping consumption.

The summer, the little doctor had at first told Peter, the

summer and the long rest and the sunshine would surely pull her round. But that summer was long past now, and even the soft wind of September no longer fidgeted among the seeded grasses, and the warmth had gone from the evening air. Aye, and gone too, with the September sunshine, was the lung specialist from Dublin with his great frieze coat and his great brass-bright motor-car and his kindly heart behind his grand manner.

He had given the patient a brief, almost cursory examination. He had shaken hands with her very graciously. He had come carefully down the narrow stairs, pulling on his heavy motor gloves. He had followed Peter into the square parlour, talking calmly of trifles, of the long, dusty, winding roads that lay between him and Dublin, of all the miles he must travel before he would see again his tall house on Fitzwilliam Square. They swung from their talk of the roads to speak of the war, to query whether or no it would be over by Christmas.

"If the war were over tomorrow, Mr. . . . er . . . ?"

"O'Dea," said Peter promptly.

"If the war were over tomorrow, Mr. O'Dea, if travel facilities were restored the day after, I would give your wife a sporting chance of being a whole woman again twelve months from this day. A year in the Swiss sunshine, or six months in the dry deserts of California, or less, say twenty weeks, at a little sanatorium I know in South Africa's Cape Province. Any one of these places would do wonders for her. Wonders!" He refused Peter's proferred drink with a gentle motion of his hand. "But, Mr. . . . er . . . O'Dea, the war is not over. The sea-lanes are still closed. The Swiss sunshine and the Californian deserts and my little sanatorium in the Cape Province are as far removed from us as if they were on another planet."

The famous man had paused, sighed, looked steadily for a moment into Peter's fear-haunted eyes. "Mr. O'Dea," he had said softly, "I could give you a sugared answer, and I could give you false hopes. But that is not my vocation as I see it. In my opinion, your wife will never see another spring. We are all, of course, in the hands of God; but medical science can do no more for her."

Peter O'Dea had lowered his eyes, had put down the un-opened whiskey decanter with a shaking hand. "A straight answer is a straight answer, Doctor. In the present circum-stances it is the kindest answer of all." He caught his breath. "Is there no hope whatever?"

"With an Irish winter facing her? With both lungs almost gone? With every hospital and sanatorium overcrowded? With the war cramping all civilian medical effort?" The specialist had finally buttoned his gloves, had turned back towards the hall. "There is always hope, Mr. O'Dea, while life lingers on. But hope is of the heart, not of the head. I think you will find that your own doctor agrees entirely with my judgement," and he had gone out into the hall where the little family doctor waited, miserable.

Peter O'Dea flung that memory from him, crossed from the hearth to watch through his kitchen window the white pall of October fog creep up the valley from the river. He turned quickly back to the fire when the pallid fog-folds reminded him too faithfully of winding-sheets and shrouds. He strained his hearing to catch the slightest sound from the room upstairs, and the stillness of the kitchen struck him like a blow. "God, the place is a wake-house already," he told himself. To lift from his mind this grey canopy of fear and gloom, he turned sharply to Fintan Fogarty, who sat smoking his pipe by the fire; to Packey Regan, busily spelling his way through the *Freeman's Journal* where he lolled on the settle.

"What's the news from the war today, Packey?"

"What news but the one news," answered Packey. "Them allies advancin' everywhere. Advancin' every whole single where, an' damn the stand the Germans can make again them at all."

" 'Twill be over by Christmas! I said all along 'twould be over by Christmas," said Peter hoarsely, clutching at a new hope. "If it is . . ." and he fell silent.

"I doubt if it will then," reasoned Packey. "Because why? Because it could be that this is all a plan on the part of the Germans. Fallin' back on the Rhine they are! Fallin' back to the Rhine, there to stand an' wait while they call back the

143

rest of their men from the East an' get ready to fight their last battle."

But Peter was no longer listening. He had heard a step on the stairs, was already halfway to the kitchen door.

Kitty Fogarty, on tiptoe, came in from the hall.

"How is she?" whispered Peter.

"She's asleep, but, God knows, she's very weak. And she's asking constant for Markie. My mother was set on going home tonight herself, but she says now to tell Fintan to go on up at once with the trap and bring the child back down, because my father, who was to bring him home here, mightn't think fit to bring him at all. An' if Fintan meets them on his way back he can have them here all the quicker."

Fintan had his overcoat on before ever she had finished talking. "The mare is ready," he said. "She's harnessed and yoked. Even if I have to go the whole way I'll not be long above an hour." He went out quickly, quietly, without turning his head.

Kitty moved towards the stairs, Peter turned to follow her. "Will I go up with you?" he asked.

"Ah, no," she told him. "Stay you where you are. What good would your coming up do an' she asleep? You'd only be worryin' yourself. Stay you where you are. You have Packey there to keep your mind occupied." She went on up the stairs, while her brother-in-law, biddable as a child, brain numbed with grief, wandered back to the fire. . . .

As he sat on in his chair, staring with dulled eyes at the greying embers, paying no heed to Packey's forced chatter, Peter O'Dea found himself thinking long of the red hair, of the white brow, of the slim throat of laughter that had entranced him one far-gone July morning when Tessie Fogarty, gay and defiant, had come marching into his school room in Carriglea . . . had come marching into his schoolroom, and into his heart to reign over both from that day forth. . . . Throat of laughter . . . throat of laughter? Where had he heard that phrase before? Oh, it was that song Fonsy had composed about her, Fonsy's wedding-gift! . . . white throat of laughter? . . . Soft throat of laughter? No, was not this how it rhymed?

144

White throat of laughter,
  And heart free from care:
Eyes of the diamond,
  Red-auburn hair:
Lips like the roses,
  Forehead so fair:
Carriglea and the white throat of laughter!

Peter O'Dea paused among his tear-dim memories to wonder what it was that Packey Regan had been saying. Something about peace and rumours of peace. Something about conscriptions or elections. Some trite man's trite words on freedom. He heard, as a dreamer might hear, the name of Jer Coady. Even that failed to rouse his interest, and he went back again to the memories, to the thoughts of his Tessie, the Tessie he had married only five short years ago. . . .

Soft throat of laughter
  And breast of the swan,
Smile like the sunshine,
  Dimples of dawn:
Brow like the snowdrift
  And grace of the fawn,
Carriglea and the soft throat of laughter!

Above the whisper of the fire, above the muted rumble of Packey's voice, above the footsteps of the hastening wind outside, Peter could hear the solemn words of the priest who had married them and the echo of their own voices in reply— "For richer" . . . "for richer" . . . "for poorer" . . . "for poorer" . . . "in sickness" . . . "in sickness" . . . "and in health" . . . "and in health" . . . "till death do us part" . . . "till death do us part" . . . He could see again the hot streets of Dublin sticky with human blood—and then the dust of those city streets seemed to merge in some strange manner with the dust which had been so widely scattered by the car which had brought them home from their honeymoon, with the dust from the car in which he had carried Markie to be christened, with the dust from the car which had borne the famous lung specialist back

145

to some tall house on Fitzwilliam Square, Tessie's death-sentence delivered. . . .

> Sweet throat of laughter,
>   The soft summer rain
> Must make me remember
>   Your sweetness again:
> The smile of your sunshine
>   Would conquer all pain,
> Carriglea and the sweet throat of laughter.

Peter O'Dea sobbed aloud where he sat there in his chair by the fire, so that Packey Regan made a quick end of his gabbling, and silence reigned again in the darkening kitchen.

Suddenly Kitty was calling from the stairtop landing, a terrible strain of urgency in the very softness of her voice.

"Peter," she called. "Peter! Quick, Peter! I'm in dread but that she's going! Packey, run up to the Chapel for one of the priests!"

He went striding up the stairs, shocked at himself that he felt so cold and calm. Yet at the last his courage failed him, and he paused, hesitant a moment, outside the bedroom door. . . .

Within, old Mrs. Fogarty was reciting that prayer which, above all others, Tessie had loved. The tired voice was stumbling on beneath a burden of tears, but age and grief only enhanced the mellow glory of the Litany of the Virgin, so that, through the habit of years, Peter found himself repeating the responses—Seat of Wisdom . . . Pray for us . . . Cause of our joy . . . Pray for us . . . Mystical Rose . . . Pray for us . . . Tower of David . . . Pray for us . . . Tower of Ivory . . . Pray for us . . . House of Gold . . . Pray for us . . . Ark of the Covenant . . . Pray for us . . . Gate of Heaven . . . Pray for us . . . Morning Star . . .

"Peter," Kitty again called softly.

Conquering himself, he pushed the door open, tiptoed gently in. He could feel the clammy fingers of grief clutching at his heart, at his throat . . . He could see his wife, through her last agony, strive to smile at him from where she lay, there

146

beyond the candle's flame. . . . And he could hear now no single word of the litany. His brain could heed nothing, nothing but whirling lines from that song Fonsy Farrell had made to grace her bridal:

> White throat of laughter . . .
>   Red auburn hair . . .
> . . . smile of your sunshine
> Would conquer all pain,
> Carriglea and the Sweet Throat of laughter.

Heir Apparent

But where are all the loves of long ago?
  Oh, little twilight ship blown up the tide,
Where are the faces laughing in the glow
  Of morning years, the lost ones scattered wide?
Give me your hand, oh brother, let us go
  Crying about the dark for those who died.

—FRANCIS LEDWIDGE

I that should lead, so will be led
  By careless bonds that are most sweet;
Because they must not fare forlorn
  The small strong hands, the wayward feet.

—SYLVIA LYND

Chapter Nine

PETER O'DEA, quiet and all though he was before he lost his Tessie, became from that day out a man rededicated to silence and gravity. If, in the first despairing days of grief, he pined to join his wife in that green grave where, facing the sunset, she awaited Gabriel's trumpet call to Judgement, he had no option save thrust the thought from him, for Tessie O'Dea had left their son Markie to her lone man's care and keeping.

And because he was, in his sorrow, a lonely man, it was a solemn Peter O'Dea who sat huddled on a high chair before the fire in Flann Fogarty's kitchen at Clashmairead and tried in vain to ward off the ever-recurring memories of the red-haired woman but three months dead. Beyond him, old Flann Fogarty, snug in a corner seat, spun the wheel of the fan-bellows to boil the potatoes which would provide the fattening pigs with tomorrow's dinner. Behind them in the flame-bright kitchen, Mrs. Fogarty, slow-moving but efficient, prepared the table for the evening meal.

The old man ceased from his fire-raising, took the pipe from his mouth, screwed up his lips, spat into the ashes. "These elections took a queer turn, masther. Didn't they now?"

"A very queer turn," answered Peter without enthusiasm. "Sinn Fein surprised everyone, including themselves."

"A clean sweep they made. Divil ever anyone witnessed the like before. Myself, I voted for th' oul' Party, while ever I had the vote, an' when a man has my stock of grey hairs, 'tisn't so easy to change. Then Fintan here is such a mad Sinn Feiner always that I swore to God I'd never turn. I said to myself that if I voted Sinn Fein 'twould be admittin' that Fintan is a wiser man nor I am. An' when you advance to my age, Pether boy, you'll find out how necessary it is to prove, an' to keep on provin', that you are, an' that you always were, an' that you always will be a better an' a wiser man nor any son of yours can ever hope to be."

"Yet you changed," said Peter, who cared little whether or no, but dreaded lest the old man fall silent again.

"I had to," stated Flann Fogarty bluntly. "A week or two before the elections I was above at a fair in the town of Carrick, the worst fair, you, sir, for forty year—this peace is after ruinin' the price of cattle. I dropped in to Kinsella's for a pint or two after I had my business done, an' when I came out the Sinn Feiners were speechin' just forninst the town hall."

"A good place for it," said Peter.

"The chairman was just gettin' up on his hind legs. 'The next man to address ye,' says he, 'is a man well known in these parts. A life-long Fenian rebel. A man who was turned seventy when he carried his gun to Dublin in Easter Week, but who plans to strike many a stroke for Ireland yet before the Lord calls him. There should be no need, people of Carrick,' he says, 'for me to stand up here an' introduce to ye the well-known Jeremiah Coady.'"

Peter O'Dea sat upright in his chair but made no comment.

"Locky Quinn was with me," went on old Fogarty, garrulous. "Locky takes a squint out of one eye up at Coady, raises the slow hand to the head, takes off the hat. 'Gloryo to you, me bould Fenian man,' says he. An', bedad, when I myself saw Jerry Coady at this hour of his age, standin' there like a pike staff, with the wind whippin' through 'the white beard, I tell you what, Pether, by the Lord God, but the tears came blindin' the two eyes of me, an' I off with my hat an' cheered with the best of them." He spat again. "An' that was how I came to vote for Sinn Fein."

Peter O'Dea roused himself, turned his head towards the older man. "The tongue was lively as ever with him, I suppose. And 'twouldn't be like him to leave the tears stand long in your eyes."

"Tears! Damn the tear was left inside five minutes, barrin' tears of laughter. 'All my unfortunate life through,' starts Jer,

152

'I've listened to the praises of the Carrick fighting dogs and the Carrick fighting men. Carrick for a man or a dog,' says he, 'that's a proverb known the world over. And there's another saying I've heard down in backward places the like of Carriglea. Carrick, I dread you, they say; Waterford, I fear you, and clouded Clonmel, sure I'll never go near you. Now,' says Jer, 'I want ye, my good people of Carrick, to live up to that reputation by voting so solid for Sinn Fein that "Carrick I dread you," will have a new meaning for our opponents from this election out.' "

"Father Time must have left Jer off his roll altogether," decided Peter.

"Oh, Jerry Coady will never die," stated Flann Fogarty with conviction. "Damn the ever. The disease was never yet invented that could put him in a coffin. Six meetin's he addressed that day, travelled all over the County Tipp'rary, aye, an' at the day's end, when two detectives came to question him at his lodgin's in Cashel, he drank the both of them blind an' sent them back to barracks with green, white, an' goold ribbons pinned on their hats an' they singin' *We'll crown De Valera King of Ireland*."

The kitchen door opened, and Kitty Fogarty came laughing in from the early murk of the January night, so quick-fallen, her young nephew tight-clutching at her skirts as she came.

"We milked the cow an' the two strippers, Markie an' myself did," she cried gaily. "Didn't we, Markie? Ah, we'll have a right farmer made of him, Peter, in less than no time."

The child looked shyly round at all the smiling faces, then hid his head in the folds of his aunt's apron.

"Come on, Markie!" Kitty ordered. "Speak up now an' tell us the truth! Which would you rather be, here with all the sucky-calves an' the pigs an' the dogs an' the cows an' the pussy-cat an' all, or below in Carriglea with nothin' near you only that old school?"

Markie stared solemnly at where his father sat half-hidden amid the flame-flickered shadows of the chimney corner. "I'd rather to be below in Carriglea, if only my mammy would come home from Heaven," said the child with a sudden rush of candour. Then, quickly conscious from the stricken faces of his elders that he had said something very wrong, he hid his face again in his auntie's apron, began to cry and to kick the floor with one small foot.

The old woman came quickly across the floor and gathered him into her wide arms. "Hush, alannah," she soothed, "don't mind what that oul' Kitty does be sayin' to you! Hush, now, an' your Granny will give you the grandest piece of applecake for your tea that ever you set a tooth in. Run over there to your father an' soak some heat into your bones while the kettle is boiling." She steered him across the kitchen. "Perished the poor child is, out there so long in the cold cow-house, an' half-starved, too, with the hunger. Bad luck to you, Kitty! You should never have kept him out there so long on such a per-ishin' evenin'!"

Peter O'Dea opened his knees wide to afford his son a safe refuge between them. He linked his hands together in a firm semicircle round Markie's waist. Kitty, crestfallen at the failure of her attempted gaiety, moved slowly away towards the room beyond the kitchen, pulling off her apron as she went. By the room door she paused. "You know what, Peter? The next time Fintan is below or that you yourself come up, you'd want to send or bring us the rest of Markie's clothes. He'll have high-roads made through every stitch he has here before another week is out. As for stockin's! Eeyah, he'd manage to hole them even if they were made of bell-metal."

The schoolmaster cleared his throat, slowly, deliberately. "'Tis very thoughtful of you, Kitty. But there won't be any need to bring or send up his clothes. Fintan will be coming down to me tomorrow, and I want him to bring Markie down with him."

"For good?" asked Mrs. Fogarty sharply.

"For good," replied her son-in-law.

There was silence in kitchen for a little while, the women immobile where they stood, the men staring at the glowing fire, the child closely watching his granny, waiting, anxious, for the promised applecake. The old man was first to speak. "'Tis no easy matter," he said, "for a man who was never

154

tutored in that particular brand of business to set about rearin' a child on his lone."

"There's not much more rearing to be done on him. He's all but fit for school. And rearing my child shouldn't prove hard for me, seeing as how 'tis for dealing with children that I draw my day's pay. Wouldn't it be a shameful thing if I failed to do for myself what I'm doing all my life for other people?"

There was silence again in the fire-bright kitchen. Markie, puzzled a little by his elders' solemnity, conscious that he himself was in some way the cause of it, stirred uneasily between his father's knees. Then the old woman came over to the fire, bent to pour a splash of boiling water from the black kettle into the brown teapot. " 'Tis, maybe, a harder task than you think, Pether," she said soberly, "to try an' raise a child without a mother."

Her son-in-law answered without looking up. "If by care and attention a son can be reared, ma'am, I'll stint neither attention nor care in the rearing of mine."

Mrs. Fogarty shuffled to the door, threw out the water with which she had rinsed the teapot. From the shadows of the room beyond Kitty said her say. "You need never fear, Peter, that Markie will lack care or attention if you leave him here to us. If we wouldn't stint ourselves for Tessie's child, we'd be a poor breed."

Her father spoke in slow anger. "There's no child of Tessie's bein' discussed at all, miss. This child we're speakin' of is Pether O'Dea's child, an' the only question for to be discussed is whether it would prove handier, both for Pether an' the child, to have the boy raised here or below in Carriglea. If Pether think it would be fitter for himself to rear up his son, I see no reason for any further argument at all." He turned to the silent man beside him. "When I say you're welcome to take the boy, Pether, 'tis undherstood, of course, that we'd be only too glad to rear him for you. The missus an' Kitty there were as heart-set on keepin' that child as I was myself. But your word, Pether, is the last word."

Mrs. Fogarty had come back from the door and stood behind her husband, teapot in hand, patiently awaiting her turn to speak. "There's very little for me to add to that, Pether," she said. "God knows but we'd like to have a child of our own blood with us an' that we'd not like to see you overreachin' yourself to rear him while there's idle hands here that could ask for no more pleasant work. Besides, I suppose our pride doesn't like to let it be said that we'd leave a lone widow-man to rear a Fogarty woman's orphan. But I know too, and God knows, how lonely 'tis for you now that Tess is gone, an' the great difference 'twill make to have the child runnin' around the house. An' I'll promise you this much, boy, if you do bring Markie down with you, you'll never be short of someone from here to do a hand's-turn for you while we have breath an' strength to do it."

Peter O'Dea looked thoughtfully over at the old woman. "The day I got married, ma'am, that very morning, I got a letter from old Jer Coady, abusing me, of course, for getting married at all, for letting down his principles, he said. But he put in this bit at the end. 'Anyway,' he had, 'if you must demean yourself by matrimony, I'm glad you're marrying a Fogarty from Clashmairead. They're a decent breed of people.'" He paused; his listeners waited. "Jer Coady," said Peter slowly, "was a great man always for telling out the truth."

Markie, tired of the serious talk and the slow silences, whispered across to his grandmother. "Granny! Granny! Is the applecake boiled yet, Granny?"

"Baked it is! 'Tis baked, alannah!" she whispered back. "Markie will have his applecake now in one minute."

Peter spoke again. "For two reasons I want to have the rearing of Markie myself. In the first place, he's the only link I have with Tessie."

"A damn good reason if you never had another," said Flann Fogarty.

"And the second reason is this: Let him turn out good or bad in the years to come, I'll have no one to praise or to blame but myself, because, whatever he'll be, 'tis I will have made him so."

Kitty came back into the kitchen. "Wouldn't it be well to

156

let us bring him on for another year or two before you start your training on him?" she asked as she set about lighting the lamp. "Sure, he's only turned four."

"My mind is long made up, Kitty," answered the schoolmaster slowly. "But I'd not wish ye to think that I'm not grateful for all ye've down ever since Tessie took sick, or that I'm not thankful to ye for offering to keep Markie. Venomous people will comment, and 'tis ye who'll suffer most from their tongues. Yet, whether I'm right or whether I'm wrong, and only time can tell that, I'm going to keep the child and the child's future tight in my own two hands."

"Yerrah, never mind about people talkin'," cried Mrs. Fogarty, picking up the teapot. "Them that wants to understand will understand, an' them that don't want to understand would be talkin' anyhow." She filled up the teapot from the jigging kettle. "Eeyah, Pether, who has finer right to rear your boy than you have yourself?"

It was a nine-days' wonder in Carriglea and far beyond when the schoolmaster brought home his son from Fogarty's to rear him, womanless, under his own wing. But nine-days' wonders and ninety-days' wonders all reach the hour when they are wonders no longer, and the time came also when, if people thought at all of Peter O'Dea or his Markie, they accepted the widower's masculine house as a commonplace, a workaday fact of life.

And, if people's minds and talk turned often enough to the teacher and his son, it was not because they any longer thought strange of Peter's plan of life but because the whole parish was interested in young Markie O'Dea's progress and welfare. For, as the months went by and the child was growing up, there wasn't man or woman in that countryside, from young Father Hahissey above in the parochial residence to Maggie the Rags begging her way along the roads, but whenever they met the master must stop him to enquire how Markie was getting on. Nor did anyone who could claim even a nodding acquaintance with the rearing of children ever fail to demand full particulars as to the state of Markie's health or could be prevented from advising his father how best to keep Markie free from worms, or how to give him speedy relief when he had the earache, or how to ensure that Markie would not heg himself to death in a severe bout of the whooping-cough.

Peter would smile a little, would listen to all their lecturings in that grave, understanding way of his. Then, thanking them very kindly for their hints and their recommendations, he would slip away home and there continue rearing Markie according to some well-thought-out system of his own. Aye, and despite the blatant way in which all the sound advices and all the wise counsels were neglected, the lad never saw a sick or a sorry day.

It was agreed around the firesides of Carriglea that a finer boy than the master's Markie had never been reared by Suir Water. From the first day Peter brought his son home from Fogarty's, he brought the lad everywhere he went himself, whether to the school or to the chapel or to the town, and, no matter where the pair betook themselves, even black strangers would turn in the street for a second look at the grave man and the handsome child. Markie O'Dea inherited his mother's warm hair and his mother's merry laugh and all his mother's gay ways, but it was his father who had gifted him with the kind eyes and the quiet smile, who had taught him that confidence in himself which came as natural to him now as the jaunty spring in his walk, and which lent a grand air of manliness to the quaint set of his erect little head.

The Fogarty aunts, and some of them were mothers and some of them were yet single, and some of them were pledged to celibacy, but all of them clever and clear-headed women, were ever and always scolding Peter for all the ways they said he had of spoiling the child—for the way he'd stint Markie nothing the boy wanted; for the way he'd gratify his son's every wish and whim. The Fogarty aunts never grew tired of foretelling to Peter how dearly he'd pay for all his pampering yet. But the master paid no more heed to the Fogarty aunts than he did to anybody else. He put his faith in his son and in his own methods of training and teaching the boy. Aye, and it is often he must have felt proud of that son and of that training.

There was no lad of his years so sturdy or so well mannered, while, in so far as knowledge was concerned, it was common gossip round the fire at the forge that, before Markie had ever reached his sixth birthday, he was well on the way to being more learned than his father. But they were ever inclined to exaggerate a little by the fire at the forge.

Those very years in which Markie O'Dea grew from baby ways to boyhood were bright and hopeful years for Ireland and the Suirside, but they were black, bitter years as well. No sooner had the Great War ended than the Little War began. While rifles crashed and houses burned, young men, aye, and men who are youthful no longer, died gladly for an old ideal behind blood-slippery barricades, on dew-sweet hillsides, in crowded streets, on lonely scaffolds.

Yet the troubles and the crossness remained remote enough from easy-going Carriglea. No raiders came to break up the little circle which gathered round the schoolmaster's fire at nighttime, and, if Ned Gorman and Packey Regan were seldom to be found there, none passed comment on their absence. Fonsy, though the years had greatly tamed him, and Ritchie Roughane, the sage sexton, and Paddy McKeown, the blacksmith, and Jamesy Hearn, the farmer who lived just across the fields, would drop in to pass an hour or two by the teacher's hearth. Andy Gorman, too, had become a more frequent visitor as the war grew more general and Ned was more and more often away with the flying column on the hills; for, though Andy disagreed with his brother's politics, blood still ran thicker than water, and it was to O'Dea's in Carriglea that news of Ned's safety was most likely to come.

There, among his elders, Markie would perch nightly on his little stool, solemn and sage, listening to high talk that should have been far beyond his years. So that there was more headshaking among the Fogarty aunts and more and direr prophecies as to the ultimate end of their orphaned nephew. But damn the hair did Peter O'Dea care, only let the boy be, and if Fonsy Farrell taught him rebelly songs and encouraged him to sing them in front of Andy Gorman and Roughane to rouse their loyalist sympathies, ah, well, thought Peter, 'tis little enough amusement the child has, and he could be learning worse things than what Fonsy the Rhymer teaches him.

But even into that quiet village above the river the echoes of the crossness, aye, and the crossness itself, penetrated once in a way. There came a raw and blustering night in winter when Peter, on his way upstairs to bed, was halted by a knock on the front door and came back down to find District Inspector Lalor of the Royal Irish Constabulary impatiently awaiting him on the doorstep, in mufti and in haste.

"Indeed and you're out very late, Inspector," said Peter, shielding with his hand the guttering candle flame.

"Better be out late than not be able to venture out at all," answered Lalor grimly. "I'm sorry for disturbing you at such an hour. I'm in need of a bicycle pump. I was dashing to Waterford, and of course my damned bike had to go flat before I even got this far."

The schoolmaster bent down, dragged out a pump from among the miscellany that littered the hall stand. "Is your car out of order?" he asked.

"Blast you, O'Dea," snapped Lalor, "will you mind your own business? You'll soon be as accomplished a spy and a pry as the rest of them."

O'Dea flushed, but his slow temper did not flare. "I didn't mean to stick my nose into your private business. I meant no harm," he said quietly as they walked down to where the offending cycle rested against the gate. "It was only a friendly query, to pass the time, to make conversation."

Lalor felt for the valve on the back wheel, pumped for a moment or two, did not speak until he straightened to test with his thumb the hardness of the tyre. "Ah, well," he began softly, "I suppose I was a bit snappy. I'm sorry, Peter. My nerves are like fiddle-strings nowadays. Between rebels and Sinn Feiners,"—he drew a breath—"aye, and bankers and bailiffs, I'm harried from pillar to post till I don't know which end of me is my head and which is my heels." He finished his pumping, followed Peter back to the house. At the door he buttoned up his heavy black coat, pulled the incongruous check cap still further down over his eyes. On an impulse he held out his hand. "Good-bye, Peter. You may as well know now what the rest of the country will know tomorrow. I'm clearing myself out of here, lock, stock, and barrel. The bank is closing on Moonbawn and there's damn-all else I can do but let them take it."

They gripped hands. Said Peter slowly, "I'm sorry to hear such bad news, Inspector. But surely you're not leaving the force?"

Lalor turned away. "I'm leaving it, Peter. I'm leaving it while the going is good and I can take a whole skin into retirement. I've been a loyal servant to the Crown all my life, sir, but I have a very good idea as to the way the wind is blowing, and I think that life in this country won't be overpleasant for any servant of the Crown in the time that's coming. I'll lose money by retiring now; but a smaller pension, and life to enjoy it, is a sight better than a bullet in the back some dark night from Ned Gorman or Packey Regan."

He was going out the gate when Peter, still striving to be sympathetic, said, "I'll be very sorry to lose young Gregory. I hadn't a brighter boy above in the school. I think as badly of seeing him go as if he were one of my own."

"He's better away," decided the policeman. "He'd never get anything hereabouts except abuse and impertinence from people who wouldn't scruple to take out of the son what they'd fear to do to the father." Suddenly, while he backed his bicycle away from the pier, Din Lalor laughed aloud. "Do you call to mind all the times, Peter, that old Jer Coady stood on the hearth inside and swore before God that he and his rebels would run me out of Moonbawn yet? And 'twas little either of us thought then that it wasn't the rebels but the bankers who would send me slinking from Moonbawn in the dark of the night." He wheeled his machine a step or two, turned back to speak again. "Take a last word of advice from me, Peter O'Dea. Stand well clear of the Stock Exchange! If you want to get rid of your money, there's a dozen more pleasant ways of achieving that aim. And here's warning number two: If ever you're misfortunate enough to own land, don't mortgage it to

161

the bank! 'Twould be more profitable and a damn sight more pleasant to sell your soul to the devil."

Then he was gone into the darkness and the rain.

If the Lalors' departure brought the first ripple of war to the schoolmaster's door, the coming of the Tans brought something more than a ripple. For months before their actual arrival the mothers of Carriglea were wont to frighten the bold ways out of their children by threats of throwing them to the same Tans. In that Carriglea was blessed, for there was many a home in Ireland where the Tans, so far from being a vague threat, were a very substantial terror. Hopeful people, and Peter O'Dea was one, sometimes maintained that, with such as Ned Gorman and Packey Regan active elsewhere, there was small reason why the Tans should ever visit Carriglea.

But come they did, and, to the worried Peter, marching home from the school, leading small Markie by the hand, the emptied lorries in front of the public-house, the black-and-khaki-clad drivers lounging by the doorway, pint-pots in hand, boded ill for the immediate future of the village. Inside the tavern, raucous voices roaring out a Flanders ditty pursued the schoolmaster as he hurried homeward.

> "Three German Officers crossed the line,
>   Parlez vous.
> Three German Officers crossed the line,
>   Parlez vous.
> Three German Officers crossed the line,
> To court the women and drink the wine,
>   Inkey pinkey parlez vous."

Peter O'Dea had eaten his dinner and was busily instructing Markie in the subtle art of dishwashing when he heard, from the village above him, the snarl of motor engines, the bang of a rifle, the sound of drunken laughter. He was folding the tea-towel, and was folding it neatly, even though his heart was pounding in his ears, when he heard a sharp bark of command and saw that the lorries had come free-wheeling downhill to halt at his own gate. There was no chance of rushing the child to some place of safety, for already a dozen bravoes were ap-

162

proaching the front door. Warning Markie for his life not to leave the kitchen, Peter strode across the hall, met the invaders on the doorstep with a brave face and a queasy stomach.

The Tans, despite their bad reputation, were in high good humour. The leader swung his rifle level with Peter's face. "'Er 'ighnesses butler, I presoom! I say, 'Enery, just trot right back to yer little ole kitchen an' tell the ole Duchess as 'ow me an' me pals 'as dropped in to tea."

Peter, backing before their onset, found himself in the centre of the kitchen floor with Markie clinging to his knees and a crush of ribald, tipsy riflemen crowded in on top of them.

"Wot's yer name, chum?" demanded the tea-seeking spokesman, one chevron of his sergeant's stripes dangling loose from his left arm.

"O'Dea," answered Peter calmly as he could.

"A good naime for a bleedin' shinner," said one of the men and spat noisily on the floor.

"An' wot do they call you when that bad beer is goin' ahround in the little ole boozer up the street?"

"Peter," stated the master solemnly, his eyes fascinated by the wavering muzzle of the sergeant's Lee-Enfield.

"Peter O'Dea! An' wot do you do for yer livin' when you ain't aht with the murder gang?"

"I have nothing to do with murder," answered Peter firmly. "I am a loyal subject of the Crown and a faithful employee of the State."

"Stow it, chum," the sergeant warned. "Every bleedin' Shinner in this bleedin' country is a loyal bleedin' citizen an' a bleedin' servant of the bleedin' State. Blime if we've met one bleedin' rebel yet. 'Ave we?" winking at his men.

They guffawed dutifully. One of them, impatient, tired already of the crowded kitchen, rubbed his scrubby chin, suggested fretfully, "Ah, hell! Give him what's comin' to him, sarge. We're long enough here."

"A loyal bleedin' citizen an' a bleedin' servant of the bleedin' State," repeated the sergeant, who had no intention of letting

163

so profound a phrase be too easily forgotten. "An' all those murder-gang pals of yours? All loyal bleedin' citizens too, I'll take my bleedin' oath! Who else lives in this 'ouse?"

"No one," Peter replied, still acutely conscious of that ever-threatening rifle. "No one except the child and myself."

"Garn," said the sergeant, spitting towards the range. "Mean to tell us you got a bloomin' baby an' no bloomin' missus? Bleedin' wonder, you are." The men guffawed. "Bleedin' wonders, all you bleedin' rebels," said the sergeant, greatly pleased at his own wit.

"She's dead," snapped Peter, a bubble of anger rising red in his brain at the thought of these thugs making merry among his memories of Tess.

"She's lucky, she is," commented the sergeant. "Women always turns sentimental like when we 'as to shoot their murder-gang hubbies. 'I know it's a dirty job, missus,' I always say," continued the sergeant with relish, " 'but then this is a dirty country,' a dirty bleedin' country," affirmed the sergeant, and waited, a shade longer than on previous occasions, for his men's laughter.

"Ah, come on, sarge," urged a melancholy corporal from the door. "There's a better boozer further up the road. We're wastin' time crowin' at this dodo. He's only the bloomin' schoolteacher. He ain't got the guts to be a murder-gang. He ain't even got any whiskey in his parlour. Only bloomin' bad port." He made a wry mouth. "I've 'ad a look," he ended despondently.

"Bleedin' loyal bleedin' citizens of the bleedin' Crown," repeated the sergeant, baffled now. "We'll soon see 'ow bleedin' loyal you are. Say 'God Save the King.' "

"God save the King," said Peter without fervour.

"Louder!"

"God save the King!"

"Sing it!" suggested the weary corporal.

"Sing it!" ordered the sergeant.

Peter strove to gulp down his anger.

"Sing it," and the rifle swung round again.

164

> "Send him victorious,
> Happy and glorious,
> Long to reign o'er us.
> God save the King.
> God save our King."

"You may be no bleedin' Shinner, chum," commented the corporal, "but, believe me, you're no bleedin' singer either."

Angry voices called from the waiting lorries. The sergeant had forgotten whatever mad impulse had first brought him stamping into the teacher's kitchen. He glared round, baffled, reluctant to leave until he had accomplished something.

"Garn," he said at last, "this bleedin' blighter ain't worth shootin'. Bleedin' loyal men without the bleedin' courage of their bleedin' convictions." He turned to his troops. "Back to our little ole battle-waggon, boys, an' we'll look for some perisher that is worth a bleedin' bullet."

Muttering, they filed out before him, clambered one by one into their places. The sergeant marched Peter and the scared Markie before him to the gate. Still covering them with his Lee-Enfield, he lumbered into his seat beside the driver.

"Loyal men!" said he and spat. "Loyal men!" and spat again. "Oh, give me an honest-to-gawd rebel every time." The engine started. The other tenders were already moving away. "Up the bleedin' rebels," cried the sergeant as the lorry ground into gear.

The men broke into song. Clouds of dust fanned out from the departing wheels.

> "I called you baby-doll a year ago,
> You told me I was very nice to know.
> I soon learnt what love was, I thought
> ... you taught ... how to love you."

The voices trailed off into a confusion of receding sound. Some warrior fired at a circling crow.

Peter O'Dea heard the bullet drone past high overhead. He stood silent, Markie's small hand clutched tight in his own. Then, relief boiling up within him, he beamed down on his son.

"Aha, Markie," he exulted, "we're two right heroes! I'm telling you, boy, 'twould take more than the Black and Tans to frighten the two of us. We stood up to the old Black and Tans, didn't we, Markie?"

"We did." Markie was all enthusiasm. "We hunted the old Black an' Tans, didn't we, Daddy?"

"We hunted them," echoed Peter. He threw back his head, looked down the valley to where the cloud of dust from the lorry wheels was approaching the highroad a mile away. He shook his fist at the distant dust cloud. He used strange language for one who had always been a quiet, unpolitic man of peace.

"Up the Rebels," roared Peter. "Up Dev! Up the Republic."

Markie caught a spark from his father's fire. Markie remembered the sergeant. He shook a chubby fist at the wide distance.

"Up the bleedin' rebels," screamed Markie.

Although the Fogarty aunts often accused Peter O'Dea of allowing Markie to stay up overlate listening to the old men goster round the fire, it must be admitted, in all fairness to Peter, that the first time the boy ever heard the chimes of midnight, and was yet from his bed, was on the night the Truce was signed.

Carriglea, in all the memory of the generations, had never known that night's equal. Before the slow June dusk was yet grey, the blue smoke of bonfires was high over every hill. From village and lone farmhouse hobnailed boots beat in dance time on cement floors, while the flying columns of fighting men came up from the dugouts, came down from the hills, came back from loneliness and fear and the shadow of death to light and life and laughter. It seemed as though some evil spell had been lifted, as though the whole world had suddenly been flooded in sunshine and song, had been wondrously changed into that Tir na n-Óg, that Land of the Ever Young, which the olden legends had so often described.

On the wind of the word of peace the forge was cleared for dancing, and the smith deemed it but fitting that the best melodeon-player in the countryside should be invited there to fulfill an oldtime promise. And so, though Peter O'Dea had fingered no tune or known little gaiety since his wife's death, yet he never played more easily or more tunefully than he did at that victory dance in the forge, and many a man and woman who heard him could never again recall the night the Terror lifted without remembering also the haunting softness of the Schoolmaster's music.

Fonsy Farrell, whose laureat poem on such an epoch-marking event as the Truce should have proved the peak-point of the celebrations, was unfortunately absent; but his poem was there, and right well did Peter O'Dea deliver it in Fonsy's stead. And, had anyone queried his right to do so, Peter's answer was ready and apt, for the poem had been written in Peter's own kitchen where Fonsy now slept, sodden, on the broad settle, having long ago freed Ireland in Sullivan's public-house. But, if Fonsy himself was silent, his verses spoke for him, and the full of the forge hushed to hear.

> The dear, dark head is raised today,
>   That long was bowed in tears,
> Bright in the light of Freedom's dawn
>   From all the war-dark years:
> And glorious her reign will be
>   Now Right and Truth prevail,
> Sweet Roisin Dhu, Dark Rosaleen,
>   Our deathless Grainne Wail.
>
> Ah, Rosaleen, you're proud this night,
>   Your beauty ne'er will pall:
> We'll keep the flag of freedom high
>   Tho' all the world should fall.
> We'll keep the flag of freedom high
>   And every land will hail,
> Sweet Roisin Dhu, Dark Rosaleen,
>   Our deathless Grainne Wail. . . .

Because of Markie, or because of those long-tongued Fogarty aunts, Peter O'Dea came home at midnight from the festivities at the forge. He was surprised to find a light before him in his own kitchen, to find Ned Gorman sitting there in the arm chair by the fire while Fonsy still snored on the settle.

"Bedad, Peter," greeted Gorman, caustic, "I didn't think you'd be out wrappin' yourself in the green flag with the rest of the fools. I didn't know you were another of the men who saved Ireland."

"Aha, Ned," crowed Peter, achuckle with joy to find his old friend safe and sound, "we don't get a free Ireland every day of the week. They tell me 'tis seven hundred years since we had the like before."

"It might be another year or two before ye get it yet. For all any of us know, the war might be on again tomorrow."

The schoolmaster stared, then said quietly, "We'll have no war tomorrow, Ned, nor the day after either. The celebrating shows you how badly the people needed peace." He turned to his son. "Light the candle now, Markie, and off with you to bed like a good boy. You're nearly asleep in your standing."

"Good night, Markie boy," said Ned Gorman and watched the youngster stumble sleepily upstairs. Then he turned to Markie's father. "The drink is gone to all yer heads, Peter. Listen, you haven't got peace. God knows, if this was peace, I'd shout and sing as loud as the next, and louder, maybe, because I might have better cause. But what ye have is only a truce—a truce, remember that! There might a peace come after it if we get what we fought for, an' there might be no peace at all if things took a turn otherwise. But, one way or the other, this is only a truce."

"It will be a long truce, then," Peter informed him. "The people have had many a black day. They backed up the fighting men well for the past couple of years. They suffered a lot for ye. They look upon this truce as victory, and you're going to have your work cut out to convince them otherwise."

" 'Tis I that know it," admitted Gorman wearily. He rose from his chair, tightened the bandolier round his waist, slung the brown rifle by its strap over his shoulder. "More than the people have lost their heads. My whole column is melted away like the snow. Even Packey an' Fintan Fogarty are away, struttin' before the women, gauchin' around with heads like balloons, listenin' to everyone tellin' them they're the men who won the war." Ned gave a hitch to his rifle, gave a tug to the battered brim of his muddy black hat. "God help the poor fools, but I fear many a mother's son will die yet before the last shot in this war is fired."

"Yerrah, cheer up, man," advised Peter. "This is a damn queer humour for you to be in tonight, Ned, after battling so long and achieving so much. Take that gun off your shoulder, for the Lord's sake, and wait for a drop of tea."

"I have tea enough," answered Gorman gruffly. "They were shovin' tea into me below in Donegan's for a solid hour an' tellin' me what a fine fellow I am an' what a grand thing it is to have Ireland free. An' only yesterday not one of them same Donegans would lift a hand to help us even if they were to get Ireland free on a plate with their dinner." The cynical soldier of Erin turned towards the door. "I'd better be off home, that's if my brother will leave me in. But I suppose, by now, he's a wholetime patriot like the rest of ye."

By the door he paused to laugh at Peter's glum face. "Aha, who's gloomy now? Do you know what's wrong with me, Peter? I've been too long on my keepin'; too many nights lyin' down to sleep without knowin' whether I'd wake in Carriglea or in Eternity." He glanced over at Fonsy, still blissfully unconscious on the settle. "Look at him, though! Look at the Donegans and their likes, with all their airs and graces. And then ask yourself one question, Peter. Was it for this we fought so long? Was it for this so many good men died?"

Peter O'Dea rubbed his forehead, considered carefully. "Well, maybe it was, Ned. Perhaps it was. Freedom is a thing that every man is inclined to use in his own way."

Chapter Ten

CIVIL War! First it was a phrase spoken half in jest, a brake on the headstrong, a spur to the faint-hearted. Then it grew to a black threat which darkened every rood of Irish sky, which clouded over the gold sun of freedom with a direr menace than Ireland of the Sorrows had yet known. And now was it an awesome reality. Now, blind with rage, athirst for blood, brother struck brother down and gloried in the deed.

Ned Gorman stood, laughing, by the door in the teacher's kitchen while Peter O'Dea stared across at him. A troubled frown gathered above the schoolmaster's soft eyes.

"I'm afraid you were a bit high-handed with him, Ned," said Peter uneasily. "You gave His Lordship no quarter at all. The wonder was that he didn't excommunicate you on the spot."

"He got little chance! Oh, I saw to it that he got no chance at all of producin' candle, book an' bell. The very minute he said to me, 'Now, Commandant Gorman, if I'm to arbitrate between the warring factions in my diocese, you must first order your men to lay down their arms,' as soon as I heard that, Peter, I jammed on my hat. I picked up my gun. I slung the rifle on my shoulder. I gave him a full military salute. 'Lovely weather we're havin', my Lord Bishop,' says I, an' marched out the door."

"You should have tried to work him round a bit." Peter shook his head. "He's a very sound man, you know, and straight as a die. If you, though a Republican colonel or general or whatever you are, don't wish to fight the Free Staters and yet wish to keep your principles, the Bishop is your only hope of settling things peaceably."

"How soft I was!" Ned Gorman shook a long forefinger at

Peter's face. "If we laid down our guns don't you know that the peace which would follow would be short an' sweet?"

Peter O'Dea came to join Gorman by the door. Together they watched the lazy rain clouds drift slowly across the troubled August sky. " 'Twill all have to be settled up sooner or later," announced the schoolmaster, examining his pipe bowl critically. "The sooner ye do settle it, the more bitterness will be spared, the less destruction will be done, the more good men's lives will be spared on both sides. Now or never is the time to settle."

Gorman turned, laughed. "To cap all your other qualifications, Peter, you have the second sight." He paused, licked his dry lips. "Jer Coady, in spite of his years, is night an' day workin' for peace. I had word from him yesterday to say Mick Collins, on his way back from Cork, has agreed to have a quiet little chat with Coady an' myself in Clonmel tomorrow night. If we can come to any understanding, Collins will notify the Free Staters here, an' we'll have a truce in this area for a start-off. If peace can be declared in one county, the rest of the country won't take long to follow the lead, so that, in another week or two, when this bloodshed is all over, I'll have a nice quiet laugh of my own at His Lordship the Bishop."

Outside someone jumped off a bicycle, began frantically to rattle at the front gate, shouting the while. "Ned! Ned! Is Ned Gorman there?"

"That's Regan," Gorman cried, rushing through the hall to the open front door with Peter on the wind of his heels. "I'm here, Packey! What the devil is wrong?"

"Good news!" yelled Packey. "Great news! Mick Collins was shot dead in an ambush last night in County Cork."

"God help us all this day!" prayed Peter.

"God be merciful to a good man," said Ned. "Friend or foe, that's not the death I'd have wished him."

" 'Tis the same end as is comin' to every other Free Stater who stands where he did," declared Regan bitterly.

" 'Tis the same end, Packey, that faces every one of us now," Gorman told him. "There can be no peaceful settlement with Collins gone. There can be nothing now only vengeance an'

171

blood. Off with you up to Fogarty's, Packey. Fintan may be neutral, but he'll have a good idea as to where most of our lads are. Get every man together an' I'll met ye at Rathcash Cross before the moon rises. An' you can inform anyone who's inclined to show the white feather that we may have been fightin' for a Republic these past few months, but we're fightin' for our lives from this day out."

"No need to tell them." Regan picked up his bicycle while he spoke. "They're not that thick in the head."

"I'm off to the dugout myself," Gorman continued. "That place is safe no longer. 'Tis too well known. I'll have the few men from there at Rathcash before dark. If there's no word from headquarters by then, we'll only have to plan out something on our own."

Packey prepared to mount his machine, threw back a word of warning. "Be careful, Ned! There's a few lorries of Staters roamin' round all day, an' 'twasn't out to pick mushrooms they came."

"I've been takin' pretty good care of myself this many a year, Packey boy!" answered Gorman sharply and had gone back into the house before ever Regan's ramshackle bicycle had borne him away.

Silently Ned Gorman gathered up his rifle, his hat, his trench coat. He was strapping on his bandolier before he spoke, smiling, to Peter. "So My Lord the Bishop is goin' to have the last laugh after all."

Peter O'Dea, though long accustomed to stifling his emotions, found trouble in phrasing his thoughts as he watched his friend work the rifle bolt up and down. "You're one damn fool, Ned, going off to fight your own countrymen in a war you hate as much as I do. You can't win, boy, and you yourself wouldn't want to win this way even if you could. Irishmen won't solve this problem by killing fellow-Irishmen. The more men ye kill, the bigger the problem grows. This 'Free State or Republic' dispute should be settled by cool heads round a table, not by hotheads with guns."

"That was how I wanted to settle it, round a table." Ned Gorman gave a final snick to the rifle bolt, then snuggled the butt under his oxter for easy carriage at the ready. "But will you tell me this, lad? Where can a cool head be found in Ireland this day an' Mick Collins dead in Cork? There's no drawback now for either side, no matter how much some of us might wish it. The bullet that killed Mick is not done with its killing yet."

He walked out of the kitchen, the gun as easy under his arm as if he were off for a day after snipe on the bog. At the gate he turned. "You've always been a damn good friend to me, Peter. If only we got the same loyalty from men who claim to be on our side as we got from you who was never with us, I'd hold high hopes for Ireland yet. If every man in this country was as sound as you are, we'd have no excuse for gun work. A few more quiet, sensible men today, Peter, would steady up the lot of us."

"Aye," the master agreed. "But 'tis mighty hard for a quiet man to make himself heard once the guns start talking."

"The guns will fall silent yet, lad," answered Gorman soberly, "an' then the quiet men can say their say. But the pity of the whole thing is, that maybe if the quiet men had been let say their say in the first place, the guns need never have spoken at all. Besides, when ye quiet men do get a hearin', some of us won't be there to listen to ye."

Peter laughed to cheer him. "Ah, now, Ned, you won't hand in your ticket that quickly. We'll laugh at this day yet when the mad times are all over. The calm heads will soon make the guns close their mouths."

"A calm head can't argue with a hot bullet. Not till the bullet cools, even if it takes blood to cool it." Gorman swung round to greet Markie, who came romping down the road. "Ah, the hard Markie! Where were you roamin' all this day?"

"I was hunting water-hens, down by the stream," cried the boy. "And where are you going to, Uncle Ned Gorman?"

"I wish to God I knew, Markie!"

"When will you be back? Will you be long?"

"I might be a long time away," the fighting man told him. "You see, Markie, I promised to meet an old friend, an' now he's gone a far way off."

173

"What's his name?" queried Markie, curious.

"Mick Collins," answered Ned Gorman softly, and then went marching away down the long, dusty road.

It was almost an hour later when Peter heard the faraway hum of lorry engines, the bark of a rifle, an angry crackle of machine-gun fire. There was a minute or two of nerve-racking silence before the engines ground into gear once more.

To him it seemed that a shadow came, unheralded, across the sunshine, so that he crossed himself where he stood, troubled, in his garden.

They knelt to say the last silent prayer around the graveside, and so still were the people that Peter O'Dea could hear the soft wind fret and fidget through the seeded grass that waved about him where he prayed for the soul of the man who lay there beneath the red earth, silent forever in that brass-bound coffin.

Beyond the crowd, beyond the graveyard wall, the sunlight glinted on the dull steel of bayonets to prove that even in death the men who had killed him feared Ned Gorman still. He wondered, since the body had been delivered up only on the understanding that there be no demonstration at the funeral, what action the officer who commanded the Free State troops on the road outside would take when he, Peter O'Dea, rose to address the crowd.

Was he a fool to let himself be dragged into this at all? Was he a fool to have listened to Fintan Fogarty's urgency? "It's up to you, Peter, as Ned's friend, as a strictly nonpolitical man. I'm neutral in this quarrel. I'm workin' hard for peace. If I speak at Ned's grave, neither the one side nor the other will count me neutral any longer. An' if someone else doesn't speak, Regan will break loose an' give a fiery oration an' try to fire three volleys over the grave, an' the result will be panic an' slaughter in Carriglea. It's up to you, Peter. Outside politics, you were his best friend. No one, Free Stater or Republican, can question your right to say a few words."

And not because of Fintan's importunities and not through fear of any slaughter which might threaten the folk of Carrig-

174

lea, but solely because of the bond that had been between Ned Gorman and himself through all the years, Peter had consented, and doubted his own wisdom now as he saw the multitude of mourners rise up from their knees, as men looked towards him anxiously, enquiringly.

He stood up, brushed a few blades of damp grass from his trousers, took two steps forward to the head of the grave, turned to face the south and the gateway, for there the crowd thronged thickest. He was very conscious of the red-eyed grief of the youngest Gormans, Andy's children, who blubbered ceaselessly despite their father's face of stone and their mother's air of melancholic disapproval; very conscious of the Free State officers who stood, holstered revolvers dangling at the thigh, amid the crowd's foremost rank. Across all the miles from Killrone he could hear the noonday Angelus ring. He spoke quietly, earnestly.

"I have been asked to say a few words here by the grave of one who was my true friend. Beyond that claim of friendship I have no right to stand here and speak of the man who is gone. Ned Gorman was a fighting man: I am a man of peace. Ned Gorman was a Fenian man while I was, until a few short months ago, a loyal, or fairly loyal, subject of the Crown. Ned Gorman believed in ideals and in ways of achieving them in which I have never believed, in which I never could believe. But Ned Gorman was my friend, and I would be poor friend to him if I did not, here today, pay tribute to my friend and to his friendship."

He paused, licked dry lips. The crowd stood silent. The children had ceased their blubbering. The Angelus bell rang no longer.

"Three days ago when he walked into my kitchen, full of the zest of life, I little dreamed it would be necessary for me or for anyone else to pay him this last sad tribute so soon. And never did he or I imagine that such tribute would have to be paid in these sorry circumstances. It is heart-breaking to think that a man who fought so long and so well against the Black and Tans should die in arms against his own, shot down by fellow-Irishmen in Civil War."

175

Here and there through the crowd men growled in anger. The officers' hands dropped nearer their holsters. Beyond the wall, as if by magic, the line of bayonets vanished, followed by the scattered thud of rifle-butts as the unseen soldiers grounded arms.

"On the rights and wrongs of this suicidal conflict each man is entitled to his own opinions. That is a privilege of freedom. There are many of you who agreed with Ned Gorman. There are as many, if not more of you, who did not. But here by his grave is no place for schisms and politics. We have not gathered here to give testimony of our political faith, but to pay tribute to a friend and a soldier without reference or prejudice to the cause for which he died."

He moistened his lips again.

"And, lest there be those of you who cannot for the moment see the man behind the things he stood for, I ask from you for Ned Gorman only that favour which Robert Emmet asked for himself in the dock, the charity of your silence. We are all too close to the terrible events taking place around us to judge the men, be they alive or be they dead, whose deeds have brought these things to pass. Yet I am convinced that when, in ten years or in twenty years, aye, or in fifty years from now, our children or our children's children tell with pride about Ned Gorman around the firesides of Carriglea, they will think of him, not as a Republican or as a Free Stater, but as an Irishman, as good an Irishman as ever fought and died for Ireland."

He paused, cleared his throat.

"Three days ago when Ned Gorman walked into my house, down the road there, he told me he was on his way to Clonmel to meet Mick Collins and Jer Coady and see if, between them, they could come to an understanding which would bring to an end this cursed Civil War. Three days ago when, stunned by the news of Collins' death, he walked out of my house, he said he was on his way to keep that appointment with Mick Collins. God give them rest! I doubt if there are Free States or Republics beyond the grave, and so they meet on friendly ground. And now, here where we have laid his body, I have a last request to make in the name of my dead friend. I would ask ye who are listening to me to look at this red grave and ask yourselves if this Civil War, this bitterness between brothers, be worth the lives of such men as he was. The answer I leave to your consciences if there be a conscience left in Ireland to-day." He paused again. "May the Good God have mercy on Ned Gorman's soul and on the soul of every man who dies for an ideal, and may each one of us, when we come to die, have as little reason to fear either the justice of God or the judgement of posterity."

He turned quickly away from the graveside, ashamed because there was a veil of tears before his eyes, unaware that, among those who heard him, few eyes were dry, unaware that his words would be echoed and re-echoed for many a day far from Carriglea or Suir Water, unaware that, in time to come, Ned Gorman would be best remembered by the words that Peter O'Dea had spoken over his coffin.

When, in after life, Peter O'Dea looked back across the arches of his years, he always linked together the months that followed Ned Gorman's death with those months which had followed the death of his own Tessie. And if, after Gorman's death, his personal grief was far less, yet his constant sorrowing for prostrate Ireland made it almost seem greater. To him, a man of peace and quietness, it seemed that the Civil War, which rapidly changed from war to a vendetta, would never end. The struggle dragged on, growing more and more merciless as all such wars do, while Irishmen killed Irishmen on wet hillsides, in muddied lanes, on high scaffolds, in barrack squares, while the Republic died and the Free State was born; while, true to Ned Gorman's ideals, Packey Regan and an irreconcilable few struggled on among the hills, harried night and day, ill-armed, ill-fed, without leaders.

In his age, Peter O'Dea was wont to maintain that the grand old days and the good old times had ended, once and for all, on that sunbright day when they had buried Ned Gorman in the deep grave beneath the mourning yew trees. The gaiety, the old carefree gaiety, he'd affirm, was never to be found in Carriglea from that bleak day forward. Maybe it was because the long Civil War left such lasting bitterness; maybe it was because the years of terror and trouble had broken the time-hallowed sequence of life there above the silver river so that the first years of uneasy peace which followed were dreary years of convalescence as Time, God's journeyman, picking up, ever so slowly, the broken threads, patiently reweaving the pattern of living, wove first a drab and dour mesh:

Maybe it was because so many friends of his youth had been crushed by the marching years; and those who were left had changed so utterly. Fonsy Farrell, for instance, had on a sudden grown old and turned religious in his age, drinking no beer, singing no songs, spending his nights dozing by the master's fire, waking but to mumble his prayers or to lament all the gladness that was gone.

But before the Civil War dragged on to its long-evident end, a last blow fell; for, on a day when fleecy clouds were sailing high above the river, word was brought to Peter O'Dea that Jer Coady lay dead in Dublin. Heart disease, the newspapers said, and keened the passing of a great Fenian. Heart-break, Peter told himself, as with Markie snuggled close beside him, he knelt beneath the vaulted dome of the City Hall and watched the stream of mourners shuffle in a day-long file past the open coffin. Heart-break for a heartsick country! Nor was this the place to wake heart-broken Jer Coady, where the city curious thronged to gaze at him, where the name of Carriglea was unknown, where the mountain-stepping men of Wicklow tiptoed, hesitant, on the marble floors, daunted by city manners and city splendours when they came, faithful, to say their last good-bye.

No! Jer Coady should surely have been waked in Carriglea, in his own kingdom, in that very kitchen where he had ruled so long. And there should have been a frosty moon riding high to lend a sadness to Suir Water, with Fonsy by the corpse-bed to chant a funeral ode. The men he had taught and the women he had scoffed at should be gathered there to tell of his jokes and his jollity and his laughter, to rhyme again the saga of his laundrying, to recall all his pranks and his vagaries. And next day they would have carried his coffin shoulder-high to the

178

parish bounds and there handed it over to trusted friends, well sure that loyal hearts would be round him until he was laid to rest at last by the stream in the valley where Glenealy hides among the Wicklow hills.

Suddenly, from the trending of his thoughts, Peter found that the City Hall had become an airless morgue; the shuffling mourners he saw as ghouls and hypocrites, come to smirk and scoff round the bier of the man whose heart they had broken. He rose from his place, grasped Markie by the hand, went striding out of the room, down the steps, along Parliament Street, up the quays, seeking solace for his saddened heart in the fresh sparkle of the sunshine, in the salt breeze from the sea.

Back at his hotel, Peter found Packey Regan waiting, worn and bearded, in the lounge. They talked softly for a minute or two of the man who was gone, then climbed the stairs to O'Dea's first-floor room.

"He's as well dead," said Regan, fumbling at his breast, handing to Peter a bedraggled sheet of paper.

The teacher sat down began, slowly, to read aloud.

"General Headquarters,
Irish Republican Army
May 24th, 1923.
To the officers and men of the army of the Republic, the soldiers of the Legion of the Rearguard.

The Republic can no longer be defended successfully by your arms. Further sacrifice of life would now be vain and continuance of the struggle unwise in the national interest and prejudicial to the future of our cause. . . ."

"Read it to yourself, masther," ordered Packey, his voice strangely harsh. "Read it to yourself, for God Amighty's sake! Too well I know what's in it already."

Peter O'Dea read on to the end. He folded the document with undue care, handed it back to the broken Regan. " 'Twas time, Packey," he said. "Ye'd have been wiser if ye gave in long ago."

"Give in!" cried Regan, mustering some of his former spirit. "Was it give in you said? Me give in? That saw Ned Gorman buried in his blood? That sees my own wife dyin' of the decline because I was too busy with my wars an' too much harried by my own countrymen to give her the care she needed? Ah, no, masther! 'Give in' is no part of Packey Regan's constitution. I'll obey my ordhers. I'll dump my gun. I'll do any damn thing I'm told, except one. I'll not surrender, an' I'll never surrender till the things I went out to fight for come to pass. There are more ways of fightin', masther, than with a gun in your hand."

" 'Twas a great pity then," O'Dea told him, "ye weren't aware of that fact eight or ten months ago before the whole bang lot of ye went tearing mad into Civil War."

Packey chewed on that for a moment. " 'Tis what I think, masther, that in this misforthunate country we have to learn everything the very hardest way. But, by God, when once we have a lesson learned, we can never again forget it."

Chapter Eleven

MARKIE was rising twelve before Peter O'Dea faced the first parting between his son and himself. Some of the Fogarty aunts had long been pressing him to send the lad away to the College in Kilkenny. God knows but that was a parting for which Peter had little relish. He had reared this son of his almost from the cradle. He had wrought and moulded him, and in the love of his boy had regained some of the happiness he had lost with the wife he idolised and the two friends he had most cherished.

Were Markie to go from him now, he feared that the boy's going would deal a death-blow to the deep understanding, the strong bond of unity, the great sense of comradeship which existed between them. But then Mother Mary Josephine, Julia Fogarty that was, had become a very far-sighted woman and a very wise woman, a woman with a very persuasive tongue, so that, in the end, Peter had very little option but to yield.

He sent Markie back up to Clashmairead with the aunt to spend a carefree day or two there at the hay-making. He waited till, in the cool of the evening, the kitchen had its quota of nightly wiseacres. Then he put down his paper, the *Independent* he took, now that the *Freeman* was dead, and, straight-forward as ever, asked the lot of them would he be doing the right thing in sending Markie away.

Roughane the sexton rapped his pipe bowl against his iron-tipped shoe-heel. "An' why wouldn't you be doin' right, masther?" he asked. "Sure, 'tisn't here you'd keep him to have him a country clod-hopper all his life from the dribblin'-bib to the shroud. Wouldn't it be a mortal sin on your soul to leave the likes of Markie waste his brains away an' eat his heart out in such a backward place as Carriglea?"

"I suppose the sooner we part, the better for both of us," answered Peter, doubtful enough. "The College training and the touch of discipline will make a man of him. Aye, and his going away might do me no harm. Maybe I've spent too long doing the nursemaid."

Andy Gorman spoke up, well knowing that he alone of the men there had previous experience of such problems. "Ah, the College education! You're nowhere without it nowadays. Look at me! Four children, and I can only leave the farm to one. What am I to do with the rest? Marry them off to farmers or to farmers' daughters? Have them go through the same slush an' toil an' hardship that I went through myself? No damn fear! I'll give them what education their heads can hold an' then let them take their chance." He beamed round on them all. "Look at me now sending Cissie off to Monaghan next September. All the ways to Monaghan, mind you. An' 'tis only mad to be gone she is. I don't see what doubts you should have at all, Peter. Sure, only for the bit of education you got yourself, boy, where would you be now? Draggin' seaweed, maybe, up to the few stony fields from the sea and the strand."

Peter took no umbrage, agreed quietly.

Paddy McKeown the smith, simple man that he was, cleared his throat. "I think 'twould be handier for you to send Markie to school below in Waterford. You know how fond he is of the fresh air an' the sunshine, ramblin' through the fields, sittin' by the river. Wouldn't it be a great shame, masther, to shut him up within the stone walls of the College? Locked in, you might say. Eatin' an' sleepin' an' livin' by ordher an' undher rule, an' he was always used to his freedom an' the open air."

The sexton snorted. "An' which of us, Misther McKeown, is free in this world once ever life catches up on us? Am I free to do what I like? Or are you? Or is the masther there? He's not, nor I'm not, nor you're not. Begor, we're not, but we must all go the road laid down for us." He paused, segments of all the sermons to which he had ever listened surging up within

182

his brain. "We must all work out our own salvation the way the Man Above means us to work it out, by the sweat of our brow. Rules an' regulations is for the students' betterment. Damn the loaf of bread wanderin' over green fields an' lookin' at the river an' breathin' in the fresh air an' breathin' out the fresh air ever put in anybody's mouth, an' divil damn the ha-penny any of them things will put in anyone's pocket either." He snorted again. "Green fields, how are you! Sure the boy is not a store bullock that he could fatten on them."

The schoolmaster gave a short, peculiar little laugh. "The fields and the river and the hills are dangerous things just the same, Ritchie, when a man or a boy has too much time to look at them or to listen to them. I know that." He halted, embarrassed, then went on. "I was a young man when I came here, twenty-five years ago. I was ambitious. I was anxious to get on. I thought Carriglea would be only a steppingstone to glory. And that's why I see what you mean, Paddy McKeown. If once he let them get a grip on him, a man could break his heart away from the river and the hills, thinking of them, longing for them. Twenty-five years ago they put their spell on me. Often I thought to go farther, to seek a higher place in the world; but the hills and the river came at me and fought me and bested me and would not let me go."

Jamesy Hearn, that silent farmer, so long used to holding his tongue in his own house that he seldom dared to express an opinion even when clear of his wife's jurisdiction, laughed vaguely and scratched his head. "Bedam, masther, but the half of what you're sayin' is beyond me altogether."

"Of course it is," said Roughane, "an' what's that but the result of sneakin' off courtin' out of this house long 'go, when the masther here an' Jer Coady an' Fonsy Farrell used be debatin' on poethry an' beauty an' the like? Though, I suppose, 'twas no matther whether you stayed or went. What beauty could you see in land or wather? Yerrah, 'tis true for you, masther. The river an' the hills will never bring anyone anywhere. An' wouldn't it be a fine thing if Markie took the notion of goin' for the Church? He'd make a grand priest, masther! A grand priest!"

Peter O'Dea was so slow to answer that Andy Gorman fore-stalled him. "Oh, he's cut out for the clergy, Peter, if anyone ever was. An' I have a lad above myself, young Kieran, who's stamped out for it too. He's always at the mother to make a priest out of him. An', sure, he'll be ready for the College in another year or two. 'Twould be a grand thing for the two of them, Pether, to have them goin' along together."

The schoolmaster sighed, said slowly, "I'd like well myself to see Markie priested, if God grant he be that way inclined."

"Priest indeed!" exclaimed the sexton, waving his pipe. "You'll see that boy wearin' the bishop's high hat yet, masther. An' that's something he'd never get if he were to stay mopin' around the ditches like Paddy McKeown would have him do."

"I'm not stoppin' the boy from gettin' anything," objected McKeown, roused. "I only gave me fair an' honest opinion."

"Any man, Paddy," soothed Peter, "is entitled to speak out his mind in a free country."

"If Packey Regan were here," retorted Roughane, "he'd soon point out the difference between a free country an' a free state. Ah, 'tis well for you, Paddy, that has nothin' to trouble you but the green fields. You have no more gumption in your head this minute than oul' Jamesy the Magpie below from Mooncoin. Jamesy was joggin' home from the creamery one mornin' lately with his face so long that the ass was afraid to look back at him. Who did he meet on the road but the parish priest. 'Begor, Jamesy,' says the priest, 'but you're in a black humour today. What's troublin' you at all?' 'I'm in dread, Father,' says my idiot, 'but that Mooncoin is goin' to be bet in the hurlin' match next Sunday.' 'Ah, Jamesy,' says the priest, half-laughin', 'there's more important things in this life than hurlin' matches.' Up speaks the Magpie, bould as brass. 'Leave aside the Ten Commandments, Father,' says he, 'an' then can you name out to me wan single thing that is more impor-tant?'"

The sexton drew at his pipe, listened, content in his cronies' laughter, then fired a last salvo. "Green fields, an' the hills, an' the river! Oh, God give you sense, Paddy McKeown."

184

Before he went to bed that night Peter had made his decision. He would send Markie away. He must send Markie away. But his mind was still uneasy, so that, before the week was out, he was away up to the oracle in which he placed most trust and was laying his troubles and his doubts before old Mrs. Fogarty above in Clashmairead.

The old woman, "bet in the legs," as she described herself, received him, propped up in the cushioned dignity of her wheeled chair, and listened in silence to his story. When his tale was done, she helped herself to a pinch of snuff, sneezed twice, blessed herself, blew her nose in her handkerchief of patterned silk.

"If you'll take my advice, Pether," she said, "you'll let him go. You'll send him away from you now, while he's young an' before you're old. If you hold onto him too long, you'll only ruin him an' ruin yourself. The day might come yet when he'd curse you for keepin' him, when he might walk out on you without yes, aye, or no an' never bother to come back."

"But if I let him go now, he'll be gone from me. And gone younger."

"I know Markie," stated the old woman. "An' I'll tell you this: If you send the boy away now, Pether, an' if you give him a free leg in the years to come, he'll ever an' always come back to you, barrin' one thing. Barrin' God calls him."

"Is he the makings of a priest?" he asked eagerly.

"That," said she, "is a matter for Markie an' his Maker. Make no effort to force him, an' what's more, let no one else try to force him. I'm givin' you that warnin', Pether, because I'll not be here much longer to keep my eye on the lot of ye, an' because I know that no one will try harder to force him into it than some of my own daughters."

She took another pinch of snuff.

" 'Twill be lonely below without him," said Peter.

"Wisha, God help you," said Mrs. Fogarty without compassion, "but aren't you to be pitied. A body would think you a child, Pether, to hear you talkin' sometimes. Sure you'd not find it that hard to get another woman to marry you?"

"I only ever wanted one woman," answered Peter softly, "and God thought her too good to leave to me."

"Wait, boy! Wait a few more years till Julia Stapleton is after you to take one of the daughters off her hands. An', if she misses yourself, she'll have a good try to get Markie, a damn good try. That woman, every hour she lives, regrets that she didn't snare you yourself."

Peter laughed. "You're very hard on Julia."

"I'm hard on no one," said the old woman placidly, "but I had good eyes always an' was well able to use them, thank God. An' I know, from the first day you ever had anything to do with us Fogartys, that, if looks could have killed the lot of us, Julia Stapleton would have us all dead an' buried an' the moss growin' green on our tombstones. A woman doesn't forget them kind of things, Pether. 'Tis only the fair dint of jealousy that keeps us alive."

They bade a grave "good evening" to a passing neighbour. "Anyway, there's no need for you to live there on your lone after Markie goes to the College," Mrs. Fogarty went on. "Aren't you gettin' a new assistant? Isn't Millea leavin'?"

"He is."

"An' good riddance too. A sour lad he was."

"I'm afraid the change won't make for much improvement. Cosby, who's coming, has a very gay name. I hear he'd gamble away his last penny. And he has an eye for the girls."

The old woman tapped her snuff-box with a great air of finality. "Let you bring this Cosby fellow in to stay with you. The gayer he is the better."

"I'd not fancy bringing a stranger into my house," objected Peter, stunned a little by the very suggestion. "I'm too set in my ways. Besides, 'tis against the regulations now."

"Regulations be damned," said brisk old Mrs. Fogarty. "Weren't you a stranger yourself when you faced in to Jerry Coady, long 'go? An' was ever a man set in queerer ways than he was? An' didn't the two of ye get on together like a pair of love birds?" She gathered her shawl close round her shoulders, she huddled herself up in her chair. "Wheel me in, Pether!" she ordered. "I feel the chill of death in that breeze."

Peter O'Dea, jovial, seated by his own fireside, looked up from the letter he had been reading. "In so far as I can judge from this letter, Conor, Markie is doing very well. Doing very well indeed. And he's quite happy." Then, more cautiously. "It's hard, of course, to learn all the truth from a letter."

"If Markie says he's happy and doing well, he is doing well and he is happy." After his fifteen years away from home the western accent was still broad on Conor Cosby's tongue. "He's not old enough yet to conceal his true feelings."

"Ah, but Markie was always older than his years," said Markie's father. "He was reared that way. You know, I reared him myself, Conor. Not a woman in the country but always swore I was ruining him."

"Women think no one can rear a child except themselves," stated Cosby judicially. "I sometimes wonder at them ever sending their children to school at all."

Peter fingered his son's letter, anxious to return from the general to the particular. "They all said I was ruining him. The aunts and all said it. All except his grandmother. She said 'twas jealous they were because I proved to be a better mother than any of them."

"From what little I saw of the boy, he certainly seemed a credit to the rearing he got."

"He's a credit to no one but himself," stated the father proudly. "You can't train what's not there, Conor. The stuff has to be there before it can be shaped. And, even if I do say it myself, there's good stuff in Markie."

Cosby, no flatterer, said nothing.

Peter tapped the letter with his pipestem. "He's all excitement over the entrance scholarship. I put him in for the entrance scholarship, Conor, and he tied for first place. Tied for first place! Wasn't that a fine achievement in his very first exam?"

"I'm sure 'twill be only the first success of many," said Cosby gallantly.

"It's a promising start, anyhow. And he seems to be cottoning onto the discipline quite well, too. Quite well. No complaint at all to make about the rules and regulations. And that's what was troubling me most. I always gave him such a free leg here that I was afraid the College discipline might lean very hard on him. Yet he took to it like a duck to water. But then, even though I do say so myself, Conor, he was a good boy always in that respect. Never a sulk nor a kick-up no matter what he'd be told to do."

Peter O'Dea took his pipe from his mouth, and a slow curl of smoke rose from where he held it on his knee. He eyed his assistant soberly. "You must have a hell of a dull time, Conor, sitting there listening to me psalming on and psalming on about Markie. I'm sorry. I don't often get the chance of so good a listener. And you're the only one to whom I say much about him. Except to his grandmother above in Clashmairead, I'm not given to singing his praises at all. But, the way it is, Conor, when all your hopes, when almost your whole life, is centred around one person, you have to talk to someone about him or burst."

Cosby laughed, waved a hand. "There's not the slightest need for apology. I like to hear a person praised who's well worth the praising. I can always share a man's enthusiasm for an achievement. You've put the best of your life's work into Markie, and you can be justly proud of the result. And it is the kind of me to be proud of your pride. And proud of your pride I am, sir, and proud of your boy, too. Oh, you needn't stint yourself of talking about Markie to me. I'm an audience that won't tire of listening."

Peter O'Dea put the cold pipe back in his mouth. "The schoolmaster who gets an understanding assistant," said he, "should praise God, fasting, every morning for seven years and seven quarantines. That's a dictum of old Jer Coady's with which he used honour me in days gone by. And I'm happy now to be able to apply it to an assistant of my own." He paused, looked back across the threshold of memory. "Old Jer was unfortunate in his assistants before I arrived. Or maybe the men who were here before me had more sense than I had. Anyhow, one night long ago, there was an argument here between Fonsy Farrell and himself, Fonsy claiming to be the better man because Jer hadn't the knack of writing poetry. Jer took the pipe out of his beard and without let or hindrance or one moment's preparation he rolled out as fine and as cutting a verse as ever I heard:

"Good Patrick sainted drove all things tainted
    And serpents painted from Ireland's shore:
At his sharp orders, they crossed our borders
    In ranks disordered and returned no more.
But some fool's persistence, sends me such assistants
    That my dour resistance now bends and breaks,
And each new laddie is so dull and faddy
    That I'm praying Saint Paddy to bring back the snakes."

Cosby clapped his hands in laughter. "Ah, that was a hard blow! At you, I mean."

"Impersonal, though. There was never anything personal in what Jer Coady might fling at you. The gibe came as natural to him in those days as the word of praise might come to the mouth of another man."

"He's not forgotten, anyway," was Cosby's comment. "One mention of his name, and every man I meet gives me enough queer stories about him to make a book that only Dickens could do full justice to."

"And that would be only turn about and fair play," said Peter O'Dea, "because Dickens was leading man with Jer Coady when it came to fiction. Ah, but you'd break your heart laughing to hear him argue and fight with Fonsy Farrell. Fonsy, with a few drinks in him, would give best to no one, and Jer would keep annoying him and rising under him till Fonsy would lose all patience and they'd finish up in a pitched battle. Yet, though Fonsy drove many a man into hiding with a few bitter lines of a gibing song, he never once turned a verse against Jer Coady. Maybe he was too fond of him at heart, or maybe he was afraid Jer might give back worse than he got; but Fonsy never, never rhymed him except to praise him."

"Fonsy Farrell the rhymer," repeated Conor Cosby. "Begor, but ye weren't short of talent here in the old days. And what kind of a lay did he compose about yourself?"

Peter shook his head. "He never honoured me with even

189

one line, and that's a marvel in itself, I suppose. Maybe I was too quiet a fellow always to give him any cause. But the best poem he ever made was about my wife. You've heard it?"

"I heard it, and it made me have a very high opinion of Mr. Fonsy Farrell."

"Well, as a matter of fact," said Peter hesitantly, "I was courting at the time, and you know how poetic you get when you're in that frame of mind. I had a notion to write a poem to her, but could make no creditable attempt at composing a line. I wanted to say something about 'Carriglea and her laughter,' but I could get no farther than that. Well, I was sitting here by the fire one night, when Fonsy started getting onto me about Tessie Fogarty. In the end I confessed to him my failure to compose a poem. I gave him those few words I had thought of. And he just leaned back in that very chair where you're sitting now and gave out the song to me, verse after verse."

"I'm well certain," said Conor Cosby, fumbling in his pocket for a cigarette, "that I'd be seated for a long time in this chair and that I'd lean back a hell of a distance in it before I could even make a start on a single line."

Peter O'Dea, as Conor Cosby once wryly informed Fintan Fogarty, spent eight long years preaching to Cosby the gospel according to Saint Markie. But during these years Peter learned, in return, to unload a little of his own worries and troubles onto the broad shoulders of his assistant. A gay spark Conor Cosby might be, a gambler with an eye for the girls, but whatever his faults he was a good teacher, a hard worker and willing.

Those were quiet years, broken for Peter by the blissful weeks when Markie was home on holidays. And Peter O'Dea grew more and more proud of his son with the passing years. There were no prizes to be won or no scholarships to be gained at the College in Kilkenny which Markie did not win, and before he finished his schooling there his fame for learning was known round the ring of Ireland. But by the time his years in St. Kieran's were ending and he must decide for himself the next step to take, it was many the night Peter worried and worried as Cosby sat late with him before the kitchen fire, the last stroller gone.

"Conor," he'd say, "I'm worried about Markie. I wonder will he be for Maynooth?"

And Cosby's answer was always the same. "You'll have to leave that to himself, sir. Markie will make no mistake when it comes to such an important decision."

"Nor would he," Peter would maintain, "were he left to himself. But there you have the priests of the College probably expecting him to go, and all the aunts advising him to go, and I think he thinks I want him to go. Well, I'll not force or influence him, one way or the other. The decision must be his, not mine."

When that summer ended and autumn came again, Markie O'Dea went quietly on to Maynooth to study for the priesthood. Whether the boy himself thought he had a clear call to the altar or not, no one knew. The father did not seek to interfere but, on the other hand, there you had the whole parish, in front of the lad, telling the master that the day of Markie's ordination would be a famous day for Carriglea; and there you had all the Fogarty aunts never letting Markie forget they would not rest easy until they saw a bishop's crozier in his hand and a bishop's hat on his head. So, finally, to Maynooth Markie went, but whether he went there of his own free will or because he was determined to please everybody but himself, remained always and ever a secret between Markie O'Dea and Markie O'Dea's conscience.

Markie had spent three full years away in Maynooth when, one October morning, a letter arrived from him which made Peter wriggle with joy where he sat opposite Cosby at the breakfast table.

"Conor," announced Peter, the hand that held the letter trembling a little, "we have a B.A. in the family!"

"You could have worse, begod," approved Cosby. "A B.A. degree never did anyone much harm yet. And it has a great hold on the imagination of the lower orders, myself included."

"And not only a B.A., but a first-class honours B.A. with first place in mental and moral philosophy."

"In mental and moral Philosophy!" Cosby whistled through his teeth. "Begor, sir, we'll have to get down the books ourselves this very night and strike up an acquaintance with philosophy. We'd be shamed forever if Markie walked in the door to us some day, talking mental and moral philosophy, and neither yourself nor myself knew the difference between a mental philosopher and a moral one."

Peter laughed absently, his eyes troubled as he turned over the page. "I'm afraid this mental and moral philosophy has proved to be a tough proposition, even for Markie. He's not feeling too well, he says, ever since the exam, so he had a bit of a chat with the College doctor. The doctor advised him to take a good rest, and he hopes to be down to us tomorrow on a month's sick leave."

"That's the best news of all," said Cosby, standing up from the table. "'Tis a month hard-earned. I'd better be off, sir, to open up the school. I don't suppose you'll be long after me?"

"I'll be on the wind of your heels," Peter promised him. "In all my years of teaching I never saw a pack of dunderheads to equal the Confirmation class we have this year. You'd need a hammer and chisel to drive religion into their heads."

"They know nothing, and they want to know nothing." Cosby pulled his peaked cap down over one eyebrow, then struggled into his raincoat. "Still, they'll know the first half of the Apostles' Creed before this morning is out, or else there will be blood spilt in Carriglea. Either they'll break my heart or I'll break their heads." He turned towards the door. "It's them or me this time, and the Apostles' Creed is an ideal battle ground."

Cosby gone, Peter O'Dea folded his son's letter, wondering to himself the while, wondering if it were bad health alone that was bringing Markie home from Maynooth, or if there might not be some other reason for this unexpected return. Could it be that Markie no longer wished to go on for the priesthood? If the boy baulked now, his failure would be a hard thing for the O'Deas to live down, a sore trial for Peter, a

192

sorer trial still for Markie, a bitter blow to all the Fogarty aunts. Not that this letter contained any hint of big decisions made in Markie's mind . . . not that Markie was the kind who told out his thoughts . . . and since he had gone on to Maynooth from Kilkenny he had grown all the more secretive. . . . Yet, Peter told himself, 'twas easy for his father to note the change in him, 'twas easy to sense that, instead of being all in all to one another, as they once had been, they had begun drifting back towards the normal relationship that exists between fathers and their grown-up sons.

Soon Peter's thoughts were ranging back to those days long gone when Markie had been his and his alone . . . when Markie had been his and no one or nothing else could claim any place in the boy's affections save alone the gay-voiced mother who slept with her face to the sunrise and the river in the hillside churchyard above Three Elms. . . .

Oh, God be with those early blundering days when first he had brought Markie back from Clashmairead to Carriglea. . . . God be good to those nights they had lain snug in bed while he taught to Markie the boy's first prayers . . . and God be kind to that moment of triumph when first Markie could repeat, unaided:

> "There are four corners to my bed,
> There are four angels round my head:
> Matthew, Mark, Luke and John;
> God bless the bed that I lie on."

Aye, and God be with that evening, when Markie, aged eight, had returned from browsing through a bookcase which contained so little that was suited to his age, had stumped an astounded clerical visitor with the grave query, "Canon Walsh, why do you never tell us on Sundays about the Sins of Society?"

And God be with that older Markie, cock of the National School above, the delight of every visiting inspector, with his apt answers and his charm and his almost uncanny fund of knowledge on any and every subject, so that they always said to Peter before they left, 'That's a son to be proud of, Mr.

193

O'Dea. You don't find talent like his growing on the bushes."

Oh, Markie had always, even after he went to Maynooth, been so fond of the things that his father loved—sitting round the evening fireside with the old cronies; mentally recording every line they knew of Fonsy's myriad poems; quick to learn words and music of folk-song or come-all-ye; fingering, slow but triumphant, through the *Keel Row* on Peter's brown melodeon.

And God keep the day when Peter first had realised that Markie, marching far and fast through the realms of scholarship, had won through to heights whither his father could never hope to follow; when, thumbing through the heavy Latin tomes, Peter felt for the first time since Jer Coady's death the full blast of loneliness.

Once that first intellectual wedge had been driven between them, the weakening of their comradeship had gone on, slowly but inexorably. Of St. Kieran's Peter had known much, if only by hearsay, but he had no part in the Maynooth world of books and bells and bibles, could never differentiate between St. Joseph's and the Quadrangle, between St. Mary's Cloister and St. Patrick's Walk: could take no part in the talk of *caveats* and lecterns which for the past three years he had so often heard bandied round between Markie and young Kieran Gorman, who now walked too in the corridors of Maynooth. Nor, indeed, did Peter wish to share in their talk of the cloisters. He had given his son to the church, willingly if not gladly, and he was not the man to complain if, in so doing, he must thereby renounce his own claim on the boy.

And now Markie was coming home! In termtime! Home on sick leave, it was true . . . but what had at first been half a fear in Peter's breast was now half a hope. If Markie had no vocation! If Markie were to stay at home! Let them who so wished point finger of scorn at Markie or at himself. If Markie were coming home . . . for good . . . they could, himself and Markie, build up again slowly but surely their old-time intimacy, revive again their former comradeship.

If Markie were to remain at home . . .

Chapter Twelve

WHEN first Markie O'Dea arrived home from May-nooth it was generally understood in Carriglea that he had so much taxed his strength with too much studying for the great B.A. examination that the need for a prolonged rest had been the sole cause of his homecoming. But a rest is a rest, and when one month had sped by, and then another, and when the short, grey days of December already presaged Christmas, the curious ones wondered among themselves and, finally, began boldly to say that he showed small inclination to return at all.

And while even the most curious respected Peter too well to ask him any awkward questions, they saw no harm in en-quiring casually from Markie the probable date of his own departure for the cloisters. "Next week," he'd always answer in that soft voice of his, but it was a "next week" that never came, so that, when Christmas was gone, when the evenings began to stretch and brighten out towards spring, the father's continued silence and the way the Fogarty aunts hung their heads at the mere mention of Markie's name, soon made plain to the world at large that Markie O'Dea would see Maynooth no more.

The parish, and Carriglea was always a broad-minded and often a fair-minded parish, decided at once that, if the boy had no vocation to the religious life, it was only right for him to turn back before he had gone too far on the road to priest-hood. But the parish decided, too, that even such a philosophic attitude would not lessen the sore hurt that his son's failure must inflict on the master.

Yet, through it all, Peter O'Dea kept his own counsel and kept it well. Whether or not he approved of Markie's doing,

he would hear no word against his son. When Ritchie
Roughane, the sexton, passed some remark to him about how
sorry everyone felt for the both of them, the master did not
waste one moment before giving Ritchie a straight answer.
"The boy's life is his own, Ritchie," he said, "his own to make
or to mar. It's not for me nor for you to tell him how to live
it. We'll have to let him cipher that out for himself."

If truth were told, Peter O'Dea needed neither sympathy
nor soothing. The first shock of Markie's failure had quickly
passed, and in its place had come a comforting sense of relief,
of satisfaction, because Markie was home. So, whenever sage
heads nodded and busy tongues whispered, Peter O'Dea but
held his head the higher and told himself that memories were
short, that talk was cheap, and went his way mindful of Jer
Coady's favourite slogan:

> *Sticks and stones*
> *May break our bones*
> *But words can never hurt us.*

As for Markie, a man who kept his own mind to himself
even more successfully than ever his quiet father did, no one
knew what his thoughts were. He gradually settled down to a
half-lazy, half-restless life which was ill in keeping with all the
bright promise of his boyhood. For many a year back, and more
especially since Cosby had come to stay at the teachers' residence, their housework had been done by Statia McKeown,
the blacksmith's wife. Now she found that, except the heavy
washing, there was nothing left for her to do. Every house-
hold task and chore was taken over by Markie as though it
were for that sole purpose he had spent all the years in acquir-
ing his expensive education. Even cooking, Statia was quick
to report, came easy to him. He had a hand for bread-making,
she said, light as ever woman possessed and a knack of ringing
the changes on common-place dishes that soon had Conor
Cosby boasting that no hotel in Ireland could compete with
the food which Markie O'Dea served up in the kitchen at
Carriglea.

His housekeeping was the only work Markie did, although

once, in a rare moment of self-revelation, he told Cosby that he looked laziest when he was most restless, because then his mind, ever wary and ever worrying, left his hands hang idle. He spent much of his spare time wandering through the fields, following the twisted trails the cattle had made for themselves, stalking the little streams that meandered across the valley to the broad river, daydreaming away to himself the while. Many a farmer fencing a ditch on some lonely outfarm, or cutting thistles in a field that skirted the highroad, or down on his knees thinning a last few drills of turnips up where the loam of the plain met the heather of the hills, would raise a startled head to find that Markie O'Dea, unheard and unseen till then, was passing within a yard of him, wrapped as usual in the cloak of thought.

For many a month after his sudden homecoming, Markie, except for an occasional visit to Fogartys', spent his nights reading away to himself by his father's fire among his father's cronies. A day came, however, when someone, someone it might well be with an eligible daughter on her hands and who had a shrewd idea of the size of the master's bank-balance, gave forth her duly considered opinion that four or five grey oldsters round a hearthstone were not fit and proper company for a young man already over-grave. It made no differ who first posed the question, the matter ended where such matters in Carriglea always ended, in the parish priest's parlour.

Peter had brought up some official documents for the priest's signature and, business over, they chatted of more personal things until at length Father Hahissey came to the question Peter had all along been dreading.

"And how," asked Father Hahissey, "is Markie?"

"Oh, keeping his head above water, as the saying is," answered Peter lightly. "Doesn't stir out very much, you know, except for a quiet ramble through the fields. But he looks after the house and the cooking so well you'd swear he was an expert in domestic economy."

Father Hahissey, who never hurried anyone or anything, drew thoughtfully at his pipe. "I hear he's very good at the housekeeping. And I'm told he's as good a man to buy groceries as crosses over the bridge into Waterford. But, to my mind, Peter, buying half-stones of sugar and boiling a few potatoes and baking a cake of bread are very poor occupations for a man of his brains and education."

Peter frowned, embarrassed. "Ah, well, of course, Father, the boy hasn't found his feet yet. We must give him a chance, you see, to find his feet."

"And do you honestly think, Peter, that Markie will find his feet moping around on his own, walking the country on his own, reading to himself by the fire while you and Roughane and the smith are psalming away to yeer hearts' content? Ah, by the powers, twelve months of such carry-on would turn a jester melancholy. I'm not seeking to intrude at all now, Peter, but what I want you to ask yourself is this: Markie may be great company for you, but are you and Cosby and Roughane and McKeown great company for him?"

"Well, he never complains or seeks to go anywhere else," answered Peter defensively. "God knows, there's no one stopping him from going anywhere he wants to go, and I'd be the last man in the world to put any rein on him. If he wanted gaiety he need only follow Cosby out the door any night of the week."

"Yes, but here's what I'm trying to come at." The patient priest stubbed his cigarette on a bronze ash tray. "What must be done for Markie is a simple thing, and yet a very difficult thing. His own confidence in himself has received a bitter blow. We must try and restore that confidence. No! I'm wrong there! We must help him to win back that confidence." The priest paused to marshall his argument. "He'll never get a grip on his confidence, Peter, till he manages to get out of himself. At present he's turning in on himself more and more every day, and the more he draws back into himself, the more he'll brood and worry."

"Well, perhaps I'm wrong, Father," said Peter, troubled, "but it never occurred to me that the boy was worrying at all. I thought if he once had a good long rest, a twelve-month even, he'd be fit and well again, able and ready to turn his hand to anything."

198

"And so he will, Peter," smiled Father Hahissey, firm and confident. "But we should meanwhile be doing our endeavours to help him back to his health. For the past nine or ten years, first above in Kieran's and then away in Maynooth, Markie has been accustomed to the company of young people, accustomed to a very different atmosphere from his present surroundings. What I would suggest, Peter, is that Markie should stir out a bit and mix again with those of his own age. If I were you I'd encourage him to go off to a hurling match; to join in a game of cards at the crossroads or below at Paddy's in the Glen, where, I'm told, the deck is never laid down. Aye, and a few hours at a dance from time to time wouldn't do him the slightest harm. Indeed, if he follows after our friend Cosby, 'tis trying to keep him from the ladies and the dances you'll be. Send him off to Waterford an odd time to the pictures or to a play. Oh, I needn't tell you all the ways of getting the boy interested in something besides himself," ended the parish priest, rising from his chair. "You know how best to get the good side of him."

Peter O'Dea, for all that he was a quiet man, was a shrewd man too, and who knows but that the priest's idea might not also have been Peter's own. Soon, in that easy way of his, he was suggesting to Markie that a few hours in younger company, an occasional hour of gaiety or the thrills of a hurling match might prove a quicker cure for melancholy than all Roughane's sage talk and all McKeown's slow sense and all Hearn's wise silence.

And it could be that Markie needed far less encouragement than either his father or the parish priest ever suspected. At the back of all his brooding there was much of the mother's gaiety in Tessie Fogarty's son, so that, before another few months were past, there was never dance or party at farmhouse or cottage for miles around but was considered incomplete without the master's Markie. Perhaps it was a natural gift that gave him music in his hands and magic in his feet; certainly there was no man in all Ireland so light or so neat at a hornpipe, while the living melody he could draw from the bellows

199

of a melodeon was enough to set a dead man's toes tapping. To hear him sing a rollicking song like *The Palatine's Daughter* would raise your heart from the black gulfs of sorrow. But when his soft voice went lilting through some slow air of sadness and sorrow, he could draw the bitter tears from a heart of stone. Let a dance-set once be ended in some tiled kitchen or at some wide crossroads, and you could, if you watched closely, note the girls crushing and besting one another in rivalry to get sitting next him on the chance of his asking whoever was nearest to partner him in the next lancer.

Even though he retained enough of his shyness to prevent him turning into a ladies' man, still it was small blame to the girls if many a one of them treasured even a gay word from him, for, if Markie had been a handsome child and a winning way with him, it is the hard heart which would not have softened to him now at the end of his teens and the dawn of his twenties. A tall, good-looking boy, hazel eyes shy and soft beneath the smooth curls of auburn hair, the sober black suits he yet wore lending him an added air of mystery, setting him still further apart from the sturdy, tweed-wrapt farmers' sons. There was never a lad who had so many of the things that make for success in life, brains and breeding, good looks and good manners, courtesy and an Old-World gentleness. And whence arose his failure, and how he remained a failure, or why he could not set his mind to the practical side of life, was a problem Carriglea could never solve.

That he was a failure the whole parish agreed. There he stayed, frittering away his time, a male maid-of-all-work in his father's house, when any other man with his brains and education would have been teaching or tutoring or writing for the newspapers; moping his life away around Carriglea when he could have been off to the cities or across the seas where there is always easy money for the picking up if a man but have a modicum of sense and the wit to use it.

For many a day, even though there wasn't a romantic-minded maiden in the parish but would have been glad to put the come-hither on him, no girl's name could be coupled with that of Markie O'Dea. He was pleasant to everyone, but behind all his pleasantry there lurked a share of his father's stubbornness, and if ever he hoped to pay court to a lassie he was determined that her chosing would be done by no one except himself.

By the time, however, that the winter evenings were drawing in again, Markie was often missing from his father's hearth on nights when there were no dances or card games or other organised diversion in the locality. Peter O'Dea made no protests, asked no questions. Knowing Carriglea, he bided his time. Experience had taught him that, from some gossiping tongue or other, the relevant facts would not be long to seek.

It was the source from which it came that most surprised Peter when at last the information did come. His sister-in-law, Kitty Fogarty, arrived in to him one Sunday evening in December, bursting with news and fearful lest someone else had been there with her news before her.

The house was empty. Cosby was off on some subtle mission all his own, Markie away at a coursing trial in the other end of the barony. Kitty Fogarty—she had been Mrs. Mullins this many a year—had the stage to herself, and Peter, who had a happy regard for his sharpest sister-in-law, was amused yet apprehensive as he watched her settle herself in her favourite chair.

"Indeed, Peter," she began, "there's no man in Carriglea bears the wear and tear of the years better than you do. I declare to goodness but I can see little change in you now from the day you were married."

"You're being too kind, Kitty," objected Peter, smiling despite himself. "I've sprouted many a grey rib since then."

"Grey ribs! Yerrah, who minds an odd grey hair nowadays? Sure, half the young lads are grey before they're thirty, if they have aira lick of hair at all left by then. Oh, not a sign of age is on you, Peter. You're every bit as young-lookin' as your son."

Warned by that hint of what was coming, he strove to switch the trend of their conversation. "You're only trying to cover up the fact, Kitty, that you yourself look more like a girl just left school than a woman with most of a long family reared."

"Ah, 'tis the hard work, I suppose," answered she amiable, nimble-witted as himself. "The hard work leaves us no time for growin' old. An' I'm sore afraid, Peter, that, if hard work keeps the bloom of youth on the brow, 'twill not be long until poor Markie will look old enough to be our father. Have you any eyesight left at all, Peter, that you can't see how the boy is fading away through fair dint of idleness?"

"I see no such thing." The schoolmaster was up in arms at once. "The boy is only biding his time, Kitty. Biding his time, girl, and choosing his ground. When the right time comes, when he finds out what course suits him best, Markie will surprise the lot of ye."

"It won't be easy for him to surprise some of us, Peter boy," stated Kitty, solemn now. "He's after springin' so many surprises on us by now that, no matter what he might do, he'd not cause some of us to flutter an eyelid."

"It was no surprise to me, for one, when he left Maynooth." Peter began slowly to fill his pipe. "I think myself that the only reason he ever went there was because he wanted to please every other one instead of pleasing himself."

"An' I suppose 'tis no surprise to you to have him doin' the rake of the parish at every dance an' diversion? An' I suppose 'tis no surprise to you, either, to have him gamblin' at every crossroads an' card-school? An' backin' horses, no less!"

"As for dancing and the like," said Peter comfortably, "you never said 'no' to a lancer yourself, Kitty, that I can remember. And I can't for the life of me see how he'll turn into gambler on what money he gets from me. Begor, he'll make or break no bookmaker on that capital."

Kitty sniffed. "I'm sure the parish priest doesn't like the example Markie is settin' to the young lads of the parish."

"Well"—Peter sucked at his pipe, played his ace—"if Father Hahissey doesn't like it, he knows whom to blame, for 'tis breaking no confidence to tell you that 'twas he himself was responsible. A few dances, Father Hahissey said, a game of cards, a bit of diversion among other young people would do Markie more good than all the treatments and medicines that the doctors ever thought of. And now that his theory has been put to the test, Kitty, I'm inclined to think His Reverence was right."

The baffled Kitty felt obliged to fire her heaviest gun. "I'm very glad to hear all that, Peter," said she sweetly. "An' I wonder did Father Hahissey prescribe for Markie the treatment he's takin' now?"

"Why?" asked Peter, "what treatment is he taking?"

"God Almighty," crowed his sister-in-law, happy at being the first herald of woe, "an' is that how innocent you are? I though the whole world knew Markie was takin' a course of Andy Gorman's eldest daughter a couple of nights a week."

Shaken, despite his forebodings, the master could think of no fitting reply, and Kitty was quick to drive her advantage home. "Of course, if he's doin' that on the priest's orders, far be it from the like of me to lift one single eyelash in criticism. But I must say that the clergy weren't nearly so broad-minded in my young days."

Peter, lamely and late, rallied to the defence of his offspring. "There's no great harm, surely, in being seen in a girl's company. If the like be a fault, 'tis one we all committed, your husband as well as myself."

Kitty rustled herself on her seat like a clucking hen on an egg-clutch. "You can have too much of a good thing, Peter boy. A retirin' man like you wouldn't know much about the like of Cissie Gorman, but you know her mother. An' I can tell you this: Of all the airs an' graces the mother had, for every air an' grace of them, Cissie has ten worse airs an' graces of her own. She was bad enough when she was livin' with that aunt in Tramore, but since she came home from all them convent schools, from Hell to Bedlam wouldn't hold her for grandeur." Markie's Aunt Kitty sniffed. "Off earnin' her livin' she should be, a great, strong lump of a girl like her, instead of gavottin' wild all over the country. I'd have given Markie credit for more sense than to be taken in by her flighty ways."

Peter pocketed his pipe before he answered, grave and deliberate. "Cissie Gorman is not perfect. Nor is anyone else. She's flighty and she's shallow. Like her mother, she wants every man's attention. Oh, I know her and her ways well,

Kitty. I'd know a Gorman's skin on a bush. But I wouldn't condemn the girl out and out for any or all of her faults. She's young and she's spoilt and she's foolish, but I think her heart is warm enough. When a few years among strangers have knocked the corners off her and calmed down the airs and smothered the graces, she might turn out to be very different."

"A fit wife for Markie, I suppose? An' neither of them twenty-one!" Kitty was haughty, but just a little uncertain. "An' where would they face if they did marry? An' what could they do? It's not in here you'd bring them, Peter! This place wouldn't be half grand enough for her. Oh, no! Lalor's old place beyond, Moonbawn, would be more in her line. An' do you think the bit of money you have spared for your old age would last the two of them long? With her in charge of the purse-strings?"

"Ah, now, Kitty," said the master, soothering her and searching slowly again for his pipe, "there's no need for you to be rushing all those fences in the one gallop. Who ever made mention of marriage? Julia Gorman will need a more brilliant match than Markie for her daughter. Good looks and good manners and a good education wouldn't be enough qualification to make him her son-in-law. She'd favour some steady man with a hard lump of money in the bank and a solid farm of ground at his back. There's very little danger of her encouraging the daughter to conquer my Markie."

"Hmm," commented Kitty.

"Moreover, Cissie Gorman, at her present state of development, is not my ideal of a daughter-in-law. She has no consideration for anyone except herself. She has no topic of conversation except herself. She can't even think about anything except herself. When Markie wants to marry, I'll not stand in his way. But Markie, believe me, won't marry such a scatterbrain."

Kitty, her task accomplished, rose from her chair. "I wouldn't doubt your level head, Peter. Well I knew that the Gormans couldn't fool you. That's what I said to Patsy when I was leavin' the house. 'Patsy,' I said to him, 'mark my word for it, cute an' all though the Gormans are, they won't get their clutches on Peter O'Dea's few hard-earned pounds.' Ah, no one will rush you into anything, Peter, in this world or in the next."

She had refused his offer to make a cup of tea, was on her way to the door when a new fear struck at her. "But if Cissie pays no attention to her mother, an' Markie won't obey you?"

Peter O'Dea stood in the doorway, puffing out tobacco smoke, a man at his ease. "My father, God rest him, is a long time dead, Kitty, but he had a constant saying that he believed in all his life. 'Bid the divil good morrow when you meet him, Peter,' he'd say. And mind you, Kitty, that's a very sensible advice to follow."

Yet within the next few weeks Peter O'Dea, lonely enough now by his fireside with the greybeards round him, found cause to bid many a good morrow to the Lad Below, for Markie was more and more often absent from home at nighttime. Nor, as the garlanded summer faded to an autumn all russet and rain, did Markie show sign of ever intending to work for his living.

There came a Sunday in late September when Cosby and Markie were away to a big hurling match in Kilkenny, and with them Roughane and McKeown, to whom hurling was as their life's breath. Even Jamesy Hearn had, no one knew how, evaded his boss of a wife, slipped away to the game, and damn the consequences! Sure, tomorrow was another day altogether! Thus it happened that the master sat, lone at twilight in his kitchen, the fire a dull glow in the depths of the range, and while he puffed at his aged pipe he gave his thoughts free rein to rove.

And first he thought to himself how little the kitchen had changed in all the years since first he had faced Jer Coady across that hearth one July evening long ago. The red altar-lamp that winked at him now through the dusk, the broad range, the cushioned settee and the high dresser, they were Tessie's legacy to this kitchen, and he began remembering to himself the glint of her sunlit hair across the years between.

The knock on the door took him by surprise, and Andy

Gorman, uncertain in the dusk, had to peer round the room before he saw the master in his chair.

"Begor, Peter," he complained, "I couldn't make out whether or not there was anyone here. Is it your eyes you're sparin' or is it the paraffin oil?"

"Oh, hello, Andy! You're very welcome." Peter was glad and yet sorry that he must part company from his thoughts. "Dozing off I was, here by the fire, and the night was on me before I knew."

He stood up to light the lamp.

"Yerrah, leave it so." Andy was already seated. " 'Tis homelier in the dark. Once I have the pipe steamin', an' no work to do, dark or day is all one to me."

" 'Tis wonder to me you're not gone to the match. Now that you have a car of your own and all. Sure, even Hearn is gone. Although, from the way I heard buckets banging above in his yard all the evening, 'twill be God help him when he gets home."

" 'Twould be greater wonder to me if I were at the match, new car or no new car," Andy stated, accumulated woes conquering a natural flair for keeping his own affairs to himself. "All the week I meant to go, and then, at the last minute, a bit of a tiff stirred up between Julia and myself. So that was the end of the hurling match for me." He puffed jerkily at his pipe. "I wasn't one month married to Julia, Peter, when I found out that she was a damn decent woman, easy to get on with, so long as she got everything her own way. But she's a bad woman to cross. An' bein' a man that always wanted the least possible trouble in his life, I let her boss me to her heart's content. Do you know, Peter, I never before, but once, went again her until this day."

"Indeed," said Peter.

"An' that was the day poor Ned, God be merciful to him, was killed. Now, I never agreed with Ned's politics, an' when, despite every warnin' from bishop an' priest, he went off mad to fight for his republic against his own countrymen, I was never more against him than then. But, be I against him a thousand times, he was my brother, Peter. When word came down to me that he had been killed, I never said one word. I only went straight up to the press in the parlour an' filled my pockets with cartridges an' took down the double-barrel from over the fireplace. Then I went back to the kitchen. 'Where in God's name are you off to?' says Julia. 'I'm goin',' says I, 'to show the men who shot my brother that there's a Gorman livin' yet to take the place of the man that's gone.' "

Andy seemed to have trouble with the stem of his pipe. He examined it carefully, perhaps to help conceal his emotion. " 'Twas near dusk of a grand summer's day, an' I wasn't well clear of Ballyvarna when the thought came to me that I hadn't a notion of where I was goin'. My aim was to join Regan on the hills, but I didn't know where Regan was, an' I doubted if anyone on the Republican side would tell me, because of my politics always bein' the other way."

"I see your difficulty," said Peter.

Gorman put the pipe back into his coat pocket. "I walked the fields all that night, Peter, half-cracked with grief at the thought of Ned, mad for battle an' vengeance, an' still no trace of Regan or his men. Aye, an' before the dawn was red I was half-afraid I would meet them, for fear they'd only laugh at myself an' my shot-gun an' my thought of vengeance. When the mornin' light came I was over beyond on the Knock road. I walked on till I came to the pump. The Free Staters had up a notice there about layin' down arms. I lifted my gun an' blew that notice to hell. An' then I slunk home for myself through the chill of the early day." He paused once more, feeling again for his pipe. "I was locked out, Peter. Locked out, an' Julia at the window to face me." He sighed. "That was the end of my rebellion, boy, but 'tis many the day since I bitterly regretted that I didn't face Regan an' the hills. A man can meet worse things than a quick bullet, Peter."

" 'Tis easy to die, Andy." The schoolmaster radiated sympathy and philosophy. " 'Tis easy to die well when the blood is hot, but 'tis the men who live on and bear with whatever troubles God may send them that keep the world turning."

"I suppose you're right," grudged Andy, "but a man can't keep his sorrows to himself always with the head bowed down.

'Tis hard when you have no say at all in your own house, nor power to correct one of your own children. A man can get accustomed to anything, Peter, but custom doesn't make the hard thing any easier. The way it is, boy, you keep submittin' an' submittin' an' submittin', until on a sudden you can submit no longer, an' then you kick at the traces." He lit his pipe and the hand that held the match was shaking. "I kicked today, Peter. At least, I thought to kick."

"She must have pushed you very hard."

"I've been pushed harder in my time. Maybe 'twas the way Julia had been all the week puttin' obstacles in the way of my goin' to Kilkenny that riled me. Anyway, just at second Mass time today, she called me into the parlour. 'I've been talkin' to Cissie,' says she, 'an' after all we've spent on her an' all the cravin' she had on us to let her off to Dublin, an' all the trouble we had to get a place for her in the hospital, what does me lady do now only put her head in the air an' say she doesn't think she'll go at all. An' she due to go this week!' 'Well,' says I, in no humour for argument, 'maybe she knows her own mind best.' 'Her own mind!' says Julia. 'At her age she has no right to possess such a thing. All that's wrong with her now is that she wants to stay at home to flirt with Markie O'Dea.'" Andy had further trouble with his pipe. "She wasn't too complimentary to Markie, Peter, though till today he was always the white-haired boy with her. Then she says to me, 'Out to the kitchen with you, now, Andy! Order her to begin packin' her trunk right away!'"

Peter O'Dea made sympathetic noises.

"I seen the truth of what Julia said," Andy went on. "Cissie, at the heart of her, is a fine girl, but she's inclined to be flighty, an' the trainin' she got at all them swanky convent schools the mother sent her to put too many grand ideas into her head. A few years of sharp orders an' hard work in some such place as an hospital would be the best thing ever happened her." He paused to put away his pipe. "I don't know if you think the same as me, Peter, but I think Markie an' herself would be better out of one another's sight for a few years. The both of them are too young yet for settling down."

208

The master nodded. "Too young and too foolish, Andy!"

"I'm glad you're with me there, but to come back to this mornin'. I agreed well with what Julia said. 'Twas the way she said it that galled me. I was to do the dirty work! I was to boss Cissie! I was by-the-way to dictate to the girl about her future, an' me left without hand, act, or part in the orderin' of it!" He swallowed hard on the memory. "I turned towards the door. 'Lookit here, Julia,' says I, 'it wasn't me sent Cissie to all them expensive schools. It wasn't me encouraged her to be friendly with Markie O'Dea. 'Twasn't me that got her the place in this hospital no more than 'twas me that learned her all her hoity-toity ways. An' so,' says I, 'it's not goin' to be me that'll tell her whether she's to go to Dublin or whether she's to stay at home from Dublin.'" Andy wiped his forehead. "I marched out of the house an' hid in the barn 'till dinnertime," he confessed without shame. "I kep' well out of Julia's way all the evenin' an', after the tea, I on with my coat an' footed it up here, Peter, because I said to myself if any man could advise me right, that man was you."

In his quiet way, without fuss or hurry, Peter O'Dea answered. "I think, Andy, we had better do a bit of advising on each other."

An hour later, their talk ended, they went marching up the road together. At the cross below the schoolhouse a couple stood chatting in the shadow of the tall trees. As the two men passed, Peter called out a good night. "Good night," came Markie's voice in answer. The master went two brisk steps further by Andy Gorman's side. Halted. Turned. Came more slowly back.

"I suppose, Cissie, I'd better bid good-bye to you," he said easily. "Your father tells me you're off to Dublin during the week. The healing of the sick and the tending of the suffering and the comforting of the afflicted is a great vocation, girl." He looked across at her where she stood, half-hidden in the star-studded darkness. "But 'tis a task no one should attempt till they've been well trained to it before hand."

Then he swung away to where her father waited on his coming.

Cosby was not himself tonight. Conor Cosby was moody, irritable, wandering round the kitchen, picking up papers and books, laying them down again unread, switching on the radio, switching it off again unheard. Some dog or horse or lady had played him false, Peter thought. And yet he had come early in. He could not have done much rambling or gambling this night.

The master decided to rouse him from his moodiness. "You didn't ramble far tonight, Conor. Any sign of Markie on your rounds?"

"I saw him from me," answered Cosby gruffly and said no more.

It must be some other girl, Peter told himself. Some girl Markie picked up with since Cissie Gorman went away.

"Yes, I did see Markie," burst out Cosby suddenly. "And since I came in I've been wondering should I tell you where I saw him."

"And why not?" asked Peter, amused. "I don't object to him winking at the posies of the parish."

Conor Cosby swore. "Be damn, Peter, but he could walk out every female from this to Slievenamon and I'd carry no tales. I'm not so much of an angel that I can cast stones at anyone. Ah, no, Peter. If 'twas courting or gambling or drinking I saw him, 'twouldn't cost me the second thought, for they're three fine agreeable ways of going to the devil. But here's what Markie was up to. He was drilling above in Mc-Mahon's field with Packey Regan's irreconcilables."

Father John Hahissey sat in his worn arm chair and waited for Peter O'Dea to lead the conversation round to wherever the schoolmaster wanted that conversation to go. Father John Hahissey had in his heart a great compassion for Peter O'Dea; he had always been a firm believer in Markie; he well knew that it was Markie and Markie's problems which had brought Peter here this night, and he could not escape from a certain sense of guilt, because, after all, it was on Father Hahissey's advice that Peter had turned the same Markie from his first

210

dourness into what the Reverend John Hahissey was sorry to hear were not entirely desirable ways.

Father Hahissey found himself regretting that the preliminaries, the talk of the weather and the crops and the state of the country, were over, and that the time had come to discuss more serious matters. With a sigh he asked, "And what's the news of Markie? Did he get himself a job yet?"

Peter O'Dea took a long pull at his pipe. "He has not got himself a job, Father; he's not trying to get himself a job; and, to the best of my belief, he has no intention of ever even looking for a job."

"That doesn't sound so good," said the priest.

"Moreover, he makes no statement or excuse to me as to why he shouldn't at least go in search of a job. It can't be his health any longer because, God knows, his health was never better. It can't be his nerves because he has left them behind him wherever he found them. And it can't be that he has no leisure to go look for a job because he has nothing else to do, except for whatever time he spends drilling with Packey Regan in the name of Freedom."

Father Hahissey, a tidy man, was sufficiently startled to spill his pipe ash on the floor. "Oh, now, Peter, we'll not gain anything by abusing the boy at this stage. We'd all be better employed examining our consciences as to the way we've treated him. Had we been more ready, either to lead or to drive, we might all feel far happier this night."

"I have no intention of abusing the boy, Father. I'm merely piling up all the evidence that can be piled up against him so that we can see how little it all amounts to. My only aim is to do the best that can be done for Markie." He paused. "I have thought out a scheme, Father, on which I'd like to have your opinion."

"Aha," cried Father Hahissey. "I always knew, Peter, that you'd put no foot wrong. I knew that in the end you'd get that wise head of yours to work and set Markie on the right road, once and for all."

If the schoolmaster heard the words of praise, he gave no sign of having done so. "Actually, Father, since Markie came home, I have been inclined to let things drift. I've been too lackadaisical where his future welfare was concerned, too easily persuaded to let the boy find his own feet. I failed to take into account the fact that maybe he was all the time waiting for me to give him a lead."

"Ummm," said Father Hahissey, noncommittal.

"Then, when things were going from bad to worse, instead of advising him as I thought right, I shirked away from saying anything to him at all. I made no complaints. I issued no warnings. I persuaded myself that I was leaving him to his own devices, and yet when he took up with the young one of the Gormans I used my influence with Andy to make sure she was sent away."

"I think you did a wise thing there," assured the priest.

"Whether I did right or whether I did wrong, I quashed the only sign of free will the boy had shown since he left Maynooth. And I turned him from the girls into the arms of Packey Regan." Peter O'Dea paused again. "I've been a quiet man all my life, Father, but till now I always was able to find my own way out of my own difficulties." Solemnly he put down his pipe. "And I'm hoping to fight my way out of this corner too, Father. I'm planning to lead and drive Markie at one and the same time. I'm going to buy Moonbawn."

Father Hahissey sat up. Father Hahissey stared, wide-eyed. "You're what?"

"I'm going to buy Moonbawn."

The priest relaxed a little. "That's a big order," he said slowly. "Oh, that's a very tall order, Peter."

"And because it is such a big undertaking is my chief reason for buying the place. 'Twill mean a hard struggle, both in money and every other way. But then I think that both Markie and myself have lived too easy too long."

Father John Hahissey rubbed his furrowed forehead. "Maybe so, Peter. That may well be so. But Moonbawn is a big risk. Moonbawn is a very big risk. Moonbawn will cost you a mint of money."

"Well, the bank manager was very accommodating. He told me, privately, that the bank is long anxious to get the place off their hands. Half of it going wild on them, he says, and no more hope of finding a buyer now than when Lalor left long ago. Oh, Moonbawn has proved a very poor investment from their point of view. Anyhow, if I put down a third of the money in cash, they'll give me a new mortgage against the rest. So that, with a bit of luck and a share of hard work, I don't think the proposition is nearly as foolish as it looks."

"Hmm!" commented the priest. "And is Markie in favour?"

Peter O'Dea peered busily into the bowl of his pipe. "I am not going to say a word to Markie until the deed is done. I'm going to buy Moonbawn, and if Markie likes it I'll be glad of him liking it. And if he doesn't like it, well . . ." and they were both silent a while. "The way I'd really like to have things turn out, the selfish way, I suppose, would be for me to be able to walk in to Markie some evening and say, 'Markie, I've bought Moonbawn for you,' just like that, and then watch the glad look of surprise light up his face, just like it used to do when he was a child and I'd bring him home some new toy or plaything."

"But don't you forget, Peter," warned Father Hahissey, "that Markie has left his childhood far behind him. Even if he wanted Moonbawn a thousand times over, he mightn't like to have it wished on him that way. He might even go against you, just to let us all see he's a grown man now with a mind and a will of his own."

Peter O'Dea stood up, smiling his shy, quiet smile. "If he does use his mind and his will and his brains, even if he only uses them to put as much distance as he can between himself and Moonbawn, I'll have won a great moral victory, Father. I'll have achieved the only purpose I have left in life, even if I have to gain my victory the hardest possible way. One way or the other, Father Hahissey, I'll have saved Markie from himself. I'll have made him fight and conquer his own sense of failure. I'll have put an end to his aimless drifting, once and for all." Peter O'Dea laughed a little grimly as he reached for the door handle. "Oh, I have Markie caught in a cleft stick this time, Father. I know Markie. When I buy Moonbawn he'll do either of two things. He'll either throw himself into the work there with a heart and a half or he'll throw myself and my Moonbawn to blazes and drive out into the world to earn an independent living."

The priest, dumbfounded still, could only nod silently. Peter O'Dea opened the sitting-room door, stood there a moment, hesitant. "Father Hahissey," he said, " 'twas seldom ever I daydreamed, but I've always wanted Moonbawn. One time I hoped to have Tessie in it with me. When she went I gave up the dreaming—till Markie came home. I've been dreaming ever since, Father, and yet I'll confess to you a strange thing. At the end of all my dreaming I can't for the life of me decide whether I'd rather have a docile Markie above with me in Moonbawn, doing with me the things I've long planned for us to do together, or whether I'd prefer to know that Markie wouldn't let me or anyone else shape his life for him and preferred to battle through life for himself, independent of his father and the whole world."

He came up the hill towards Carriglea through the grey gloom of the November dusk, and, though a chill breeze of winter nagged, fretful, round the naked trees, there was singing joy in the heart of Peter O'Dea. Aye, in his heart the thrushes sang, for Moonbawn was his at last, his and Markie's. "Moonbawn! Moonbawn! Moonbawn is mine," sang his heart. "Mine and Markie's! Moonbawn!" Today the bankers had signed, and the lawmen had sealed, and the bargain was made. And what though the price was stiff and the mortgage large and the interest high!

"Moonbawn!" cried his heart. "Moonbawn!"

Ah, this was surely a night for rejoicing. This was a night Jer Coady should have lived to see. Jer, who had so long striven to war down the Lalors and all that they stood for. Jer, who should surely have been here to celebrate the day which sent his one-time assistant to rule over Moonbawn in their stead. Peter O'Dea, fanciful, wondered if Jer were the happier tonight in his high place above the stars at the knowledge that right had triumphed.

Or this was a night for Fonsy Farrell, a night when Fonsy should be waiting, triumphant, by the fire in the kitchen, a pint-pot of porter in his hand and the lilt of a new song on his lips, a grand new song, the song of Peter and Markie and Moonbawn. Well Peter knew what Fonsy would name that ballad were he alive this night. *The Song of the Quiet Man*, he would call it, a song never to be forgotten while grass grew green and water ran clear in Carriglea.

And the thought came to him, too, how Tessie would have laughed, laughed, proud and joyous, were she waiting for him there in the lamp-sweet kitchen. And the Tessie of his thoughts was not the wife who had faded so fast in all the bloom of her womanhood, but the carefree girl whose auburn curls, as they danced above the white throat of laughter, had ensnared his heart one July morning long ago.

Yet, if no one else waited at home to greet him, there would be Markie; Markie, soon to be happy at his father's happiness or soon to show that he had a will of his own and the wish to use it. Peter wondered if he and his son would plan the future together; would plan how Peter, to pay off the bank's interest, would stay on at the teaching for another few years; how Markie, with the aid of a labourer or two, could take on the working of the farm; how Fintan Fogarty had promised that his horses and equipment and men would always be at their service should need arise. Or would Markie, in that easy way of his, calmly point out to Peter that he was a man in his own right, not a creature of his father's to be led or driven.

Peter O'Dea, when he reached his own gate, was smiling to himself still at the thought of the triumph he brought with him. He wondered that there was no light in the kitchen, for he had expressly asked Markie to wait in tonight until he himself returned. Perhaps, he thought bitterly, this is one of Regan's drill nights.

He had lit the lamp and was stoking the range when he saw the letter on the mantel-shelf, coldly addressed, in Markie's flawless handwriting, to 'Peter O'Dea, Esquire.' Wearily he sat down to read. Once he read it through, very quickly, and then reread, ever so slowly. He stood up again, an old man, very tired, very worn . . . but with an ever-growing spring of joy bubbling up through his grief.

So Markie had chosen to go his own road!

For a moment a wave of disappointment almost stunned him, numbing heart and brain while he went stumbling across the dim hall into the dark parlour beyond.

So Markie had chosen to go from him; had gone, the letter said, to seek the smile of fortune from the four winds of the world . . . had gone and deserted in his going the father who loved him . . . had gone because of all the rumours he had heard that his father was buying Moonbawn for him . . . had gone because he was determined to prove that he could make his own way and could live his own life, that he did not need ever and always to shelter beneath his father's shadow . . . had gone, and in his going paid his greatest tribute to the way his father had reared him, had shown by his going the real worth that was in him. . . .

Before he was fully conscious of where his feet had led him, Peter O'Dea was kneeling before his wife's picture; and if there were tears in his eyes, they were tears not of sorrow or of anger, but of compassion and of pride.

"I'm sorry, Tess," he was saying, "I'm sorry that I failed to rule him right always, that, by trying to hold on to him too selfishly, I nearly ruined our boy's life forever. But sure, Tess, I couldn't have the heart to be hard on him. I couldn't. I have to let him go from me now, Tess, the way, as your mother promised me long 'go, that he'll come back to me, for good, some other day. But I have no fear for Markie, Tess. A better lad was never born. No matter where he goes or to what he turns his hand, he's a son we can both be proud of. . . . And though he's gone from us now, he'll not stay always away. So it's up to myself and yourself, girl dear, to see that when the good day comes, his due here will still be waiting for him. We must hold Moonbawn, Tess, you and I, until Markie comes home."

He stood up, lit a match, smiled up at the face that smiled down. "I had to let him go from me, Tess. I had, you might say, to drive him from me. But I'll take my bible oath, girl, that in so doing, I've made a man of him."

END

1-17